PRAISE FOR

"Readers who crave suspense will devour Cantore's engaging crime drama while savoring the sweet romantic swirl. . . . *Crisis Shot* kicks off this latest series with a literal bang."
ROMANTIC TIMES

"A gripping crime story filled with complex and interesting characters and a plot filled with twists and turns."
THE SUSPENSE ZONE on *Crisis Shot*

"A pulsing crime drama with quick beats and a plot that pulls the reader in . . . [and] probably one of the most relevant books I've read in a while. . . . This is a suspenseful read ripped from the front page and the latest crime drama. I highly recommend."
RADIANT LIT on *Crisis Shot*

"Cantore, a retired police officer, shares her love for suspense, while her experience on the force lends credibility and depth to her writing. Her characters instantly become the reader's friends."
CBA CHRISTIAN MARKET on *Crisis Shot*

"An intriguing story that could be pulled from today's headlines."
MIDWEST BOOK REVIEW on *Crisis Shot*

"The final volume of Cantore's Cold Case Justice trilogy wraps the series with a gripping thriller that brings readers into the mind of a police officer involved in a fatal shooting case. . . . Cantore offers true-to-life stories that are relevant to today's news."
LIBRARY JOURNAL on *Catching Heat*

"Cantore manages to balance quick-paced action scenes with developed, introspective characters to keep the story moving along steadily. The issue of faith arises naturally, growing out of the characters' struggles and history. Their romantic relationship is handled with a very light touch . . . but the police action and mystery solving shine."

"Questions of faith shape the well-woven details, the taut action scenes, and the complex characters in Cantore's riveting mystery."

"[In] the second book in Cantore's Cold Case Justice series . . . the romantic tension between Abby and Luke seems to be growing stronger, which creates anticipation for the next installment."

"This is the start of a smart new series for retired police officer–turned–author Cantore. Interesting procedural details, multilayered characters, lots of action, and intertwined mysteries offer plenty of appeal."

"Cantore's well-drawn characters employ Christian values and spirituality to navigate them through tragedy, challenges, and loss. However, layered upon the underlying basis of faith is a riveting police-crime drama infused with ratcheting suspense and surprising plot twists."

"*Drawing Fire* rips into the heart of every reader. One dedicated homicide detective. One poignant cold case. One struggle for truth. . . . Or is the pursuit revenge?"

DIANN MILLS, bestselling author of the FBI: Houston series

"This hard-edged and chilling narrative rings with authenticity. . . . Fans of police suspense fiction will be drawn in by her accurate and dramatic portrayal."

LIBRARY JOURNAL on *Visible Threat*

"Janice Cantore provides an accurate behind-the-scenes view of law enforcement and the challenges associated with solving cases. Through well-written dialogue and effective plot twists, the reader is quickly drawn into a story that sensitively yet realistically deals with a difficult topic."

CHRISTIAN LIBRARY JOURNAL on *Visible Threat*

"[Cantore's] characters resonate with an authenticity not routinely found in police dramas. Her knack with words captures Jack's despair and bitterness and skillfully documents his spiritual journey."

ROMANTIC TIMES on *Critical Pursuit*

THE LINE OF DUTY SERIES

BOOK TWO

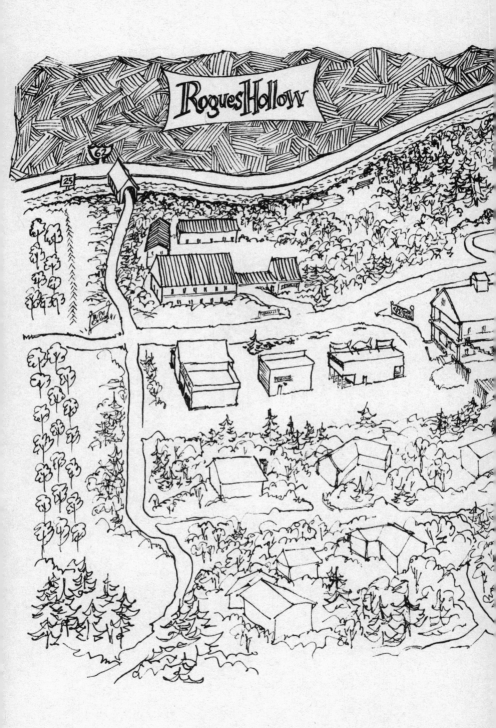

LETHAL TARGET

JANICE CANTORE

TYNDALE HOUSE PUBLISHERS, INC., CAROL STREAM, ILLINOIS

Visit Tyndale online at www.tyndale.com.

Visit Janice Cantore's website at www.janicecantore.com.

TYNDALE and Tyndale's quill logo are registered trademarks of Tyndale House Publishers, Inc.

Lethal Target

Designed by Faceout Studio, Charles Brock

Edited by Erin E. Smith

Published in association with the literary agency of D.C. Jacobson & Associates LLC, an Author Management Company. www.dcjacobson.com.

Unless otherwise indicated, all Scripture quotations are taken from *The Holy Bible*, English Standard Version® (ESV®), copyright © 2001 by Crossway, a publishing ministry of Good News Publishers. Used by permission. All rights reserved.

Romans 13:4 in the epigraph and chapter 23 is a paraphrase written by the author.

For information about special discounts for bulk purchases, please contact Tyndale House Publishers at csresponse@tyndale.com, or call 800-323-9400.

Library of Congress Cataloging-in-Publication Data

Names: Cantore, Janice, author.
Title: Lethal target / Janice Cantore.
Description: Carol Stream, Illinois : Tyndale House Publishers, Inc., [2018] |
    Series: The line of duty
Identifiers: LCCN 2018012497 | ISBN 9781496423740 (sc)
Subjects: LCSH: Policewomen—Fiction. | GSAFD: Christian fiction. | Suspense fiction.
Classification: LCC PS3603.A588 L44 2018 | DDC 813/.6—dc23 LC record available
    at https://lccn.loc.gov/2018012497

Printed in the United States of America

24   23   22   21   20   19   18
7   6   5   4   3   2   1

DEDICATED TO ALL LAW ENFORCEMENT—STATE,
FEDERAL, MUNICIPAL—WHO CONTINUE TO WORK
HARD TO KEEP PEOPLE SAFE IN THE FACE OF DANGER
AND HOSTILITY. YOU ARE TRUE HEROES.

ACKNOWLEDGMENTS

I'd like to acknowledge my church family, Trail Christian Fellowship, for showing me true fellowship and what it means to "think like Jesus."

I'M GOD'S SERVANT. I DON'T BEAR THE SWORD
IN VAIN. I AM AN AVENGER WHO CARRIES OUT
GOD'S WRATH ON THE WRONGDOER.

ROMANS 13:4

— — —

BE STRONG AND COURAGEOUS . . . FOR THE LORD
YOUR GOD IS WITH YOU WHEREVER YOU GO.

JOSHUA 1:9

1

The dream was always so vivid to Tess. The sound of a struggle, the screams of fear and anger, then the sharp report of a gunshot—they were all completely real. It was as if she'd been there, but of course she hadn't. The fake echo of sounds didn't wake her up. Even in her sleep, it was the blood that woke her, the thud of a body hitting the pavement and the spatter of blood all over the sidewalk.

Tess's eyes shot open. She sucked in a shuddering breath as the nightmare faded. Feeling sticky with sweat, she sat up and threw the blanket off. She knew it would be no use to try to go back to sleep.

She placed her feet flat on the floor and sat with her head

in her hands as her heart rate settled down to normal. It had been more than a decade since the nightmare had shredded her sleep and she'd thought she was well past it. Why now?

It had started years ago, on her birthday. The nightmare smashed her sleep in some form or another for a long time after the incident that sparked it. The PD shrink had said it was a kind of PTSD that would fade with time, and it had. Here she was in a new home, in a new place, miles away from Long Beach, years older, so much perspective behind her, and she never expected the dream to resurface.

She was wrong.

It was a little after four in the morning. Chief of Police Tess O'Rourke flipped on the lights and decided that her day would start now. She showered, scrubbing her head with shampoo, working to wash the remnants of the dream away. There was no date on the calendar that affected Tess more than her birthday, June 1. Birthday—one day out of the year to celebrate however many years a person has been alive. Some people hated it because they hated the thought of getting older, but aging never bothered Tess. It was something else about the day that tortured her.

Her birthday was also the anniversary of her father's murder. He was shot and killed while on duty on her sixteenth birthday. He died on a dirty sidewalk in Long Beach. For Tess, the day was never a celebration. It was a day to get through, nothing more.

- - -

The phone rang when Tess was halfway through her first cup of coffee, studying a folder of paperwork she'd received from the DEA. Routine helped dispel the fog that came after the dream. The routine of police work was good medicine.

Caller ID told her it was Becky Jonkey, the graveyard patrol officer. Tess frowned. Becky would be EOW in a little over an hour; her call now meant something unexpected had happened. She grabbed her phone.

"O'Rourke here."

"Chief, I've got a situation. A dead teenager. Looks like a drug overdose."

Tess heard the uncertainty in her voice. "Looks like?"

"It's complicated."

"I'll be right there. Address?"

Tess wrote down the address and closed the folder she'd been studying. It was Friday morning and, because of all the hours she'd put in at work so far this week, technically her day off, but she'd learned that the chief of police was never really off duty. And she didn't mind. Police work was her life, especially on her birthday, and the lines between off shift and on shift were thoroughly blurred already.

Besides, she'd asked to be notified of any death appearing to be drug related. Drugs, specifically synthetic opiates, were the black plague of the twenty-first century. *Drug overdose* was becoming an all-too-common phrase. There was a growing crisis in the Rogue Valley of opiate addiction and death by opiate overdose. Officers in Medford, forty minutes away and the largest city near Rogue's Hollow, carried Narcan to deal with the issue. Tess considered whether issuing Narcan was feasible for her tiny department. Given a small-town budget, it would be difficult.

The paperwork she'd been studying concerned drugs,

homemade and illegal opioids. Tess had arrested a fugitive last summer, Roger Marshall, a man who'd been smuggling drugs into Oregon from California. She and one of her officers had helped to develop the intelligence that enabled the DEA to make some big arrests. As a result, they were invited to take part in a large-scale warrant service in the early morning hours this coming Monday, led by the DEA, just over the border in Yreka, California. It was the culmination of nearly a year's worth of investigation.

But the raid wasn't until Monday. Today she had a death to investigate.

Her uniform was at the station, so she decided on jeans, a polo shirt, and her duty belt. As she dressed, Tess considered the address Becky had given her for the call, a high-priced location. She wasn't that familiar with this particular number, but it indicated to her that this wasn't some street person. The homes on Broken Wheel were the most expensive in Rogue's Hollow. Was that why it was complicated?

A passing glance at the digital clock on her mantel, one that also gave the temperature and the date, gave her pause.

It was bad enough the sun was just dawning on her birthday; now she was heading to a death. She'd never be free of the clutches of this day. It was a cool, dry morning, and Tess shivered with foreboding as she locked up her house and climbed into her patrol SUV.

2

Rogue's Hollow was still asleep, the streets dark and quiet, as Tess drove across town to Broken Wheel. Tess never would have picked this small town to call home, but that was exactly what it had become. She'd come to know the place and the people, and she felt a protective pull tug at her. Maybe it wasn't as fast-moving and busy as Long Beach, California, but it was her responsibility now, and she took her responsibility seriously.

The green glow of the computer told her that Eva Harper, the calling party, had tried to wake her teen son up and couldn't. She feared aneurysm. Mercy Flights responded and cleared the call, subject DOA. She wondered at the difference. Jonkey was leaning toward drugs and Mom was thinking natural causes. Tess passed the Mercy Flights ambulance going back the other way and nodded at the driver.

A crease of light showed in the distance as the sun began to rise on what promised to be another beautiful day when she pulled next to Jonkey's cruiser. All the lights were on in the house. Tess didn't know the Harpers, but she knew their next-door neighbors, Delia and Ellis Peabody and their son, Duncan. Seventeen-year-old Duncan had witnessed a murder last year, and it seemed to change him. He'd turned from a thorn in her side, because of his propensity for teenage high jinks, into a valuable witness.

Tess walked up several steps and paused at the front door, rubbing her hands together against the early morning chill. This was a part of the job she hated, mostly because she knew what it was like to be on the other side, what it was like to lose someone violently and unexpectedly. It wouldn't matter to this mother that her son died at home and not in the street. He was gone just the same, and nothing would change that fact.

She sucked in a breath and knocked on the door. To her surprise, Duncan Peabody answered. Fair-skinned, his face was red and blotchy, eyes bloodshot, straw-colored hair wafting in all directions.

"Chief, aw, man, I can't believe it. It's Timmy, my best friend. He . . ." Duncan choked up and shook his head, wiping his eye with the palm of his hand and stepping aside for Tess to enter.

Delia Peabody approached. She spoke in a whisper. "Chief, Officer Jonkey is in the bedroom; she asked me to direct you there. Eva . . . well, Eva is having a hard time at the moment. Ellis is trying to get ahold of her husband, but Drake's deployed right now."

Tess's eyes raked the living room. There were three women on the couch; Eva Harper was in the middle. She was sobbing. The only man in the room, Ellis Peabody, was on the phone.

"I can talk to Mrs. Harper after I speak with Officer Jonkey."

Delia nodded and led Tess down a hallway. She pointed to a door. Tess thanked her. Delia went back to the living room and Tess opened the door.

The body of a young man lay sprawled diagonally on the bed, wearing only boxers, his head where his feet should be, at the corner near the edge. His chest was a dark, mottled purple, telling Tess he'd died facedown and the blood had begun to pool. Medics, or his mother, had probably turned him over. There was a pool of vomit on the floor beneath his head.

Tess had seen this before—too many times, really—and for her the scene pulled back a curtain on a big-city problem that had invaded her small town. Though the postmortem would have to say definitively, this certainly looked like a drug overdose.

"What do you know so far?" she asked Jonkey.

"He was supposed to be up early. It's his birthday today."

Tess rocked back with that revelation and Jonkey noticed.

"Something wrong, Chief?"

Shaking her head and chastising herself for the lapse, Tess reined in all the swirling emotions threatening to overwhelm. Just a coincidence. "Go on."

"He and his mother planned to drive to Portland for the weekend. When she found him, he was already cool to the touch. She called in a medical, Mercy Flights responded, and I rolled up with them." She shook her head. "He was obviously beyond help, so I called you and they left."

"How old was he?"

"Eighteen."

Back in control and on her game, Tess looked down at the body. "What a waste, dead on your eighteenth birthday."

Jonkey held out two evidence baggies in her gloved hands. In one was a needle and in the other was a white powder residue. "I called you because his mother freaked out when I found this. It looks like he was a user. I never would have guessed. She's adamant it's not his."

Tess looked at the baggies and studied the residue. It could be several things, but four previous deaths in the valley had been caused by an illegal drug called acetyl fentanyl. A relative of the powerful prescription painkiller fentanyl, it was five to fifteen times more potent than heroin and a hundred times more powerful than morphine. The stuff was bad—a small amount could produce a euphoria like heroin or oxycodone. But the cost of that euphoria was often death.

It was so dangerous, she'd received a law enforcement alert to use caution when dealing with anything suspected to be fentanyl. An officer back East overdosed when his bare skin accidentally came into contact with the substance he'd confiscated at a crime scene. He had to be treated with Narcan, spent a couple of days in the hospital, but was expected to recover. Not even police dogs were immune; several throughout the country had overdosed doing their jobs sniffing for narcotics.

Tess had read up on the compound because of the previous deaths linked to its use in the valley. The illegally produced product could be mixed with heroin to make it an even more potent product, or it could be sold in pills disguised as oxycodone. If the needle was his, it told her that Tim had likely mixed it with heroin.

But something was off here. Rogue's Hollow was a small town. Tess had, by now, learned who the druggies were and who the problem children were. Tim Harper wasn't one of either set. This family had not been on her radar for any reason.

"You've never come across this kid with drugs?" Tess asked Jonkey.

She shook her head. "He wasn't even one of the kids who ran with Duncan when he was off the rails."

"Did his mother say who she thought the paraphernalia belonged to?"

"No. She was distraught. She believes he must have had an aneurysm or stroke, anything but overdose. When the medics asked her if Tim did drugs, she denied and just about fell apart. I didn't want to make things worse. But aren't the parents the last to know? Duncan said they were best friends; maybe he would know."

Tess nodded. "I'll talk to Duncan and Mrs. Harper. ETA on the coroner?"

"Hour."

Tess stepped forward and looked at the boy's outstretched arm. Could that be a needle mark? she wondered when she spied a small, dark spot in the crook of the arm. She couldn't be positive. It was prudent to wait for the postmortem to confirm her suspicions or completely cancel them out. There might also have been some scrapes and bruises on his hip and thigh, but with the lividity, it was hard to tell. She then did her own brief visual survey of the room. It looked like a typical boy's room: sports posters on the wall, computer with game controllers, and a couple of bumper sticker sayings about beer and parties. But when she turned, the wall behind her caused a "Whoa" to escape her lips.

"Kinda cool, huh?" Jonkey said. "Tim was known as the photog."

"I'll say."

The wall was covered with photos, mostly four-by-six, but a few blown up larger. Tess stepped closer and saw a range of nature shots, candids with friends and family, and pics of the town of Rogue's Hollow and other places she didn't recognize. They were all quite good to her untrained eye, happy and positive depictions of a kid who had a full life. In one corner of the room a small table contained an older film camera, a couple of digital cameras, and several lenses.

The only thing out of the ordinary that caught her eye was the open, screenless window. She walked to it and looked out, not sure why it bothered her. Late spring nights were cool, but not freezing, so windows were often open, especially to take advantage of fresh early morning air. Because the house was on a sloping hillside, even though Tim's room was on the first floor, there was quite a drop from the window to the ground.

"Problem with that, Chief?" Jonkey asked.

"Not sure. The screen is down below. It's about a ten-foot drop. Doubt anyone climbed in, but someone could jump out. I'll ask his mom if this is normal." She gave the closet a once-over, then turned to her officer. "Check around for any other contraband and photograph everything. I'll be back."

Tess left Jonkey and returned to the living room to talk to Tim's mother. It was never easy to talk to someone who had lost a loved one. Though this wasn't a notification, Tess would never forget the first time she'd had to deliver the news about a death. A man high on meth had stabbed his live-in girlfriend to death in a violent altercation. The woman had put up a horrific fight and the house was a bloody mess. Tess had been on the sidewalk when the woman's adult son came running home because news had reached him that something had happened to his mother. He couldn't be allowed in the house, and she was forced to tell him right there on the sidewalk that his mother was dead.

The sound he made would stay with her forever. It was a strangled cry, a hideous, pain-filled howl. Then with a bare hand he punched out the window of the car closest to him, probably breaking his hand, and took off down the street the same way he came.

And for Tess, violent death always brought back memories of the day she'd been told about her father, killed in the line of duty. She truly felt Eva Harper's pain, understood the hurt, the shock, and the loss. True, Tim didn't die in a violent shooting, but he did die in a senseless, unexpected way that his mother would never make heads or tails of.

As Tess stepped into the living room, she saw that another man had joined the mix. Not surprisingly, it was Pastor Oliver Macpherson. He was on one knee, holding Mrs. Harper's hands, and he appeared to be praying.

He, too, understood the pain of loss. His wife, Anna, and her cousin Glen had been murdered nearly a year ago when Tess had only been in town for two months.

Oliver's presence was a given. She'd learned in the past year that he was always there when people needed help, support, even those who didn't attend his church. She'd seen him at the scene of a drowning, offering a shoulder to a foreign tourist, heard that he helped make a house wheelchair friendly after a man was severely injured in a car crash. A month ago in the early morning hours he showed up to help when a local couple lost everything in a house fire.

Tess paused, never truly certain how to approach Pastor Mac, as he was called. The man confounded her. She considered him the crazy friend she couldn't figure out. The fact that his faith hadn't seemed to waver, even after the murder of his wife, left Tess scratching her head.

"How can a supposedly good God keep letting people die horrible deaths?" she'd asked him once over coffee.

"Tess, the world is broken, and everybody dies. I don't blame God for Anna's death; I blame Roger Marshall."

"Certainly he pushed, but God could have stopped it, if he's God."

"If we were puppets, and God the puppeteer. People are free agents; they make decisions for good or evil." He'd shrugged, stormy green-gray eyes clouding briefly. *"God has a greater knowledge of everything than I will ever have. I can't question his will or resent circumstances over which I have no control. All I can do is live my life the way I'm called to live it."*

Tess had changed the subject after that. Her mother often said something similar, and it made Tess angry. The attitude was so *passive*. She still seethed at times over the loss of her father.

It was incomprehensible that after his loss Oliver could

still believe and tell people a good God existed. But she did agree on one point—the world was broken. You couldn't be a cop for eighteen years and not know that. Broken with a lot of pieces missing. And what was it they said about Humpty Dumpty and all his pieces?

Despite the snag over faith, she considered Oliver a good friend and valued his help, especially in situations like this. He could calm down a crisis without saying a word. She didn't want to interrupt his comforting Eva and she didn't have to. Duncan stepped up to Tess before she could say anything to the pastor.

"Tim was going to college in the fall. . . . How?"

Dressed in baggy shorts and a green Oregon Ducks T-shirt, Duncan was tall and slim. Tess had to look up to hold his eyes. She could see the pain there.

"When was the last time you saw him?"

"Last night. We had a party for Greg."

"What? Where?" Tess knew Greg Nguyen, a local high school baseball star. Because Rogue's Hollow didn't have a high school, teens from the Hollow and Shady Cove attended Eagle Point High, making Greg a celebrity in the entire Rogue Valley.

He shoved his hands in his pockets and looked sheepish. "You know, the Spot."

The Spot. The kids had partied in the woods, in a popular place she'd learned about early on in her tenure as chief. The Spot was across Midas Creek, on Bureau of Land Management property, and across from the location where Anna and Glen had faced their killer nearly a year ago. Like a shadow of the old postal delivery creed, neither snow nor rain nor heat nor gloom of night, nor a murder, had made the Spot any less attractive. In fact, knowing that a murder occurred across from their favorite party spot had made it more popular in a *Walking Dead* kind of way.

Tess pulled Duncan out the front door to speak to him on the porch. "Duncan, was Tim an intravenous drug user?"

Shock too real to be faked exploded on his face. "A what? No. No. Not Tim."

Tess raised an eyebrow. "We found paraphernalia."

Duncan shook his head. "No, Tim didn't do drugs."

"What went on at the party?"

"Beer and some pot—that's all I saw. I swear." He held his hands up.

Tess studied the kid. She knew he'd been a pot smoker when she first arrived in Rogue's Hollow. But the last few contacts she'd had with Duncan had been positive. He'd cleaned up his act and impressed her with his newfound maturity. She believed he was telling her the truth.

"Who was there?"

"Just the guys. Me, Greg, Trace, Josh, and Tim. Greg just signed a letter of intent; he's getting a full ride to college. And Coach Whitman was there, for a little bit, at the beginning."

Tess recognized the names, all Rogue's Hollow boys. Jocks mostly. She had seen some pictures of sporting events on Tim's wall. Tess loved baseball and had managed to attend the last regular season game Greg pitched. The talented all-American, all-state athlete was electric for a high school player, really fun to watch. If she remembered right, Whitman was the assistant coach.

"I'm only speculating here, but it's possible Tim died from

a drug overdose. If so, he had to buy the stuff somewhere. Did you see anything that looked shady at the party?"

Duncan blanched in shock. "Honest, Chief, I didn't see anything that looked like Tim or anyone was buying drugs."

"But what? Something crossed your face just now—what?"

Duncan wiped his palms on his thighs. "Aw, he talked . . . a while ago . . . I thought it was just talk . . . about celebrating getting out of town and into college in a special way. He wanted to try something like ecstasy. But he didn't spell it out. Maybe a few months ago he would have told me, but now . . ."

"He knew that you were trying to stay clean and straight?"

Duncan nodded, head down. He raised his head slowly. "You're sure he died from an overdose?"

"No, I'm not sure. The autopsy will give the official cause of death. I'm just asking questions. Do you think he might have experimented?"

Duncan winced. "He might have. And maybe a few months ago I would have tried it with him and we'd both be dead."

Tess let that pass, hoping Duncan's newfound law-abiding personality would stick. She doubted it was ecstasy that Tim tried, but there was no point in getting into that with Duncan.

"He had to buy it," she said. "Drug dealers don't generally give people birthday presents. Was anyone else at this party?"

"Uh . . . there were some older guys."

"Who?"

"Couple guys from the Hang Ten. I think one of them was called Eddie. I don't know the other. And Dustin Pelter was there . . . you know, Pig-Pen?" Duncan scratched his chin. "I didn't count. I was just listening to Greg talk about baseball." He shrugged.

Dustin had been friends with Anna's cousin Glen. He was a semi-homeless guy who would show up wherever he might get free pot or beer. Tess also knew that at one time he was a heroin addict, though supposedly clean now. He'd have to be interviewed.

But it was the mention of the Hang Ten that caught her attention. Of the three pot farms in her jurisdiction, the Hang Ten was the biggest. Could they be dealing more than pot? Tess wouldn't doubt it, but she'd have to prove it. Legalized recreational pot was not something she thought was a good idea, but the people of Oregon had voted.

"Was there anyone at all there you think could have been dealing hard drugs? Maybe to Tim?"

"I can't believe Tim did drugs. But I didn't stay till the party ended. I made so many mistakes in my past, I'm trying to keep my curfew. I left before midnight."

"I want you to talk with Officer Jonkey, write down everyone's name."

He nodded.

"Let's go back inside. I'll get Officer Jonkey."

They stepped through the front door and Tess went back to Tim's bedroom.

"Anything else?" Tess asked.

Jonkey shook her head.

"Send what you have to the lab. And ask for prints on the syringe."

"You think there's a problem?"

"I don't know; something is just off. No harm in covering all the bases." Tess considered Jonkey for a moment. She'd been on for twelve hours; it was her end of watch. Gabe Bender would be logging on any minute. "How tired are you?"

"Chief?"

"Do you want some overtime and to see this investigation through, or do you want Bender to relieve you?"

"This is my first death investigation that's not a car crash. I'd like to finish it if you'll approve OT."

"Consider it approved. I'll wait for the coroner. Duncan tells me that Tim partied last night at the Spot. I want you to head up there and look for evidence."

Tess noted the surprise on Jonkey's face. In the world of investigations, sitting still and waiting for the coroner was grunt work. Searching a scene for evidence was police work. That Tess, *the chief*, would opt for the grunt work and let the lowly *patrol officer* do the police work probably rocked her back a bit. But Tess had to learn to trust her people. So far none of them had let her down, and Jonkey needed the experience.

"Um, sure, but . . ."

"Yeah?"

"Well, is there anything in particular I should be looking for?"

It was Tess's turn to shrug. "If it's okay with his mother, why don't you take Duncan with you? Get an idea where everyone was while they partied. If Tim purchased drugs, my bet is he got them from someone there."

Jonkey nodded and together she and Tess left the bedroom. Tess explained the idea to Duncan and his mother.

"While this isn't a homicide investigation," Tess told Delia, who'd agreed to let her son go with Jonkey, "maybe Duncan will remember something that at the time seemed unimportant, but now might lead to an answer concerning Tim's death." She turned to the kid. "Help Officer Jonkey with where everyone was and what exactly went on at the party."

He bobbed his head up and down. "I will."

"Becky, rule #4: 'Always trust your gut.' Look for anything off, suspicious. Maybe something will jump out at you; maybe it won't. But give it a good going-over."

She nodded. "Roger that. Come on, Duncan; let's go."

Tess asked communications to check on the coroner's ETA. She had about twenty minutes to wait, and she wasn't going to complain. In Long Beach, it was not uncommon for officers to wait ten to twelve hours for a coroner's van.

Delia Peabody overheard the call. "Chief, there's coffee in the kitchen if you want it."

Coffee sounded heavenly to Tess. "Thanks."

Pastor Mac had finished praying with Mrs. Harper. He was sitting next to her on the couch and she was doing the talking now. Briefly he looked up at Tess and gave a slight nod of acknowledgment. She continued into the kitchen. She poured herself some coffee, thought for a moment, and filled a cup for the pastor. When she walked back into the living room, Delia and Ellis were saying their good-byes and Eva was gone.

"She had to use the restroom," Oliver explained when he closed the door. "Delia is leaving to organize some women to stay with Eva until her husband gets home."

Tess handed him the coffee.

"Thanks for this." He sipped the brew.

Oliver Macpherson was tall and broad shouldered. He'd never looked to Tess like a pastor. She could see him working outdoors with physically challenging labor, chopping down trees, fighting fires, but it was difficult to see him in her mind's eye behind a pulpit. There was a bit more white in his close-cropped beard since Anna's death, but his stormy green-gray eyes, though muted by grief, were just as bright and alive as ever.

"Sure. Thank you for coming over. I don't know what to tell her."

"That's not been my experience." Pastor Mac offered a somber smile. "It's been my experience that you know just the thing to say to people in extreme grief."

Tess felt her face redden and she looked away. True, she'd offered Oliver heartfelt advice following the death of his wife, Anna. But she'd felt a connection then because of how hard Anna's death had hit, and the words had come easily. But discussing death and loss always came back to faith for him and churned up anger in Tess.

"Does Eva attend your church?"

"She does, her husband also when he's here. Ellis was able to get ahold of someone in authority in Drake's Army unit. He will likely be given compassionate leave."

"That's good to hear." She sipped her coffee. "Did you know Tim well?"

"I did. He was our resident photographer. He was quite good. As I understand it, he wanted to study art in college and make photography a career."

"No hint of drug use?"

His brows furrowed. "You're thinking narcotics. Eva thinks he had an aneurysm because he vomited."

"I could be wrong, but we found paraphernalia."

"Don't tell me this is related to the other deaths?" His face went rigid with disbelief.

Tess remembered that Oliver had presided over two of the recent drug-related funerals. He was up to speed on the poison that had found its way into the valley.

"The coroner will have to say for certain," Tess sighed.

Oliver shook his head, eyes darkening with anger. "Roger Marshall is gone. How did another supply line pop up so fast?"

When she arrested Roger Marshall for murder, and he was ultimately found responsible for Anna Macpherson's death last summer, they'd discovered that he smuggled into the state stolen prescription drugs like oxycodone, receiving them from California and sending them north. He wasn't a cooker; he distributed. This conduit for illegal narcotics was the reason she and Bender would be working with the DEA. A year later they were still trying to uncover all Marshall's connections.

"Drug dealers are like cockroaches—you stomp out some, but others just keep oozing up out of the cracks. All I can do is put a finger in one hole among dozens in the dike."

"It's a testament to your dedication that you keep trying." He offered her a tired smile.

"Or to my hard head."

"That too, but in a good way. You remind me of an ancient warrior in stories of old, a dragon slayer, committed to killing the beast no matter the hardships or setbacks."

"But in those ancient stories there's always a good end: the dragon is slain. I don't see that end here. If I could find a way to take away the desire for drugs, that would be a dragon worth slaying."

"True. Only a heart change can take that away," Oliver said, and Tess flinched.

She'd heard her father say that exact thing so many times. She held Oliver's gaze, saw the compassion and the pain there, and felt a connection return. They both wanted the same thing: to end scenes like this where people grieved over a senseless loss.

Oliver started to say something and stopped. The spell was broken. Eva came out of the bathroom, wiping her eyes. This conversation could be saved for another day.

"Mrs. Harper, do you feel up to a few questions?"

The shattered woman nodded and sat on the couch. Pastor Mac sat next to her and placed a supportive arm about her. Tess faced them, sitting on the edge of the coffee table.

"These questions are hard, but they have to be asked. Was Tim involved in drugs? Did he use?"

Eva Harper shook her head. "No," she said with ultimate certainty. "I know my son. He would not do drugs."

Tess feared she was wrong but let it go. "When did you last see him?"

"The boys met here before they left to celebrate. He went off with his friends around 9 p.m. I went to bed before he got back from the party. I woke up when he and Duncan came in, but I didn't get out of bed."

"He and Duncan?" Tess frowned. Duncan had told her that he left the party before Tim.

"I think it was Duncan. . . . I mean, I heard Tim talking to someone, and I assumed it was Duncan. They made a lot of noise. It was around one o'clock. I yelled for them to quiet down, and they did. I should have come downstairs. Maybe if I had . . ." Her composure fled and she leaned into Macpherson.

"Don't blame yourself. I hate to say it, but you probably couldn't have changed anything." Tess waited a beat. "Was there a reason Tim took the screen off his bedroom window?"

"Why no, I didn't know he had. It's off?"

"It is. It's too high for anyone to get inside without a ladder, but you'll probably want it back on."

"If you have a ladder, I'll put it back on for you," Oliver offered.

There was a knock at the door, and though the day was beginning and it was time for people to be off to work, Delia had returned with several other women from the area. They all surrounded Eva Harper, and Tess was glad the grieving mother had their support.

Tess had nothing else to ask, so she left them to it and went to sit with the body until the coroner arrived. The wheels were turning in her mind, the dream forgotten and her birthday as a consequence. So many denials about Tim and drug use. Did Tim experiment one time with tragic results? It wouldn't be the first time a kid played with fire and got burned. But it seemed so off to Tess.

Yet, barring natural causes, what were the options? Intentional overdose, accidental overdose, or murder. What possible motive could there be to kill an eighteen-year-old kid set to leave for college?

3

Oliver stayed with Eva until the coroner came and Tim's body was removed. It always hit home with those left behind when the body bag was wheeled out. Already fragile, Eva crumbled, and Oliver did what he could.

He thought about Tess, someone who knew all too well what Eva was going through. She'd looked tired this morning, a little distracted, but she did her job well. She left when the coroner did, following behind his vehicle. Oliver had an image of her in his mind with her finger in the dike and knew that she would hold the line to the last. Even with the hint of fatigue, she projected such a strong, assured, and professional presence. The green in her eyes was vivid, and her gaze observant and alert, because she had a dragon to slay. He told Eva that she could rest in the knowledge that Chief O'Rourke would do everything in her power to figure out exactly what happened to Tim.

Once the bedroom was empty and there was support for Eva, and since Tess had given him the green light, Oliver closed himself inside and cleaned up the vomit as best he could. He stripped the bed and started the laundry. The last thing he wanted was for Eva to have to worry about those menial chores. The mindless work gave Oliver time to pray for her and ponder the chief's conclusion that this was a drug overdose. It didn't make any sense, not with the Tim Harper he knew. Tess had good reason for considering narcotics, he knew, so they would have to wait for things to play out.

As soon as he was certain Drake was on his way home, Oliver pulled the Harpers' ladder out of the garage and put the screen back on Tim's window and then said his good-byes, assuring Eva that he'd be available if she needed him. Oliver had a busy schedule and considered canceling the first couple of appointments in his book. But with all of Eva's friends arriving, she was well taken care of.

This opiate epidemic bothered him to his core. It wasn't only because Anna died at the hands of a drug trafficker; it was simply the waste of life. But the more he thought about it and Tim, the more he believed it was unlikely that drugs had claimed the promising young man's life.

He hoped to be able to talk to the chief more about the subject. A stop at the Hollow Grind was called for. Listening to Eva had been more important than drinking his coffee. He felt the need for more caffeine before he went to work, and as he approached the coffee shop, he stepped right into the middle of an argument.

"Stop trying to pressure me. You've no business knowing how I'll vote." The normally easygoing, mild-mannered Arthur Goding, one of his parishioners, squared off with a much younger man, one of the many who'd shown up out of the blue to work at pot farms. Oliver knew full well Arthur hated pot and pot farmers; he'd gotten an earful from the man many times.

The youngster would not back off. "All I'm saying, pal, is that we've got a moneymaking business. If we do well, that's money in the town coffers, not just our pockets."

"I'm not your pal. You're pushy and rude." Goding shoved the coffee shop door open but stopped before stepping inside. "You pot farmers are out there buying up good farmland and planting stinkweed. Don't see that I have any common ground with that on any level." Arthur continued into the coffee shop.

The young man shook his head, looking around at all the people who'd watched the confrontation, including Oliver. "A vote for pot sales is a vote for revenue. Even you must admit that money is good for a small town like this, right?"

Oliver smiled, knowing that the point of contention was an upcoming election. They'd been without a mayor for almost a year. The last one resigned after it was discovered he'd been sheltering a fugitive. Senior council member Addie Getz was serving as interim mayor, but she didn't want to serve the full remaining two years. The city finally decided to conduct a special election, which was scheduled to take place next month. A second item on the ballot was an initiative for allowing the sale of recreational pot in the city limits. While it was legal in the state, some municipalities had chosen not to allow its sale in their jurisdiction.

"No, I wouldn't admit that," Oliver said pleasantly. "Ill-gotten gain is never a good thing."

The guy rolled his eyes. "Old dude, you need to step into the twenty-first century. Vote yes on Measure A." He shoved a flyer into Oliver's hands and then continued down River Drive.

Oliver crumpled the flyer up and tossed it into the trash before entering the coffee shop. Arthur was putting cream in his coffee.

"I wouldn't worry, Arthur. The feeling I get is that they'll lose. Not many people in this town want to see cannabis for sale on Main Street."

"I hope you're right." He sighed, calmer now and back to his levelheaded self. "But these potheads don't stop bullying. Suppose they scare people into changing their minds? Now that they think they have a chance, they'll apply pressure everywhere. The fellows at the Hang Ten are the worst," Arthur noted derisively. "Those are some unsavory characters, I'll tell you. Hired muscle. You better believe they'll keep pushing, keep threatening, trying to change votes in their favor." He held his hand up in frustration. "I hope our side isn't intimidated."

"If they do threaten, then it becomes a police matter." Oliver knew it was true about the bullying; the entire council had complained about this.

"I wish the stuff had never become legal," he said with a

resigned sigh. "But the genie is out of the bottle now." He pushed the door open and was gone.

Hands in his pockets, Oliver watched him go. Arthur was right; the people who wanted recreational pot sales legal in the Hollow were often bullies. Would losing the election fair and square stop the nastiness? The whole issue would probably be a small thing in any large community, but in Rogue's Hollow it was pitting neighbor against neighbor. That was Arthur's problem; his neighbor happened to be the largest pot farm in town. Every day Arthur witnessed firsthand the pot business in operation. A couple other people Oliver knew who hated the new pot legalization had actually gotten into physical fights.

The tranquility of the town had been shattered.

"Hate to see that." Pete Horning, owner of the Hollow Grind, walked from behind the counter and gave Oliver a cup of coffee. Pete was one of two people running for mayor. "But he's got a point—the pot guys are a bit obnoxious."

"And it works against them. Thanks for the coffee."

"I just think the chief should be a bit more proactive."

This gave Oliver pause. "What do you mean?"

Pete shrugged. "The Hang Ten would have been out of business after that incident a couple months ago. She should have left things alone."

A couple of months ago the Hang Ten had been the victim of a robbery. Several greenhouse seedlings, some packaged pot, and a large amount of cash had been stolen. The farm's owner was on record saying he'd have been out of business if Tess hadn't been able to return the stolen goods and cash. As Oliver understood it, that incident was in part why the Hang Ten had taken on "hired muscle."

"Wait a second. Are you saying she shouldn't do her job? That she should look the other way?"

Pete arched an eyebrow. "All I'm saying is any cop has discretion. She could have used a little in that situation; then there might just be one less pot farm here." He went back behind the counter, leaving Oliver flabbergasted.

The issue was doing more than shattering peace; it was shattering the character of some good people.

4

There were discrepancies in Duncan's story, and it bothered Tess—almost as much as the circumstances surrounding Tim's death did. Eva was certain someone had come home with Tim. If it was Duncan and he'd lied, what was he hiding? Tess found more that rubbed her the wrong way when she followed the coroner out of the house. She stopped to look under Tim's window and didn't like what she saw. The bush underneath was smashed as if someone had jumped from the window to the ground. The breaks in the bush were fresh; they hadn't yet dried out in the warmth of the sun. She photographed it with her phone.

She thought about going back inside and questioning Eva

further but then decided not to put her through any more trauma. She'd talk to Duncan again, clear up the story he'd already told her. He should also know if Tim made a habit of jumping out of his window in a teenage thrill-chaser sort of way, something maybe his mom wouldn't know.

Her mind rumbled with a budding volcano of questions. If Tim or Duncan hadn't jumped out, then who? And why leap out a window unless you were fleeing detection? And if fleeing, why? And from what?

Duncan was in the station with Jonkey when Tess arrived.

"Find anything useful?" Tess asked.

Becky Jonkey was working on the computer, utilizing some new crime scene software. The department had been given the software as a free trial, and as the resident computer expert, Becky used it whenever she could. The jury was still out as to whether it would be useful to purchase. Tess could see that she was constructing a picture of the Spot. She'd also listed the names of the partygoers on the side.

"Duncan gave me some good descriptions of the unknown subjects. I'm setting the scene just for the practice." She didn't look up. "List of party people is on your desk."

"Thanks." Tess motioned to Duncan. "I have a couple questions for you."

"Sure, Chief."

"Think carefully, Duncan. Were you telling me the truth when you said you left the party before Tim?"

"Yes, absolutely!" He frowned. "Why?"

"Where'd you go?"

"My curfew is midnight. Mom and Dad were waiting up for me."

That would be easy enough to verify.

"Someone went home with Tim. Mrs. Harper heard another guy come in with him, and she thought it was you."

"It wasn't, honest. Wait, do you think Tim was murdered?" His eyes went wide.

Jonkey looked up. "Murder?"

Tess held her hands up. "Hang on; I'm not sure. It's still undetermined until the postmortem." She told them about the window.

"Tim never jumped out that window that I know of. Who would want to murder Tim?"

"Don't jump the gun, Duncan. I'm just dotting all the i's."

"But—"

"No buts. We need to be sure before we say something definitive. Don't say anything that might get back to Eva Harper, understand? It could only cause more pain."

"Yeah, I get it."

"Now, if you've assisted Officer Jonkey all you can, maybe it's time to go home?" She looked at Jonkey, who nodded.

"Thanks for all your help, Duncan," Jonkey said.

Duncan shrugged, looking exhausted and deflated. "I didn't help much." His voice wavered. "I can't believe this is happening. Tim's gone—" The voice broke and he took a second to compose himself. "You'll let me know what happens with this, I mean if it really is murder?"

"Yes, I will. Thanks again."

Duncan left and Tess went into her office.

Officer Bender, on for day shift, poked his head in. "Anything I should know about Harper?"

Tess sighed. "Nothing certain, just a gut feeling that there's more going on there than we know. At the very least, if it is drug related, I want to find the dealer. If you can help identify all the partygoers, that'd be great. Get a copy of the list from Becky. We need to talk to everyone. Especially Dustin Pelter."

He nodded and left her office.

"If it don't feel right, then it ain't."

One of her dad's expressions came to mind. It was the one that had led her to pen rule #4: "Always trust your gut." A rule Tess lived by.

A lot of things surrounding the death of Tim Harper were unsettling. It was also distressing to Tess that this death warranted a call to the sheriff's department to ask if they had any leads about where the illegal opiates were coming from. That meant Sergeant Steve Logan. She and Steve had dated for six mostly good months.

Tess's thoughts went back, unbidden, and she reflected on their time together. He'd been her rock through the holidays, helping her navigate the first winter she'd had to work in the snow. It was a whole new world fighting crime in the snow and ice. And it wasn't all work; they'd played too, skiing on Mt. Ashland, snowshoeing at Diamond Lake, and snowmobiling at Lake of the Woods. It had been really *fun*.

Through all of it, Steve had dropped hints about their future. He was ready to settle down, start a family—it was obvious. Tess ignored each and every hint, changing the subject when he got serious, preferring to take things one day at a time and hold lightly. Then the death knell came—she remembered it as if it were yesterday. The snow had melted and spring was in the offing. Her house was coming together and she'd made dinner for him. Afterward, they sat in front of the fire, and she could still feel the warmth of his embrace and the heady feel of his kiss, when he asked her point-blank: "Where do you see this relationship going?"

"I like things the way they are."

"But nothing stays the same forever, Tess. I'm ready to take the next step."

She'd gotten up, irritated when thoughts of Paul, her ex-husband, and his betrayal flashed through her mind. *I don't want to be hurt like that ever again.*

"I'm not there yet—"

"Will you ever be?" He stood and faced her, and Tess saw the hurt in his eyes. "We have a good thing . . . at least, it feels that way to me."

"It does to me as well, but I . . ." She struggled to find the right words and then felt awkward when all that came out was "I like things light and noncommittal."

She saw anger replace the hurt and he stiffened. "That's just not good enough for me." He grabbed his coat and was gone. Tess remembered watching the door close and wondering why she didn't try to stop him.

She really did like Steve, but the thought of making a commitment turned her feet ice-cold. They'd spoken on the phone a few times since that night when they realized they both wanted different things. He couldn't understand her reticence completely, but neither one could say the words "We need to break up." And now they were navigating the murky world of "taking a break." At first, it was relatively easy. Steve was reassigned to a desk job for training purposes for four months, and their paths never crossed at work. He'd only recently returned to working in the field. So taking a break would get harder to do in a small valley.

Rubbing her forehead and feeling like she could use another cup of coffee, like maybe a gallon size, Tess decided she could wait until the coroner's report came in to call Steve. Knowing the exact cause of Tim's death would be helpful.

Relieved for the moment, she stood up to pace and think about this drug problem and possible suspects. The Hang Ten came to mind. Even though it was legally licensed by the state to grow pot, the pot farm was a headache in a lot of ways. On the surface, there was no evidence that the Hang Ten was involved in anything illegal. But Tess wondered. The legalization of pot was a kind of new gold rush, and it created a whole new class of entrepreneur. Tess had been amazed at the different classifications of workers on the farms. It was big business for sure. Besides the master cultivators, there were trimmers, budtenders, and people who supervised the drying. But these weren't stable, year-round positions. Law enforcement had discovered a new subset of migrant workers with these farms, nicknamed trimmigrants or scissor drifters. These pot workers migrated between jobs, not exactly homeless, but not exactly laying down roots anywhere either.

Added to the mix was the fact that pot was still a federal crime. Money made from and associated with pot sales couldn't be deposited in banks. That meant a lot of cash floating around, which in turn meant a lot of thievery, attempted or successful.

The Hang Ten's owner, Gaston Haywood, moved from Southern California about a year before Tess. He'd established the farm and by all accounts had done well with his first harvest. She'd dealt with him a couple of months ago after he was the victim of a robbery. Two armed men assaulted him in his garage, beat him up pretty good, and stole several young plants from the greenhouse, some ready-for-sale pot, and a whole lot of cash—nearly $75,000. All told, Haywood estimated his total loss at close to $100,000. It was the kind of attack that was becoming common where pot farms were concerned.

In this instance, Tess caught the crooks before they could even smoke a joint or spend a dime. Like an event from an episode of *America's Dumbest Criminals*, one of them had dropped an ID card at the Hang Ten. She and two of her officers arrived at the address on the ID as the guys were removing what they'd just taken from their truck. It was a laughable law enforcement story she and Bender would probably tell over and over. Since then, Haywood had improved the security at the farm, adding cameras and a gated entry. He and some of his workers took to wearing handguns openly, legal in Oregon, an open carry state. He also hired two scary-looking guys, Eddie Carr and Don Cherry, ostensibly for security.

She wondered if the two at the party were really a couple of Hang Ten employees. She chewed on her bottom lip. It was an easy jump to make because she'd yet to totally adjust to pot being a legitimate business. Her law enforcement mind classified them as drug dealers and often feared that pot farms could easily be fronts for dealing harder drugs like fentanyl or heroin.

A knock at her door broke her chain of thought.

"Sorry to interrupt. Thought you could use a little more coffee."

It was Oliver, holding out a welcome sixteen-ounce cup of coffee from the Hollow Grind. His gaze was warm and friendly. "You take it black if I remember right."

Tess nodded. They had shared many cups of coffee in the past year, both before his wife's death and after. Not always the wonderful stuff the Hollow Grind produced.

Grateful, she stepped forward and took the coffee. "Thanks. I was just thinking I needed more caffeine. How is Mrs. Harper?"

Oliver gave a tilt of his head. "Devastated. Several of her friends are with her now. And her husband will be home as soon as he can."

"Good." She sipped her coffee, realizing that she wanted to talk to Oliver about anything but a death. Their last long conversation had been about his wife's death.

He started this conversation. "I have a couple questions— that okay?"

"Go ahead."

"Is something bothering you? You seemed a little distracted this morning."

Tess couldn't suppress a smile. "And I thought I had such a cop face."

Oliver grinned. "My job is to read people. And friends . . . well, I tune in to them."

Tess considered what she wanted to tell him. She'd made certain her birthday didn't show up anywhere at work. She'd learned in her first month here that the people she worked with liked to celebrate each other's birthdays with a potluck or pizza. She'd participated in several celebrations so far, dodging inquiries about her own. She was determined that her birthday would remain uncelebrated. She wondered about mentioning it to Oliver. With him, she knew it would go no further.

"The date is bothering me."

"The date?"

"Tim and I share a birthday. Only I haven't celebrated mine since I was sixteen, and I have no plans to start."

"Your—" His face told her he realized exactly what she meant. "Hmm. I can understand why you don't see the day as something to celebrate. Even with the passage of time."

Tess shrugged, now uncomfortable. The last thing she wanted was pity. But as she held his gaze, she saw no pity there, only understanding.

He cleared his throat and changed the subject. "I put the screen back on Tim's window for Eva. . . . Uh . . . Are you thinking foul play?"

"It just struck me as odd, that's all. I have a suspicious nature."

He smiled. "I suppose that's why you're good at your job. But I'm not normally suspicious, and the circumstances with this bother me. Maybe I'm naive, but Tim and drugs aren't two words I would put together."

Tess sat, sipping her coffee, and contemplated for a moment. "If you're right, and the next choice is foul play, then it begs the question: who would want to hurt a kid like Tim?"

He puffed up his cheeks and blew out a breath. "That I can't say. In this day and age, murder doesn't seem to need a specific reason."

"Now you're talking like a cop."

He smiled. "I'll, uh . . . I'll leave you to your day. Mine is busy as well. But if you need something, I'm always available."

She nodded and he left.

5

Tess had developed a simple routine since her hire. It developed out of something she'd done last summer when she was trying to find a killer. Back then, she'd walked the town, talking to shop owners and anyone she thought might have been able to help her solve a homicide. After the killer was caught, Tess thought about the walk-through and decided it would be a good practice to continue. So three days a week, if weather permitted, at random times, she'd leave her office and walk the town, talking to people, stopping in at businesses, being visible. She didn't want the walk to become a rut, hence the random times, and quickly discovered that she liked the interaction. She got to know people and places and felt that it helped her to be a better chief.

After finishing her coffee, she needed fresh air, so Tess went out on her walk. It had been a long winter. Rogue's Hollow had gotten snow, sleet, and everything in between, so the warm sunshine was very welcome. River Drive was busy; the rafting and fishing on the river was ramping up. Tess walked to where the businesses began and then headed down River Drive, a spring in her step and the nightmare a distant memory.

She poked her head into the bookstore, owned by her friend and council member Casey Reno. Casey wasn't there, but Tess said hello to the woman behind the counter before continuing down the street. Hotshot Fishing was busy; she merely nodded to some tourists, not wanting to interrupt the business. After Hotshot, she walked past the station and post office.

Then came the Hollow Grind, which was busy also, though it was long past the morning rush. She continued to the latest new business in town. Pizza and Things had opened after the first of the year, filling a space that had long been vacant. It smelled great and her stomach rumbled. Maybe pizza would be her late lunch.

"Chief!"

Tess turned to see Arthur Goding coming out of the pizza place, sandwich bag in hand. He was a retired postal worker and a great friend to police.

"Arthur, what's up today?"

"Glad I caught you. I've got those ATVs ready to go for you."

"Already?" The man's hobby was repairing and refurbishing off-road machines like ATVs, snowmobiles, and dirt bikes. He'd told Tess over the winter that he had a couple to donate. She'd been thankful; the one off-road vehicle the PD owned had come in handy over the winter, but it had reached the end of its useful life. Thanks to Arthur, next winter they'd be better prepared.

"Yep. It'd help me out if you could come get 'em. I'm heading down south soon for a wedding. I plan on picking up a couple of machines on the way back, so I could use the space."

"Okay, I'll get ahold of Gabe—he's got the trailer—and we'll come get them today. That work?"

"It does." He saluted her with his bag and walked off to his truck. His dog was hanging out the passenger window, tongue lolling.

Cutting her walk short, Tess sent Gabe a text. He indicated he'd go hitch up the trailer and meet her at Arthur's. Gabe's patrol vehicle was a four-wheel-drive pickup with towing capabilities. The ATVs would be stored in a maintenance shed at the end of Midas Drive. They could be used to search trails, if need be, or to get to remote rural properties. They'd had to travel to some out-of-the-way properties to check on a couple of elderly widows during the winter.

Tess headed back to the station to pick up her car, reflecting on the fact that Arthur's property was on Chainsaw Ridge, next to the Hang Ten. Duncan had said two guys from the Hang Ten were at the party. Did that mean they brought more than pot with them? There wasn't enough evidence at this point to search the place or drag any of the employees into the station, but it warranted questioning the men. As much as Tess wanted to visit the place herself, she'd leave it to Jonkey. This was her case right now, and Tess wasn't going to micromanage. She trusted her officers, and she wanted to make sure they knew that.

— — —

As Tess drove up Chainsaw Ridge, the elevation was such that she could look right and see Gaston Haywood's pot grow area, secure behind eight-foot dog-eared redwood fencing. From what Tess had read, outside pot went in the ground the end of April, beginning of May. She couldn't yet see growth from this far away but knew the weed would grow fast. The plants had been huge last October, or Crop-tober as she'd heard some people call it.

Arthur and Haywood had isolated, relatively private pieces of property, with astounding views of the valley and the Rogue River. Identical seven-acre lots on Chainsaw Ridge, they backed up to a narrow canyon that was BLM forest. Arthur's property sat a little higher than Haywood's; he was the only one with easy access to the canyon.

Tess pulled into Arthur's driveway and parked in front of the house next to Bender's truck and trailer, then walked back to where a large metal garage stood. Arthur had the garage built behind his animal pens and barn, specifically for his hobby. The large structure was filled with ATVs, snow-mobiles, and Jet Skis, some operational and some not.

She found Bender and Arthur bent over an ATV partially taken apart. They were talking about repairs, and to Tess it might as well have been a foreign language.

"Hey, Arthur, Gabe, what's going on?"

Both men looked up, Arthur with a smudge of grease obvious on his coffee-brown cheek.

"Chief, just working through a problem with Gabe here." He wiped his hands on dirty coveralls and pointed. "Those are your babies."

She looked in the direction he pointed and saw two ATVs, one a two-seat Kubota with a cargo bed on the back, the other a single-seat QuadRunner.

"Wow," she said as she moved toward them. "These are used? They look brand-new."

"I fixed 'em up and painted them. They're running like new as well." He stepped next to her. "I heard the Harper kid died today."

Tess jerked toward him, almost forgetting how fast news traveled in a small town, especially bad news. She nodded. "Waiting for the coroner to say the how."

He tsked and glanced toward the Hang Ten. "It's 'cause of them, I know it. Not directly maybe, but it's never a good thing when a vice becomes legal."

Tess said nothing because nothing was definitive yet. Drugs were on people's minds because of the opiate deaths in the valley.

Arthur shook his head and pointed to the ATVs. "Why don't you take them for a spin?"

"I've never driven one of these," Tess said as she put a hand on the Kubota and took a closer look. It appeared powerful and well-appointed. The back section would hold a lot of gear.

"Aw, it's just like driving a car." Bender handed her keys

and then walked around and jumped in the passenger seat. "Let's go. We can check out the old logging camp."

Tess climbed behind the wheel. "I've wanted to see that place." Tess had heard about the remains of a logging camp from several people since she'd come to town. She loved learning history and local lore and had read a little about the place, called Midas Camp. The area had been actively logged from the late 1800s to the early 1900s.

"Wow, this is fun!" Tess said as she stepped on the accelerator and shot up the canyon on the peppy ATV.

It was Bender's turn to grin. "Kind of makes you wish we had more calls in the forest." He spoke loudly to be heard over the engine.

It was warm and dry and the vehicle climbed easily.

"The camp is about a mile and a half up the canyon," Bender said.

In a short time Bender pointed out the first structure. Tess pulled up to it and killed the motor. They both climbed out and Gabe gave her a tour. There were five discernible buildings and four piles of graying wood indicating structures that had already been compromised by time and weather. She could make out a discernible pattern, the smaller structures in a semicircle around the large one.

"The large log cabin over closest to the millpond, that was the mess hall. It's in the best shape."

Best was relative, though. While the building he indicated was surprisingly intact, parts of the roof were missing. Of the other four cabins, some roofs looked ready to cave immediately, and all the windows were missing. Tess doubted it would be long before nature recovered all the ground.

"The smaller structures were living quarters?"

"Yeah, and over there by the large pile of wood, if you dug down a bit, you'd find the last remaining railroad tracks. A sawmill used to stand there, and the timber would be taken down the canyon by railcar and sent to the larger mill in the Hollow. You know that the church at one time was a sawmill."

Tess nodded; she'd heard that story.

Bender continued. "Once the area was logged out, they just shut everything down and left it."

Tess looked around at the beautiful forest surrounding them. "Hard to believe that this area was ever logged out."

"Nature comes back quickly, that's for sure."

"Kids don't bother the place?"

"There's been a little vandalism over the years, but it's not easy to get here unless you cross Arthur's property. There are some roundabout ways in if you take the trail at the end of Midas Drive and go south, but it's only hardy hikers that find the route down, and they are inclined to respect it, for the most part."

They wandered around for a bit. Tess noted that a lot of grass was crunched down, so some hikers had obviously found their way up here.

"Let's head back," Tess said.

"Okay if I drive?" Bender asked.

"You bet." Tess hopped in the passenger seat.

Coming down the canyon, Tess had a clear view of the pot farm and saw that Haywood had someone hard at work on fencing in their entire acreage. That cost a pretty penny. She knew he'd gotten a little paranoid since the robbery and really didn't blame him. The fence must be an extension of his security plan.

As Tess and Bender made the turn from the trail onto Arthur's property, they found themselves in the middle of a dispute: Arthur in a heated discussion with Gaston Haywood.

"What do we have here?" Tess asked, half to herself and half to Bender.

"Aw, that Haywood guy thinks Arthur is spying on him when he rides his ATVs up the canyon," Bender said. "He gets all fired up because of the robbery. Probably thought we were doing a little spying."

"What?" Tess gave a laugh of disbelief. "What possible reason would Arthur have to spy on him?"

Bender shrugged. "Who knows what goes through a pot grower's mind."

Tess had to admit, from the lip of the canyon, she could clearly see Haywood's home and the two travel trailers he kept on it, not to mention the fenced-in pot grow area and the large greenhouse. It'd be easy to spy if Arthur wanted to. And Haywood's agitation brought up the thought she'd had earlier: What if the fentanyl and opiates plaguing the valley were coming from the Hang Ten and that's what he had to hide?

Bender pulled the ATV close to the two men and Tess could hear the argument. She worked hard to listen and not take sides until she heard both perspectives.

Arthur was a genial man and good friends with several of her officers. Tess knew him as well as she knew anyone in her new town. He was generally well thought of and always involved if something called for volunteers. It was highly unusual to see him get upset.

Gaston Haywood looked every inch a Southern California surfer, with his blond, nearly white hair, washed-out blue eyes, baggy board shorts, Vans sneakers, and a La Jolla sweatshirt. He'd moved from California to Oregon specifically to grow and sell recreational pot. Tess had heard that after she'd recovered the loot taken from the Hang Ten, he'd marched next door to Arthur and offered to buy his "piece of junk home" for cash outright. That served to widen the chasm between the neighbors, something that was already Grand Canyon–size.

At least today, Haywood was not wearing a sidearm.

"I don't want your people crossing my property to go up the canyon. If you were neighborly, I might not mind, but you're not neighborly," Arthur was saying as he shook his head.

"The canyon is public property. If you can go up it, so can we."

"Not on my land. Go around."

"You're not going to tell me what I can or can't do. I don't appreciate you spying on me." Haywood was red-faced.

"Why would I spy on a bunch of lowlifes?" Arthur was calm and matter-of-fact.

"Okay, okay." Tess raised her hands as she walked toward the men.

She had read reports written by her officers who had mediated several disputes between these two. She knew that when Arthur refused to sell his property, Haywood had begun a harassment schedule, playing his music loud, speakers directed toward Arthur's home.

Arthur was not amused and took to letting his dog defecate on Haywood's property, and a feud was begun. Tess wondered when they'd get to the respective restraining order stage.

"Chief, I'm more than willing to let bygones be bygones, but this kid, he's ruining my quality of life. He plays that stuff they call music so loud I'm afraid my ears will bleed. He puts a notice in my mailbox every day telling me to sell. I ain't selling. He won't back off."

"'Cause I'm tired of stepping in dog poop! Old man, you got one foot in the grave. My business is growing and you're fading. I'm looking to take on a partner. I want to expand. Sell me your house and move into one of those assisted-living places."

"Enough!" Tess stepped in before Arthur could respond. "Mr. Haywood, Arthur is not going to sell; stop asking. And he's not spying on you. Keep your music down. I can issue citations for that."

Haywood rolled his eyes in disdain and Tess added, "Believe me, the fines will add up." Turning back to Goding, she said, "Arthur, keep your dog on a leash or in your yard; that is also a citable offense. Let's all behave like adults."

"Figures. You're taking his side," Haywood said. "Just remember, Chief, my taxes pay your salary, and I put a lot more money into this community than this dried-up old man." Haywood harrumphed like a spoiled brat and stormed away, back toward his home.

Tess watched him go. That was the first time she'd heard the "I pay your salary" rant since she'd come to Rogue's Hollow. Different state, same bluster.

"Chief, I'll do my best to get along," Arthur said, shaking his head. "But that kid is a pain in my neck."

"Arthur, I can't go there unless there's evidence of a crime."

"I trust you. But like I said, me and my dog are leaving soon to head south for a nephew's wedding. Be gone a few weeks. Kind of worried about the place. Don't want to come home and find a nasty surprise."

"We'll keep an eye on your home."

"Appreciate that. I have a neighbor kid coming over to feed my livestock. All I can do is hope that Haywood doesn't offer him more money than I got to do some mischief." Arthur held out his hand and she shook it. "I'll try to stop being a nuisance. But can't say I'll be supporting cannabis anytime soon." A pensive look crossed his face. "On a more positive note, how do you like the vehicles?"

"Love them. Thanks again. Both vehicles will be a welcome addition to the PD."

"Let's get them loaded on my trailer," Gabe said.

Tess drove the Kubota and Gabe the single up onto the trailer. As she watched them tie the vehicles down, she considered the dispute they'd just mediated. She knew Arthur had a legitimate beef with Haywood over the music and the pressure tactics—not to mention the man's obnoxious personality—but Haywood wasn't breaking any serious law that she could see. The whole situation was a mutual combat, mutual nuisance type of deal.

Why was he so bothered by Arthur's forays into the canyon? Was it the robbery or something more? Was something else not kosher going on at the farm?

But the biggest question on her mind at the moment— did the activities at the Hang Ten have anything at all to do with Tim Harper's death?

6

Saturday afternoon, Oliver sat in his office and listened to Drake Harper pour out his grief over the loss of his only son. Drake made it home sixteen hours after his son's lifeless body had been removed from the house by the coroner.

"I can't believe this is happening." He closed his eyes and rubbed his chin, fatigue and grief seeming to crush the strong man who'd been serving in the Army for twenty years now. "I raised Tim better than that. Drugs?" He cursed and stood to pace.

"That's a preliminary finding."

"It makes no sense." He threw his hands up in frustration. "The chief said she found paraphernalia? Someone planted it. Tim would not do drugs. I need to get to the bottom of this."

"I agree with you—this is senseless. But I trust the chief to work it out."

"She's already made her mind up. Tim's dead and she's going to take his reputation away by saying he was a drug addict."

"No, I don't believe that. Chief O'Rourke only wants the truth. She herself said the coroner's report would tell us what happened."

Drake sat back down, tears evident. "Tim was a good kid, Pastor Mac. A good kid. Why? Why?"

Oliver got up and sat next to the broken man, placing a supportive hand on his shoulder while he cried. His own chest tightened. He'd asked that question a million times. It was the question he heard most often from hurting people . . . and the question God was least likely to answer.

- - -

Bryce Evergreen hurried and finished up the list of things his employer had asked him to do. Yesterday his boss had had a run-in with the local PD at the neighbor's, and fearing that if there were some problem with the cops, his afternoon off would be canceled, Bryce did everything as quickly as he could. The running feud between his boss and the neighbor was no secret, and Bryce bet the cops' presence up there the day before had set his paranoid boss off.

All Bryce wanted to concentrate on was seeing Tilly. He washed up and changed his clothes to head into town. All he had to wear was either a beat-up pair of jeans or a not-so-beat-up pair of jeans, so the not-so-beat-up pair would have to do. He brushed them off as best he could. His boots were the newest things he owned, and he stomped the mud and gunk off and did his best to spruce them up. He'd just been paid, so he had the means today to take Tilly to dinner before she had to go to work.

He checked his watch. If he hurried. It was at least a twenty-five-minute walk to the inn. He needed to get going. Bryce grabbed a cap, set it on his head, left his trailer, and walked down the driveway toward the gate. He heard a car start up behind him and moved to the side so the car could get by. But it didn't go by; it slowed when it reached him.

"Hey, Evergreen, want a lift?" It was Don Cherry, another employee at the farm, although what he did, Bryce didn't really know. He was a big man, an ex-con, and he gave Bryce the creeps. He'd nicknamed him "the Hulk."

Even though he wanted to hurry, Bryce said, "Nah, I don't mind walking."

Cherry stopped the car. "Get in."

Bryce stopped. The Hulk was still smiling, but his tone told Bryce it wasn't a request. He opened the door and got in the passenger seat.

"Where're you headed?" Cherry asked after clearing the gate at the end of the driveway.

"The inn."

"To see that girl?"

Bryce flinched and shot Cherry a glance, not at all sure he wanted the guys he worked with to know about Tilly. The Hulk was grinning. Or at least Bryce thought it was a grin.

"Secret's safe with me, dude. I saw the two of you go to church last Sunday. I figured you're close."

"She's a friend. We grew up together."

"That's cool. I didn't really want to talk about her. I was wondering about the church."

"The church?" Bryce's eyes narrowed. Was the Hulk going to tease him about going to church?

"Yeah. I went to chapel in the joint."

His tone was matter-of-fact, not mocking, and Bryce relaxed.

The big man continued. "That holy stuff helped me get early parole for good behavior. I just wonder if the local padre is as good as the jail padre was."

Bryce cleared his throat. "Pastor Mac is a good guy. I, uh . . . like him a lot."

"Hmm. Might give the place a try." He came to a stop across from the inn, and Bryce hopped out, still nonplussed by the odd conversation. Up to that point, Cherry hadn't spoken more than three words to him.

"Thanks for the ride."

"No problem," Cherry said, then continued down the street.

- - -

Saturday night, Oliver got home for dinner a little after six. He felt drained after his interaction with Drake. The man's grief hit like a blast of air from a furnace, blazing hot. In the best of times, he never really looked forward to eating alone but decided a while ago that he needed to get used to it. And today for the first time since Anna's death, he came home happy that she wasn't there. The murder of Tim Harper would have broken her heart.

There was still no pressing need for him to learn to cook,

however; even after a year, the meals ministry saw to it that he would never go hungry. Tonight he was looking forward to heating up some homemade enchiladas. One of the women in the church made some great hot sauce, and he was thinking about that when he stepped up on the porch.

He went to open the door—he never locked it—and for some reason the hair on the back of his neck stood up. He turned to his right. Someone was on the porch, in the shadows.

Suddenly fearful, Oliver stepped back from the door. "Who's there?"

A large man moved to where Oliver could see him. Oliver almost relaxed. He knew of the man, had heard people talking about a big scary guy who worked at the pot farm on Chainsaw Ridge, but he'd never met him. What made the apprehension linger was that he'd also heard the term *ex-con* in relation to the man. Why was he hiding in the shadows?

"Evening, padre," he said as he stepped forward, holding out his hand. "Name's Don. Do you have a minute?"

Oliver appraised the man for a few seconds, working to relax completely. He shook the offered hand, and his own was engulfed by Don's large, rough mitt and firm handshake. Don let go and held Oliver's gaze. Oliver couldn't read him, but there was no malice obvious. He thought about telling Don he usually counseled at the church and stopped. Why was he a pastor if not to reach the lost? And from what he'd heard, Don Cherry was lost.

"Hello, Don, nice to meet you. I was just going inside to heat up my dinner. Care to join me?"

The big man looked Oliver up and down and then looked away. "You aren't afraid of me?"

"Should I be?"

"No." He rubbed his chin. "But if I come in, can we keep this to ourselves? Don't you have to be quiet about anything we talk about?"

"I'm not a priest, so this isn't a confessional, but if you want to keep our conversation confidential, I can do that. Unless you tell me something I'm required to tell the police, like you're planning to hurt someone or yourself."

He grinned, a gold tooth on the far right side of his mouth showing. "Nothing like that, padre. Nothing like that. My coworkers just won't understand you and me conversing."

Oliver moved forward and opened his door. "Then come on in. I hope you like enchiladas."

7

Tim's death occupied the weekend for Tess, though technically she was off. After speaking to Drake Harper, which was difficult, she kept track of the investigation as Bender and Jonkey worked to find and talk to everyone who was at the party. Nothing surprising or damning came from any of the interviews. The only mystery was one older guy everyone saw there, but no one knew his name. And they had no luck contacting Coach Whitman. Tess tried to shelve her unease about the case because of the upcoming raid. She wanted to be all in for that.

At 1:30 a.m. Monday, Tess shifted gears and picked Gabe up at the station and began the drive to Yreka. This bust was something she'd been looking forward to since she arrested Roger Marshall last year and found out he was a pipeline for illegal drugs. Two weeks ago, DEA Agent Marcus Ledge had told her that they were getting close to Marshall's supplier.

"We had a breakthrough. A snitch came through with some good information. We took down a drug house in Rio Linda. More information came from those we arrested. Now we have two more targets to hit up your way, in Yreka, California. We think it's the heartbeat of the operation, at least in the northern part of the state."

For Tess, it was great news for two reasons: first, it tied up loose ends regarding Roger Marshall's arrest, and second, too many people were dying because of illegal drugs. She wanted to stop whatever she could.

"Opiates seem to be everywhere lately," Ledge noted. *"The group we're taking down is tied to the Mexican mafia and was probably supplying Marshall. The cartels shifted to fentanyl production a few years back. It's cheap to produce and gets them more bang for their buck. One gram of pure fentanyl will make a hundred grams of fake heroin. I've got people in Yreka getting things ready for an early morning warrant service."*

He'd initially said they would hit the homes in the middle of the week but moved it up two days to Monday.

"Just a gut feeling," he'd said. *"Something tells me that we need to move faster. Can you move it up and still join us?"*

"You bet." She carefully took notes as Ledge outlined the operation.

Now, as she remembered the call, she wondered if they could really stop the illegal drug flow and save kids like Tim. This was one dragon Tess really wanted to slay.

— — —

"Wow, look at these guys," Gabe Bender said as Tess pulled into the parking lot where the DEA's takedown teams were staging. "They look as if they're going to war."

Tess nodded as she took in the scene herself. DEA entry teams were suiting up, readying weapons, and completing last-minute equipment checks. You couldn't be too careful when dealing with drug dealers in general and the Mexican mafia in particular. The sight was welcome and familiar to Tess; she'd been involved in many such high-profile operations with Long Beach PD. This was a first for Gabe. They were here because after Marshall's arrest, both Gabe and Tess put in a lot of hours working out the drug trafficking operation Marshall had been involved in. Some of their investigation helped the DEA get to the search warrant stage.

The early morning search warrant strategy was to capitalize on surprise and overwhelming force to avoid resistance that would be a danger to officers as well as suspects. Tess had seen the confusion generated after a couple of flashbang grenades went off; they typically paralyzed people and allowed for their safe apprehension.

"We are going to war," she said as she parked the car. "I, for one, want to win it."

"Won't argue with that."

They found Agent Ledge at the communications vehicle, studying a couple of maps. Next to the maps were wanted flyers with photos of the targets, a handful of men they'd discerned were heading up the drug operation. Tess had the posters up on the wall in her office. One had no photo because they only had a possible name but no positive ID. José Garcia was the name that popped up most often. While that was the equivalent of a Mexican John Smith, Ledge was fairly certain it was correct. Garcia was slippery, the subject of rumors and tall tales. He went by the moniker "Fantasma," or "Ghost" in Spanish. He was short. Some descriptions gave him a jagged scar on one side of his face; others just called him scary-looking. They got a little more information on him every time someone in his crew was arrested.

Tess knew that arresting these most wanted individuals wouldn't end the drug trade completely, but it would plug some big holes.

The communications vehicle was set up like a compact comm center, complete with computers and TV monitors and a dispatcher to help with the raid. The police action would be carried on an off channel. Most bad guys now had scanners or apps that monitored police activity. Tess knew Ledge and his team would take every precaution to prevent the targets from being tipped off.

"Ah, Chief O'Rourke, Officer Bender, glad to see you made it." Ledge extended his hand and Tess shook it. "We're buttoning everything down now."

Tess liked Marcus Ledge. The man was about as thick as he was tall and all solid muscle. His voice was a combination of Bruce Willis's and Clint Eastwood's. He was easy to work with and very good at what he did.

"Any questions?"

"Just one." Tess pointed to the map. "At house number one, that field behind it—it's lumpy. What's under the lumps?"

He grinned. "You studied the intel I sent—"

"It's a dirt bike course, that's all," a different voice interrupted Ledge.

Tess turned to see Ledge's partner, Sal Hemmings, approach. Unlike his partner, Hemmings was not personable, he did not play well with others, and Tess didn't care for him. As usual, his cheek bulged with sunflower seeds, which he saw fit to spit anywhere and everywhere. Tess had worked with guys who smoked and guys who chewed tobacco, but none of them were as annoying as Hemmings was with his seeds.

The field still bothered her and she wasn't going to drop it. "We're dealing with people who like to dig tunnels. Is it possible the lumps are hiding something?" Tess knew they'd found tunnels in Rio Linda.

"You questioning my expertise?" Hemmings was tall and lanky, easily six-three to Tess's five-foot-six-inch frame, so it was natural for him to look down at her. He spit seeds out the right side of his mouth as he did so.

"I'm making an observation." She held his gaze, ignoring the seeds and refusing to back off.

He looked away first. "I was against you even being here. Like pretend cops from a Podunk town are going to be any help," he mumbled as he stomped away.

"Ignore him; he's grumpy. He didn't want to move up the raid." Ledge gave a wave of his hand. "You and Bender follow me. I'll put you in the field as part of the perimeter team—that work for you?"

Tess glanced at Bender, who nodded. "It does."

"Then saddle up; we're ready to go."

— — —

Excitement mixed with apprehension once Tess and Bender were in place behind the main target address. Ledge and Hemmings were part of the entry team. If she couldn't breach the door and storm the inside with them, Tess was glad she was in a position to keep an eye on the lumpy lot. Even if it was like being the grunt waiting for the coroner.

Despite everyone's assumption that this field was simply a dirt bike course, Tess was on edge. The last search warrant she'd served was on a property in Rogue's Hollow where they'd found a hidden man cave. Suppose these guys had a tunnel into the field?

They wouldn't get far, she thought, unless . . . What if they had resources hidden? Maybe distance wasn't the plan but damage to law enforcement personnel was. Tess played out a lot of scenarios in her mind as her eyesight adjusted to the darkness.

She and Bender were parked at the rear northwest corner of the house. Their windows were down, and though it was cool, she could feel the sweat beneath her vest. It was warmer here than it had been in the Hollow. Ledge gave the call to move, and a few seconds after that she heard his voice, though distant, shatter the early morning quiet.

"Police! We have a warrant!"

She looked over at Bender as they listened to what sounded like the splintering of a door under the force of a battering ram and a cacophony of loud voices.

The entry team would move in and secure all the occupants, clear every room. She didn't realize how tense she was until she heard muffled gunshots ring out—*tap-tap-tap*—and she jumped.

She reached over and turned up the radio, hoping she didn't hear an officer down call. All the while her eyes scanned the dark field. They could still hear audible law enforcement orders and the sounds of glass breaking. Was that more gunfire?

"Suspect down. We need medics," someone said after what seemed an eternity.

"Are you code 4?" dispatch asked.

Tess didn't hear the answer. Bender tapped her arm and pointed. "There, I saw movement!"

She clicked on her spotlight and her heart leapt into her throat as at the end of her light's glow, in the middle of the field, a head popped up out of the dirt.

Tess cranked the ignition and pressed the accelerator hard as she keyed her radio. "Edward-1, suspect fleeing in the back field. In pursuit!"

Teeth jarred as the SUV roared over the lumps. The head became a fleeing figure, who turned their way, and a gun glinted in the headlights. All she could do was hit the siren, hope the lights blinded him, and step on the gas. His muzzle flashed and the windshield spiderwebbed. Tess ducked on reflex.

"You okay?" she asked Bender.

"Fine!"

He fired again, but the shot must have gone wild; there was no impact. The suspect jerked right toward more lumps, and Tess moved to cut him off, accelerating. She went airborne over one large bump, fear biting when she realized that she had no control and might accidentally run the guy over.

"Hang on!" She braced herself for impact. When the SUV hit the ground, the seat belt tightened and snapped her back into the seat, she bit her lip and tasted blood, and though the air bag didn't deploy, the impact disoriented her for a moment. At the same time, she felt something snap under her and then a thud against her right fender.

The SUV jerked to a stop, dead and listing, and Tess blinked back to orientation. Bender groaned but he was moving.

She unsnapped the belt and bailed out the door, drawing her weapon and flashlight at the same time. She stumbled to a knee and dropped her gun. Rising quickly with only her light, breath coming hard and fast, she directed the beam to the right side of the leaning vehicle. A figure was there, on the ground. She guessed he'd run right into the passenger-side front fender.

There was no time to look away and find her weapon. He was moving, pushing himself to his knees. She glimpsed a gun on the ground in front of him, visible in the dusty glare of her headlights.

"Freeze! Police!" she bluffed, shining her powerful flashlight in his eyes.

The man squinted and lurched toward the gun, and so did Tess. As his hand grasped the grip, her booted foot came down on his wrist.

He screamed and cursed, yanking the hand back without the gun. He then lunged at her, grabbing her around the knees, lifting and dropping her hard against a mound of packed dirt. Her breath fled, and she brought her hands up to protect herself from further attack.

The man released her legs and reared back. Her raised hand partially blocked the backhand he sent toward her face, but it still glanced across her jaw and she grimaced in pain. He cursed in Spanish and leaped away from her—he was going for his gun.

Tess fought disorientation in the dusty, dry air, wondering where Bender was. Pushing herself up, she grabbed her Taser and shifted left as the suspect turned toward her with the gun in hand.

Tess aimed and pulled the Taser trigger, the fishhook barbs glinting in the murky light as they impacted the suspect in the chest and abdomen at the same time he fired the gun.

8

The Taser did its job. The electrical current caused a complete neuromuscular lockup, and the suspect went down, dropping like a tree. Vaguely aware of a sharp pain in her shoulder, Tess moved forward, knowing she had only a couple of minutes to restrain the guy.

Just then Bender appeared at her shoulder, face bloody. "Sorry it took me so long," he said in a nasal tone. "I couldn't get out my side of the car, had to climb over."

Together they handcuffed the suspect and secured his weapon. Breathing as hard as if she'd just sprinted fifty yards, Tess stepped back and studied her officer's bloody face. "Are you sure you're okay?"

He wiped his face with the back of his hand. "That'll teach me to not fasten my seat belt. Think my nose is broke." He pointed to the radio. "They're calling you."

The suspect's body began to relax from the muscle-tightening shock, and Bender turned his attention to him.

Tess stepped back and retrieved her own weapon about the time the guy snapped out of the stun and exploded in a string of Spanish curses.

Tess grabbed her radio, swallowed, and took a deep breath before pressing the button. They were asking for Edward-1.

"Code 4 in the field, one in custody. He popped out of an escape hatch under one of the lumps." She was ready to relax, counting her lucky stars and content with the victory, until DEA Agent Hemmings came roaring out of the waning darkness, face contorted with anger.

"Just what in the devil do you think you're doing?"

"What do you mean? Ledge asked us to watch the field. I saw this guy pop up and went after him."

Hemmings looked as if he might explode. A vein pulsed in his forehead. "Why didn't you notify dispatch?"

"I did. I told them we were in pursuit." Tess was perplexed as to why he was so angry.

"You're reckless!" He threw his hands up. "Look what you did to your own officer!" He blustered for a few more minutes and then stormed away.

Tess turned to Bender, who shrugged. He'd wiped the blood from his nose, but Tess could see it was beginning to swell. He'd have two shiners as well.

"Don't worry about me. Maybe we stole his thunder?" he suggested.

Tess watched Hemmings leave. "Maybe." She'd obviously accidentally stepped on his macho in some way. "Forget him—do you need to see a medic?"

"I'll be fine. What about you?" He pointed.

Tess looked and saw blood running down her arm from under the short-sleeved shirt. "Huh?" She pulled at the sleeve and saw the tear in her shoulder patch and the crease in her arm. "He must have grazed me." She looked over at the suspect.

He grinned. "Next time I'll kill you."

"You have the right to remain silent; exercise it," Bender said.

The man spit on the ground next to Bender's boot, then said, "Lawyer," and turned away.

Tess saw Ledge coming their way. He passed Hemmings and they shared a brief, heated exchange that she couldn't quite make out. Ledge continued toward them.

She leaned against her listing SUV, wondering what Ledge could possibly add to the tirade of his partner. She thought Hemmings was a hothead, but Ledge was a good, solid investigator.

"Well, well," Ledge said as he looked their suspect over, "you caught a big fish."

"What?" Tess frowned and looked closer at the dirty, sweaty man. Recognition dawned as she remembered him from the wanted posters. This was Javier Alexander, aka Shorty, a member of La Eme. He'd added quite a few more tattoos; they snaked up the side of his neck to his jawline.

"You'll be in jail for a good long time, Mr. Alexander. Doubt there will ever be a next time between you and me."

The man gave her a vintage hate stare and said nothing. Tess returned her attention to Ledge.

The agent folded his arms and sighed. "Sal will get over his miff. I knew you had brass, Chief. That's why I asked you along." He smiled but it faded. "You two okay?"

"Just a little banged up, along with our vehicle."

"I see that."

"Think the axle is broken," Bender said.

"Think Forest can fix it?" Tess asked.

"Forest can fix anything."

Ledge chuckled at that and radioed for a vehicle to come get the arrestee. "Good work anyway." He jabbed a thumb toward Alexander. "We found his escape hatch in the basement. Also found a map of the field. Care to guess what he was running to?"

She shook her head.

"Under a lump out here is a hidden motorcycle and a bunch of guns and explosives. It wouldn't have been pretty if he'd gotten there. There might have been pipe bombs flying and lots of casualties. As soon as it's light, we'll get a backhoe out there. I wish the rest of the raid had been successful."

"What happened? Who got hurt? I heard the shots and the medical call."

"No good guys are down. One of the worker bees got off a couple of rounds before he went down. He was probably trying to slow us up to let your hombre get away. He's circling the drain right now. There was some other incidental physical resistance." He shrugged, fatigue and disappointment showing. "But it appears as if they were tipped off. The guys we caught were cleaning out the last of what was probably a big operation. From the intel we had, there should have been more people here and more product. Ditto at the other locale. If we'd come in later in the week like we originally planned, everything would have been gone. Hemmings had to eat crow over that as well as what was in the field."

"Is there enough to make sure everyone involved goes away for a long time?"

"Yes, but the big guy is in the wind. He earned the name Fantasma today." Ledge's face scrunched in disgust.

"He's not superhuman, just good at staying off the radar," Tess said.

"Yep, and it's frustrating after all these months."

A DEA vehicle came bouncing across the field, and Bender stood Alexander up and secured him in the backseat.

"Come on, let's get your guy booked and order a hook for your vehicle. Sal will calm down. His ego is bruised that he was so far off the mark about this field. And we may not have cut off the head of the serpent today, but his day will come."

9

The full light of day revealed that Tess's vehicle had indeed broken an axle.

"I called Forest," Bender said as he and Tess surveyed all the damage to their vehicle. "He's sending one of his tow trucks down here to get us." Forest owned Wild Automotive in Rogue's Hollow and was a wizard with mechanical things.

"Great," Tess said, happy that they'd be able to stick around and see the DEA dig up everything hidden in the field.

Search of the residence complete, they'd learned the full extent of the raid, and sadly, Ledge was right—the bad guys must have been tipped. There was some fentanyl residue, some pot, and some heroin, but not the huge quantities the

DEA expected from a major hub. Also, there were indications that machinery used to manufacture pills had been recently removed.

"They relocated someplace else," Ledge said. "And we'll have to develop the intel to find that place as well."

"We always seem to be playing catch-up," Tess said.

Hemmings stayed in his funk, but the sunflower seeds were back with a vengeance. He was across the field, talking with another officer near the large lump concealing the escape hatch. Bender sat with an ice pack on his nose. Tess saw him keeping one eye on Hemmings.

After a minute, Bender faced her, lifted the ice pack, a grin playing on his lips. "How is it that the chief of a Podunk PD in Oregon outcopped the vaunted DEA? Hemmings was certain the field was nothing more than a dirt bike track. You proved him dead wrong. Kind of makes me proud."

Tess laughed. "Never underestimate a small-town PD."

Bender replaced the pack of ice on his nose and leaned back in a chair an agent had brought for him. She herself sported a bandage for the crease in her upper arm. It almost required stitches, but luckily Steri-Strips worked. Tess considered the wound par for the course, and she was glad at what she and Bender had accomplished today. In fact, she was proud of all her people and her PD. She'd stack them up against any agency.

— — —

LONG BEACH, CALIFORNIA

Hector Connor-Ruiz took a seat at the bar and ordered a Bloody Mary. He'd partied way too much the night before because the booze was free, and now his head was pounding.

Thankfully, the sound on the TV behind the bar was muted and he had some space to himself. His drink came, and he nursed it as he watched the screen, occasionally reading the closed-captioning. Nothing seemed to keep his mind off his problems. He'd just received a thirty-day notice from his landlord to quit, and all his freelance contacts had dried up.

Hector specialized in sensationalizing police brutality and found that there really wasn't a lot of work when the police decided not to be brutal. At least that was what he tried to explain to the landlord when he begged for more time. The jerk was not sympathetic.

Just then the words *police*, *raid*, and *dead* caught his eye.

"Hey, turn the sound on." He waved to the bartender, eyes now intent on the screen.

"How about please," the guy said.

Hector ignored him because he turned the sound up anyway.

"*We're awaiting a briefing by the DEA agent in charge. But to repeat, three search warrants were served here in the small town of Yreka, California. Agents were looking for opiates and a drug operation with a connection to the Mexican mafia. What we know so far is that one person was killed by DEA gunfire. What is notable about this raid is that a former Long Beach police officer took part. Viewers will remember Tess O'Rourke and the shooting she . . .*"

Hector stopped hearing as his pulse began to pound and he saw red. He remembered the shooting, and of course he remembered Tess O'Rourke.

That woman was responsible for all of his bad luck. Maybe it would change if she were involved in another shooting.

Then people would see that he was right all along—Tess O'Rourke should be in jail, not working as a cop.

Headache forgotten, Hector felt infused with new energy. He'd failed to get her fired last year, but maybe he'd get another shot. And maybe this time she'd go to jail.

- - -

Tess and Bender were not able to leave right away, even after Forest's flatbed had loaded her sad-looking SUV onto its bed. Because of the officer-involved shooting, reporters descended on the location with a vengeance. Especially since the person who'd been shot had died, and it was discovered that he was only seventeen.

Geraldo Herrera had gotten off four rounds from an assault rifle before law enforcement gunfire took him down.

True to form, the news media was calling him a "teen victim"—never mind that he'd had enough guns and ammo at his disposal to kill every law enforcement officer who'd served the warrant. Annoyingly, Tess found herself the center of attention at first.

One reporter called out a question before the press conference had even began. "Chief O'Rourke, did the fact that your last job ended because of a shooting keep you from firing your weapon today?"

"The Taser was all that was called for today," Tess said, not wanting to talk about dropping her weapon.

A bunch of questions came her way after that and she did her best to explain what had happened in the field. Several photographs were snapped, and it got Hemmings's nose out of joint.

"People, people, people, Agent Ledge will begin the conference shortly. He is the agent in charge." He shot Tess a glare and she hiked a shoulder. "Chief O'Rourke simply assisted here, that's all," he said with a wave of his hand.

Tess turned to Ledge. "I'm sorry, Agent Ledge. This is your rodeo. I don't want to take the spotlight."

He grinned, not bothered at all like Hemmings was. "I knew I was taking on a celebrity when I asked you along. Just hang out for this circus, answer specific questions about today if you want. If they get overzealous, I'll redirect them."

Tess smiled and nodded.

Tess and Bender stood in the background while Ledge ran the press conference. Even after the field was dug up, for all the resources involved, it was a disappointing outcome. The agency was, however, playing up the raid as a huge success, exaggerating a bit here and there in a psychological warfare kind of way. When another agent showed up with pictures of some of the contraband they'd recovered from the houses they had raided, the media lost interest in Tess. The photo spread of weapons and drugs confiscated, though minimal, helped to calm some of the outrage over a dead teen drug dealer.

There was bomb-making material, several assault rifles, and fentanyl. But the agency had expected a lot more. Even in personnel, they arrested only six people. Alexander was the only one on their most wanted list; the others were low-level workers without serious police records. But when the floor was opened for questions, the first reporter was not interested in the topic of drugs.

"How is it that Chief O'Rourke was involved in this operation? She has no jurisdiction in this state anymore."

"Chief O'Rourke was instrumental in developing the intelligence that led us here. As you may recall, she arrested the person running things in Oregon last year. We couldn't have gotten to this point without her. And where we are today is at the conclusion of a successful, multiagency drug interdiction operation."

That was it. Ledge, true to his word, redirected the reporters, and the focus returned to what they'd done today, not what had happened in Tess's past.

"This is our outstanding suspect." Ledge pointed to a sketch of Fantasma. "I asked an artist to draw something up with everything we've discovered about the guy to this point. Someone in the viewing audience knows this guy. There's reward money for information leading to his arrest."

Tess studied the rendering. He came off as sinister and dangerous. He was smart, though; Tess knew that. He'd been running a criminal drug cartel for too long to be stupid.

"We're asking for the public's help and we're setting up a tip line. José Garcia should be considered armed and dangerous. Take caution and call police if you see him."

Tess wanted to be the one to take him into custody. She wanted to be the one to close the book for good on the bad actor but doubted he'd ever show his face in the Hollow.

10

Oliver looked at the calendar and a profound sadness enveloped him. It had been nearly a year since Anna's death, and he was running out of firsts without her—first Thanksgiving and Christmas, first birthdays, first wedding anniversary . . . The realization hit like a punch. He filled his coffee cup, then went to his study and sat at his desk to steady himself and let the sorrow volcano run its course. A deep sense of loss hit him occasionally but had lessened with time. This one was strong. Tim's death had stirred up memories and stoked a fire causing him to feel Anna's death all the more completely at the moment. It was always tempered by the knowledge that she was whole and happy in heaven, but he missed her deeply.

He thought of Tess, losing her father on her birthday and now being unable to celebrate the day because the two events would forever be connected. Anna had barely gotten to know Tess, but she'd liked the new chief and believed she'd be a good fit for Rogue's Hollow. As usual, Anna was spot-on. Tess had fit in and Oliver was glad she was here. He felt a connection with the woman; in a short time they had gone through a lot together. He knew that she understood his loss, but he wished she had the same peace that his faith gave him when the loss weighed down like an anchor.

He believed that was the problem the other day, on her birthday—the loss was smothering her, after all these years, because she'd never really come to terms with it. He hated the word *closure* because there never really was closure for such a profound loss, the wound was forever. But he knew personally that there was hope, the hope of heaven and eventual restoration. Tess couldn't move on because she didn't have the same hope he did. Oliver wondered how he could help her.

A glance at the clock reminded him that she was in Yreka, helping the DEA. He prayed all would go well with the operation. And then he prayed for Tess, that somehow he'd find a way to help her find peace with the loss of her father and maybe, one day, be able to celebrate the day of her birth for only that.

— — —

Tess and Gabe got back into town late Monday night. Her disabled unit was dropped off at Forest's repair shop and Tess took the keys for Gabe's truck. She doubted that Gabe would be able to work for a while. After filling out all the associated injury-on-duty paperwork, she talked him into letting his wife take him to the emergency room for his nose. Despite putting ice on it right away, it was swollen and he was having trouble breathing. His wife texted a while later that surgery was scheduled for sometime Tuesday, but it was expected to be routine and easy.

Tess got a few hours' sleep and made it to the station on time and had to right away deal with Bender's absence. It was going to take some schedule juggling.

She was in the midst of plugging holes in coverage when she realized that she hadn't heard anything from the coroner about Tim Harper.

Sitting back at her desk, she wondered if she should call. True, it had only been a couple of days, but things generally moved faster here than in Long Beach because there wasn't the same volume of bodies making their way to the coroner's office. There, an autopsy for someone like Tim, with no glaring signs of foul play, could take a couple of weeks.

She called and the coroner spoke to her himself.

"Sorry, Chief; there are some anomalies here. Hate to be mysterious, but I'm not making a determination until I'm certain. I've asked the coroner up in Multnomah County to consult. I promise to get back to you ASAP."

He would say no more, and Tess was left to ponder the word *anomalies*.

11

"I hate cops." Hector Connor-Ruiz slammed the newspaper down on the table, spilling his coffee and garnering him dirty looks from several coffee shop patrons. He glared back and they returned to their coffees. He'd bought the paper specifically to see if there was an article about the news report he'd seen the day before. He found the article on the front page, and it turned his stomach and killed his appetite. O'Rourke hadn't been the shooter. And to make matters worse, *she was being lauded.*

He got up, discarded his unfinished coffee with the paper in the trash, and left the shop. He'd been in a bad mood before he'd stopped for coffee, and now, after reading the

paper and seeing the one person he hated more than anyone else in the world being applauded, his mood was worse
than ever.

He climbed into his car and turned on the scanner, feeling somewhat better when he heard there was a traffic stop
happening around the corner. Hector stepped on it, pulling
away from the curb and cutting someone off and ignoring
the honk. He made a turn and saw the patrol car half a block
ahead of him on the other side of the street. He pulled over
and parked as soon as he was able, then bolted from his car,
spitting on the ground as he did, hurrying to get in position
to film the traffic stop. Quickly pressing the right buttons on
his phone, he started a livestream on Facebook, hoping a lot
of followers would tune in.

He held his phone up as he crossed the street and came in
behind the patrol car, working his way up to the car the two
officers had stopped. Whenever he happened upon police
activity, he filmed, and when filming, he always provided his
own unique commentary.

"Hello, fellow justice warriors. Hector here, live and
ready to stop injustice. Not sure what these fascists pulled
this innocent citizen over for, but we'll make sure it's all on
the up-and-up."

One officer cast a glance his way before talking to the
driver; the other kept his gaze trained on Hector, who showed
him a rude hand signal and kept talking to his phone.

"The pigs have seen me and are watching me. I'm exercising my free speech rights."

To the cops he said, "This is a public place and you two
are public servants. I have every right to be here." Then he

continued his narrative. "These two pigs have nothing better to do than harass people."

The cop on the passenger side of the car stepped toward Hector and held up his hand. "I'm asking you not to interfere, sir."

"And I'm asking you not to be a fascist. Why are you harassing this poor man? Because he's black?"

"That's not your concern, sir."

"It's everyone's concern!" Hector moved toward the passenger window. "Are you okay, citizen? Do you need my help?"

The officer stepped between Hector and the car. "You're interfering with the performance of our duty. Step back or you will be subject to arrest or citation."

Something snapped in Hector. He'd had a bad couple of months. Traffic had dropped off precipitously from his blog, he'd run up an enormous amount of debt running for mayor—a contest he lost soundly—money from outside sources had dried up, and he'd wasted hours searching fruitlessly for a cheap place to live. And all his problems he blamed on the police.

He swung his fist, but the cop was ready. He stepped back and Hector's punch merely grazed his shoulder. Before Hector knew what was happening, he was on the ground in handcuffs.

"Sir, you're under arrest for assaulting a police officer."

Hector cussed and kicked. But the cop didn't hit back. He simply held him down, kept him from landing any kicks or punches, until Hector got tired of fighting and they could pull him to his feet and put him in the police car. They were annoyingly polite and firm as they belted him into the backseat.

Hector called them names, cursed and screamed, spit at the barrier between the front and backseat.

He *hated* cops. But there was one cop he hated with every fiber of his soul.

He cursed her as he was booked in at the downtown station. Someday he'd get even with her.

Someday Tess O' Rourke would pay.

12

The week got busy being one man down. Bender's surgery went off without a hitch, but the doctor wanted him off at least a week, maybe more. Drake and Eva Harper were not at all happy with the delay at the coroner's office. They wanted Tim's body released so they could plan a memorial. Tess sympathized with them, but her hands were tied. It was Thursday afternoon before she heard back from the coroner about Tim Harper's autopsy.

"Chief O'Rourke, sorry this took so long, but frankly, you got yourself a winner. A very interesting case."

"What have you found?"

"I ran a preliminary check. The white powder residue you

sent tested positive for opiates, and Tim Harper died from respiratory failure. He was an otherwise healthy young man, so the obvious suspicion is that the underlying cause of the failure was opioid overdose. The sample has been sent to the lab for further testing." The man paused.

"Why do I hear a *but* coming?"

"Because the young man also suffered a severe closed head injury. There are some scratches to indicate a fall. I also found some gravel in a wound on his knee, indicating he might have fallen on the pavement. Now the injury to his head wasn't fatal. But he most likely had a concussion and needed medical attention. I found a single needle mark on his right arm, so if heroin or fentanyl is the culprit here, I doubt he was conscious when injected with the lethal dose. That leaves me with a homicide finding."

Tess leaned back in her chair, ears buzzing. The coroner went on with his postmortem, but knowing that Tim was murdered changed everything. She tuned back in as he finished.

"Also, since there was only the one needle mark, there is no evidence to suggest he was a habitual intravenous user. The paperwork says you found a syringe?"

"Yes, we did. I asked that it be printed."

"Wise. I'll send them Mr. Harper's prints. I doubt they will be on the syringe. I'd bet money he did not inject himself."

Wow, that was definitive. "Thank you."

"I'm inclined to release the body for burial unless you want a hold on it for any reason."

"You've taken all the tissue samples you need, correct?"

"Yes, we'll have complete tox screen results in three to four weeks."

"Then release it."

He hung up after saying she'd get her hard copy of the autopsy in a couple of days.

Tess pulled up the reports Jonkey and Bender had written, their interviews with Tim's classmates who'd attended the party, looking to see if they held a clue about who would have murdered Tim and why.

"He was excited about college." Josh Heller.

"No one was in a bad mood. It was all good." Duncan Peabody.

"Taking pictures, that was all Tim talked about, creating mind-blowing photo essays." Trace Danner.

"He barely drank one beer. He was taking pictures of the moon." Greg Nguyen.

Jonkey indicated that Coach Whitman had not been contacted. Per the boys, the reason he left the party almost as soon as it started was to drive to Salem for personal business. Tess made a note to call later in the morning and see if he was home.

Bender had spoken to Dustin Pelter. *"I just got high, that's all. Stayed long enough to get a joint. Didn't know the guy's name. Free is free. I'm not using anything stronger these days."*

"'Free is free,'" Tess muttered in disgust. Free dope would attract someone like Dustin. Though Dustin had helped Tess last year with her first homicide investigation in Rogue's Hollow, he was not what she'd ever call reliable.

Jonkey interviewed Eddie Carr, the new security guy at Hang Ten. He claimed he stumbled upon the party while hiking by himself and only stopped to smoke a joint. He denied knowing anyone, contradicting what the boys had said, that he seemed friendly with the guy giving pot away.

And he didn't know who Tim Harper was. Tess read the statement a couple of times. Jonkey had indicated that she thought the guy was lying, but there was no leverage to push him at the time, no proof of foul play.

Everything was different now. And they were almost a full week behind the curve. Tess needed to talk to everyone again.

Only one party attendee was as yet unidentified. The older man who was offering everyone pot. All the guys said he appeared to be a friend of Eddie Carr's. Tess had thought that would be Don Cherry, the other new security guard for Hang Ten. But the description the kids gave of the man did not fit the hard-to-miss Don Cherry. At six foot five, solid muscle, with prison tats covering his arms, he could never blend into a crowd of teenagers.

Tess had spoken to Drake Harper when he arrived home. He was devastated by his son's death. How would he take the coroner's news?

The parents had to be told. Tess stood and walked into the lobby area.

"Sheila, I'll be out for a little bit but listening to the radio."

"Okay, Chief."

Tess climbed into Gabe's patrol truck, missing her SUV and mentally rehearsing what she would say to Eva and Drake Harper. While she'd already considered murder, she was certain the parents hadn't, and she knew it wouldn't be any easier to swallow than overdose.

When she arrived at the house, the driveway was full of cars. Oliver had told her that some family had flown in from back East and support from the church had ramped up. She looked for his car and relaxed when she saw it. He'd help cushion this blow.

Someone outside having a smoke saw her, crushed out his cigarette, and rushed into the house.

Drake Harper met her at the door. "Chief, do you have news?"

"I do, Mr. Harper." Everyone in the living room was watching them. "Is there a place I can speak to you and your wife in private?"

"Uh, sure." As he turned, Tess could see Eva. The woman looked as if she'd aged ten years since Friday. Next to her was Pastor Mac.

"We can go in my study." Drake stepped aside for Tess to enter. "Eva, the chief wants a word."

Eva's eyes were as big as saucers. "May Pastor Mac join us?"

Drake looked at Tess and she nodded.

Once in the office, Drake closed the door and Tess gave them the coroner's news.

"What?" Drake paled and Eva collapsed into his side. "Why? Who would do this?"

"Mr. Harper, I assure you I will do everything in my power to find out the who and the why."

Color slowly returned to the man's face.

"Do you know of anyone who'd want to hurt Tim? Anyone he didn't get along with?"

"No, absolutely not." Drake was angry. "Tim was well liked. He was a positive, upbeat kid."

"Do you have any leads? Any guesses?" Eva asked.

"It's too soon. Obviously I will reinterview all the party-goers, look at everything from a different perspective."

Fury twisted Drake's features. "Yeah, you can't blame him anymore, can you?"

Oliver stepped forward. "That's not fair, Drake. The chief has not been laying blame."

"Fair? What's not fair is my son is dead. And someone used drugs to kill him. It's no leap in logic that there are drug dealers here in town hiding in plain sight. Duncan told me Eddie Carr was at the party. He's your killer—that's obvious. You should have arrested him from the get-go instead of blaming Tim."

Oliver started to say something else, and Tess gave him a look.

"Mr. Harper, I repeat, I will find out who did this and arrest that person. I'm truly sorry for your loss." She turned and left the office, walking back through a room of people with questioning looks on their faces. She saw Duncan and Greg in the corner. She wanted to talk to both boys but thought another time would be better.

Oliver called out to her as she reached her vehicle. "Tess, he's upset and hurting and only lashing out."

"I'm not bothered by his anger. I don't mind being a target if it helps him deal with his grief."

He put a hand on her truck door. "I know you had suspicions from the beginning about Tim's death; your instincts serve you well."

"Yeah, and it makes me angry as well. It's bad enough that someone in the valley is peddling death—that really fries me. Now, a promising young man is dead. I can't help but think his death is somehow connected to the opiate seller. Find him, I find my killer. So that's my target, and I will hit my target." She climbed into the truck.

"I know you will," he said.

She started the car and drove back to the station, anger building with each minute that passed.

Did Tim uncover something about the drug trade that cost him his life?

Did he take a picture of something he shouldn't have?

What in the world could he have done that was so serious murder was the only option?

The drugs were the key—they had to be. Tess chose to focus her anger on the plague of opioids invading her valley.

13

All Hector's cursing and spitting hadn't gotten the cops to throw a single punch. He'd been booked, didn't have the money to bail himself out right away, and the two people he called for help shined him on.

Then the stupid cops found some old tickets he hadn't paid. The judge ordered him remanded to custody for the fines. He knew they were just messing with him, but he couldn't even film the clown court.

By Thursday, Hector was still fuming in his jail cell, sore from being restrained and from sleeping on the hard, smelly jail bed. He'd expected to spend just a few hours in jail before being released. Now the bail was even higher and he was stuck. They were going to transport him to the county jail in

LA, and he'd be released right away because of overcrowding and have to find a way home. The cops were such Nazis. He'd been to this rodeo before. He hated jail almost as much as he hated cops.

The odor, the noise, the danger. The guy in the cell with him smelled of urine and beer and was snoring like a buzz saw on the bottom bunk. Hector paced the small enclosure, stopping only when he heard footsteps. The jailer was coming. Hector tried to think of a smart insult to hurl at the guy when he walked past. Cops were bad, but they generally had brains. Jailers were morons.

But the guy stopped at his cell.

"Ruiz?"

"It's Connor-Ruiz."

"Yeah, whatever." He slipped the key into the lock and opened the door.

Hector didn't move.

The jailer motioned with impatience. "Well?"

"Well, what?"

"You've been bailed. Do you want me to process you out or do you want to stay?"

Hector started to ask by who and stopped. Did it matter? All he wanted was out of this hellhole. He grabbed his sweatshirt and hurried out of the cell, forgetting even to insult the jailer.

When Hector hit the lobby about an hour later, still putting his belt through the belt loops on his trousers, a large man wearing a sleeveless shirt accentuating bulging, tattooed shoulders and biceps, someone he'd never seen before, was waiting for him.

"You Connor-Ruiz?"

Hector finished with his belt and pulled the court paperwork from his mouth. "Yeah, that's me."

"I'm from Andy's Bail Bonds." He held out a manila envelope. "Guy who posted your bail asked me to give you this."

"Who posted my bail?"

"Not here to answer questions, just to give you this."

For a long moment they stared at one another. Finally Hector reached out and took the envelope. The bondsman turned to leave.

"Why all the mystery?" Hector called after him. "Who bailed me?"

"Look in the envelope" was all the guy said without turning back or slowing his progress out the door.

Hector stood there for a moment staring at the envelope. He turned to his right and saw the front desk police service assistant watching him. Deciding not to open the package in the station, he followed the bondsman out into the night.

Hector walked all the way to Lincoln Park before he sat on a bench and opened the envelope. The money caught his eye first—a thousand large bundled with a rubber band. Next was a letter with instructions and a phone number pasted to a burner cell phone.

Breath coming fast with surprise and wonder, Hector jammed the money in his pocket and read the letter. He reread it twice before he allowed himself a smile. If this were true, he'd not only hit the lottery, but he'd connected with someone with whom he had a great deal in common, a person who hated Tess O'Rourke just as much as he did and had the resources to take her down.

14

Tim Harper's funeral was finally scheduled to take place two weeks and a day after his death, and it was heart-wrenching and draining. Oliver didn't remember feeling so worn-out since Anna's funeral. The church was packed. There was overflow in the fellowship hall. It even shut the town down for about two hours. Chief O'Rourke was there. Oliver knew she'd been working hard on the case since the murder classification by the coroner. But the department was shorthanded because Gabe was still off after having surgery. Oliver wasn't certain how much she'd been able to accomplish.

Also at the funeral was the guidance counselor from the college Tim would have attended. He'd really been impressed with Tim's photos and his talent. More moving than any of the eulogies was a presentation Duncan, Josh, Greg, and Trace had put together of Tim's photos of them, Tim's family, school, and Rogue's Hollow.

Oliver was dragging by the end of the weekend, and that was why he did something he rarely did—he took Monday off. His friend Victor Camus had a drift boat and fishing poles, so Oliver went fishing.

They met at the boat launch just below the dam at Lost Creek. Oliver liked to fish, but he loved being on the river. Every time he got out, it felt as if he'd never done it enough. God's hand was in the power of the current and the beauty of the passing terrain. It always energized him. And it didn't hurt to see an occasional deer on the bank, munching on foliage.

He and Victor climbed into the boat early, around 5:30 a.m., and began to drift, Oliver casting, Victor expertly rowing and steering the craft down the Rogue River. Victor worked as a fishing and hunting guide. He garnered top dollar, so Oliver felt fortunate that the man would spend his free time taking him out. They didn't speak until Oliver hooked his first fish.

"Nice one," Victor said as he readied the net.

Oliver reeled the six-pound steelhead to the side of the boat and Victor brought it in. He then removed the hook and released the fish back into the river.

Back at the oars, Victor got talkative. "Been about a year now—seems like that chief is working out for us."

"I would agree with that," Oliver said as he prepared to cast again.

"Too bad she can't do something about the pot farms."

Oliver turned from his pole and looked at Victor. "They causing you problems?"

"Not me personally, but they stir up the town. It's ironic—years ago when it was illegal and there were hidden pot grows everywhere, I had to be careful when taking people out. Always a danger of booby traps and running across paranoid hippies. But it was a problem only out in the wilderness. Now that it's legal, the problems are all front and center in downtown Rogue's Hollow."

"It sure seems that way."

"All these overdoses, I think they're a result of the proliferation of pot farms. One drug leads to another. Wouldn't surprise me if the Hang Ten guys are in some way responsible for his death."

Oliver stopped midcast. "You thinking those guys are murderers?"

"Maybe I've watched too much TV. They just seem like the usual suspects."

With the funeral preparation having occupied his time, Oliver was not up to speed on exactly where Tess was on the investigation, but she'd probably considered the Hang Ten. "The chief is on it, Victor. I have confidence she'll get to the bottom of Tim's case. Tess is dedicated. She and Gabe were just down in California last week working with the DEA."

"I saw that in the paper. She got shot, didn't she?"

"It was a graze," Oliver said, still a little shaken over how close Tess and Gabe came to getting seriously hurt. "She caught a bad guy, a big-time drug importer."

"Paper said that guy was probably the one sending stuff to Roger." Victor tsked and spit into the water.

Hearing Roger's name brought to mind Victor's sister, Helen. She'd married Roger, believing he was aboveboard, while he'd married her to simply provide cover and look respectable.

"How is Helen?"

"She's okay, likes Arizona. She thinks the world of the chief. Called me after seeing the news report. It was good to see our chief on TV being praised for her police work."

"It was, and the praise was well deserved. She works hard." Oliver thought the coverage was a two-edged sword. He was glad Tess was being recognized for excellent police work, but he worried about the chances she took, hoped the notoriety wouldn't make her a target.

He knew the murder of Tim Harper angered her. It had to be related to drugs. He remembered her frustration that all she could do was plug one hole in a leaking dike.

Tess O'Rourke was a warrior for justice—he'd called it right—a dragon slayer, a quality that made her a good police officer and loyal friend. But always behind her zeal for justice was the underlying "I need to do this because *God won't.*" She'd been railing against God and denying her faith since her father was murdered when she was sixteen.

He thought about how she'd helped him in the immediate darkness right after Anna's death, before the absolute horror of what had happened had set in, by reminding him that he needed to put one foot in front of the other and continue with the business of living. Life still had to be lived.

While her advice was sound, it wasn't what brought Oliver through the deepest valley of his life. It was remembering the Healer of souls. He'd spent a month home in Scotland after

Anna's burial and all the memorials that sprang up to honor her. The time in the Scottish Highlands cleared Oliver's head, took him back to the basics, and reassured him that no matter what pain and loss he felt in this world, God was still in control. And there would soon be a time when the pain and loss were forgotten and he would be as healed as Anna now was, and in the presence of God.

In the midst of his grief, Oliver had never felt close to losing his faith. On the contrary, it was his faith that sustained him. The more he thought about it, the more he realized that he had new purpose, something Anna would approve of. Faith in God would never insulate a person from the pain of living, but without faith there was no hope that the pain would count for something, that it wasn't all for nothing. He couldn't imagine Tess truly healing from her dad's death without relying on a faith that told her it was for a reason, it wasn't in vain.

A person could only put one foot in front of the other and honor their loss if they had faith that there was something worthwhile to come. Therefore, he knew he had to help Tess regain her faith. He must find the right way to show her that there was a God who was in everything—the good and the bad—and that he cared deeply for Tess.

15

Monday morning, two weeks and three days since the murder, Tess still had no leads, and other than her growing suspicion about Eddie Carr and the Hang Ten, she was at an impasse. Alone in her office, Tess tacked to her whiteboard a printout of Jonkey's software scene rendering of the Spot during the party. She folded her arms and studied the representation. The figures were all named as Duncan remembered them when he left. There was no evidentiary use to the depiction and really no investigative use either. It just helped Tess to put her mind there.

She jotted notes as she thought, alternately writing, then crossing out or underlining if it made sense.

1. Were there arguments or fights that night?

Murder among friends. It happened—Tess had seen it often in Long Beach, especially when alcohol was involved. But she doubted that was the issue here. Nothing she'd heard pointed to one of his friends killing Tim over a disagreement.

2. Did Tim interact in a negative way with one of the strangers?

No, everyone said the gathering was mellow, happy. Everyone was looking to the future.

3. Were there hidden family issues?

Every family had them. But Tess had seen too much raw grief from Tim's parents to go down that path.

4. What could Tim have done to cause someone to want to bash him over the head, then inject him with a lethal dose of drugs? Did he take an unwanted photo?

That seemed far-fetched, but Tess knew murders were often committed with less provocation. She needed to look at the last photos he took, just in case. She remembered the cameras she'd seen in Tim's room. Did one of them hold the evidence that would crack the case?

She wasn't sure how long she studied the artwork, but her perusal was interrupted by Sheila Cannan, her clerk, knocking on the doorframe.

"Sorry to interrupt, but Drake Harper is here. He wants to talk to you."

"Oh, okay." Tess turned the whiteboard around. "Send him in," she said as she sat down behind her desk.

Harper walked in a second later. He wasn't a big man, but he had a presence, a military bearing that made him seem tall and powerful, even with the obvious grief. Tess had noticed he'd barely held it together at the funeral.

"Have a seat, Mr. Harper."

"Thanks for letting me drop in, Chief."

"Not a problem. What can I do for you?"

"First, I wanted to apologize for my behavior the other—"

"You have nothing to apologize for. I understand completely."

"You're too gracious. Thank you. I was wondering if I could have Tim's phone back. The coroner didn't have it. I'm not sure what you need it for, but my wife and I—"

"I don't have Tim's phone."

"Didn't you take it for evidence?"

"At the time I was at your house, we were investigating a possible accidental death. The only evidence we collected was the paraphernalia."

He frowned. "Eva believed you might have it. We can't find it anywhere. He was using it to take pictures that night. It would be the last of his work, maybe a last selfie . . ."

And maybe a photo of his killer.

Tess thought a minute. She hadn't looked for a phone, and none was evident in the photos Becky had taken. If the coroner had come across anything, he would have notified her about personal effects.

"I'd actually like to see those photos as well."

Drake brightened ever so slightly. "Tim was a great photographer."

"Did he have a cloud account? It's possible the photos were uploaded as soon as he took them."

"I, uh . . . I'm not sure. I helped Tim learn about taking old-fashioned photos, even showed him how to use a darkroom, but that's obsolete now, isn't it?"

She nodded, disappointed, but she took a different tack. "Have you gone up to the Spot? Maybe he dropped it up there somewhere. Sergeant Pounder is on duty today. I'll have him meet you up there."

"Great, I'd like that." He stood. "I can also call the phone company. It's on our plan, so hopefully the GPS will tell us where it is."

His expression told her there was something else. She waited.

"One more thing. I hesitate to mention it because Eva's been a mess. But she thinks Tim's clothes are gone."

"His clothes?"

"Yeah. The ones he wore to the party, tan shorts and an orange Beavers shirt. I told her she must be mistaken . . . But first his phone, and we can't find his bike anywhere either—it's all got to be related."

"His bike also?"

"Eva initially thought Duncan brought him home from the party, so maybe the bike was still in Duncan's Jeep, but it's not. And Duncan didn't bring him home anyway."

Nonplussed by this new information, Tess remembered the boy was in his boxers. Why would a killer take his clothes?

"I'll see that the other boys are asked about the bike. But his clothes, that stumps me."

Tess walked him out. "Sheila, can you call Curtis and have him meet Mr. Harper at the Spot? He wants to look for Tim's phone. It might have some evidentiary value as well."

Sheila picked up the phone.

"Thank you, Chief." Drake faced her momentarily, then turned and left the station.

The idea that there might be something in the photos blasted some hope into Tess's thoughts. But the more she thought about it, the more her hope faded. If someone killed Tim over a photo, they almost certainly destroyed his phone.

16

Neither Curtis nor Drake Harper found the phone. And according to the phone company, there was no ping on the GPS. The bike was also problematic. Tim didn't have a car. He rode his bike everywhere. Rogue's Hollow wasn't a big place. It wasn't directly on a busy highway like Shady Cove. Tess had learned that a lot of people were comfortable riding their bike everywhere, even at night. The absence of Tim's bike said that the killer likely gave him a ride home. From where? If so, had he kept the bike or hidden it, and why?

Tess had reinterviewed all the boys after the funeral. According to them, Tim had still been at the Spot when the last of them left for home.

"I offered him a ride," Greg said, "but he told me that he'd probably ride around town to try to find the best place to shoot the moon."

"Did he tell you where the best place was?"

"He mentioned a couple of spots. . . ."

Tess had asked all the boys to come to the station; she just wanted to go over everything again. She asked Duncan how it was that he and Tim, not jocks, had become part of a group of jocks.

"We're all from the Hollow. We grew up together. We've always been friends."

Greg Nguyen was the leader of the group—that much was obvious. He looked the part of star pitcher: tall, solidly built. His father was Vietnamese, his mother white, and he inherited both light coffee-colored skin and slightly almond-shaped arresting green eyes. Tess bet the girls were all over him.

"But he wasn't sure where the absolute best location would be," Greg said. "Chainsaw Ridge was one."

Trace was next in the pecking order. He was a baseball player as well, though no scholarship waited for him. He was a lithe, rangy kid, with dark hair and eyes. He'd brought a baseball with him and was fiddling with it, bouncing it off his bicep and catching it.

"I heard him say that, but he also talked about the viewing platform at the Stairsteps."

Josh and Duncan agreed with their friends.

"Did he interact at all with the guys from the Hang Ten?"

Greg and Trace exchanged glances.

"It wasn't anything," Greg said.

"Let me be the judge of that. What happened?"

"Tim was taking photos on his phone, of everyone. That Eddie guy asked him not to photograph him. Tim didn't; that was it."

"Was he angry when he asked?"

"No," Trace said. "He was just like, 'Hey, don't point that thing toward me.'"

"What about Dustin?" Tess had been trying to find Dustin for a second interview, but he'd disappeared. She'd checked out places he often stayed and came up empty.

Trace looked at Greg, then said, "I don't remember Dustin saying much of anything."

"Yeah." Greg nodded. "He just smoked—sat next to a rock and smoked."

"How did Dustin get there? Did he come with someone?"

Duncan laughed. "Oh, that guy, he has a sixth sense when it comes to the possibility of free anything. He rides an old beat-up beach cruiser. He was still there when I left."

The other boys shook their heads.

"I don't remember when he left, or if he was still there when I left," Greg said.

"Who of all of you left the party last?"

"Me and Trace rode together," Greg said. "Duncan left first, Josh after him. When we left, Tim was the only one of us still there. Even the crashers were gone."

"Anything else you can tell me about Eddie Carr?"

They exchanged looks; then all of them shook their heads no.

She wanted more from them about Eddie Carr, but they had no more to give.

After the boys left, Tess mulled what she'd heard. She got

a little more information when a surprise showed up in her doorway. It was Coach Whitman, back from Salem. He'd been absent from the funeral. Tess thought that odd, but Greg said the man spent a lot of time in Salem.

"Chief O'Rourke, I got your message. I'm just devastated about Tim Harper, but how can I be of any help?" Whitman looked like an ex-jock going soft. Probably in his late forties, his hair was gray and a small paunch hung over his belt. She remembered reading that he'd coached college ball in Arizona before coming to Oregon to coach high school. She wondered at that. Why the comedown?

"Thank you for coming in, Mr. Whitman. I heard you were at the party that night. I'm asking everyone who was there what went on."

"I'm in an uncomfortable position here. Yes, I was at the party for a few minutes to wish Greg well. He's the best athlete I've ever coached. But if it comes to light I was present while the boys were drinking beer . . ."

"I'm trying to find Tim's killer. Getting you in trouble for bad judgment isn't high on my list."

"Ouch. Yeah, it was bad judgment. Maybe if I'd gone off on the boys and stopped the drinking and the party, Tim would still be alive. I spoke to Greg and Trace and then left for Salem."

"What's in Salem?"

"My girlfriend. She moved up there two months ago for a job and I've been trying to keep the fires burning."

"What time did you get there?"

He hiked a shoulder. "It was a long drive. I think I got there about three in the morning."

Tess considered this. Salem was roughly three hours away. Leaving here after eleven would get him there by three.

"I'll need your girlfriend's name and number."

"Am I a suspect?"

"Everyone is a suspect. Do you have a problem with giving me the information?"

"Forgive me, Chief. It's just that we're circling back to my bad judgment. Is there any way the high school will get wind of this?"

"I want to talk to your girlfriend, not your boss."

She didn't get much more out of Whitman. Even the boys had said he didn't stay long. Tess called the woman and got voice mail. She left a message and requested a timely call back. The coach bothered her, and she thought about checking into his background, but there wasn't a way to do that without notifying his work. Then again, he did come in without being asked. Maybe the girlfriend would clear everything up. She decided to wait until she talked to the woman.

Tess returned to Eddie Carr and the Hang Ten. Maybe this wasn't about the party; maybe Tim had ridden his bike to where he thought he'd get a good shot and that's where he met his killer. Haywood and his people were paranoid; maybe they misconstrued what he was doing. But why take Tim home, leave him on his bed, and take his clothes?

She'd called Steve after receiving the coroner's report but struggled with how to ask him for help.

"Good morning, Steve."

"Hi, Tess."

There was an uncomfortable pause. Tess cleared her throat. "I was calling to talk to you about Tim Harper."

"Yeah, I read about him. What a waste. He was a good kid. Hard to believe anyone would want to kill him. How can I help?"

Tess relaxed. This sounded normal and routine. "Looking to answer the 'Why Tim?' question. Assigning motive is the hardest part of this case. I keep coming back to drugs. We had a couple party crashers." She read him the description of the so-far unidentified man at the party. "Does he sound like any guys you know about who are involved in drugs?"

"Kinda sounds like a guy MADGE has been looking for. They think he's been cooking the fentanyl we've been finding." MADGE was the Medford Area Drug and Gang Enforcement task force. It was made up of several law enforcement agencies in the area. The only reason there was no Rogue's Hollow officer on it was that Tess couldn't spare the personnel.

"They think he's a retiree from California, possibly renting a house in Shady Cove. They haven't yet been able to nail down an address. Have them check out the residue you sent to the lab. They might be able to tell if it's some of the same stuff they've already confiscated."

"Great. Thanks, Steve."

"No problem. I wanted to talk to you about the press conference in Yreka a couple of weeks ago. Good job. Glad you weren't hurt too bad."

"Unfortunately, Gabe got the worst of it." With the awkwardness gone, Tess realized she'd missed him.

"You're short now, huh?"

"Yeah, till he gets back."

"Holler if you need help."

"I will, thanks."

Tess hung up and wondered about Steve. He'd been so supportive when she first arrived in Rogue's Hollow. He'd helped her navigate the new penal code, introduced her to people, shown her a little bit of her new state, and become emotional support. But as much as she pulled him close, she also pushed him away. Her ex-husband had been a cop and betrayed her. That's why she added rule #12 to her list of rules to live by: "Keep work professional, and personal life, personal."

She liked Steve. Sometimes Tess wondered if she was being too guarded. After all, they worked well together; she enjoyed his company. But there was no spark, no pull to him she felt compelling. This had made her doubt the wisdom of entering a committed relationship with him.

Still, there was nothing in the world so awkward as "let's just be friends."

She absentmindedly scratched her arm, the spot where the bullet had skimmed. The Steri-Strips were gone, and the spot itched. She was fortunate. Poor Gabe had to endure more. Typically, his PD brethren were not the coddling type.

"Look at the bright side," Curtis Pounder joked. "Any work on that nose can only improve the face."

But losing a member of her eight-man force, even if only for a couple weeks, was not a laughing matter. It meant Tess working more hours, filling in gaps. It wasn't that she minded working, but Tim's murder was getting colder by the day.

The lines between work and personal life were so blurred right now, she was taking work home with her as she pondered Tim's murder and all the other drama in a small town. But at least it distracted her from the nightmare still haunting her sleep, and that was a good thing.

17

Wednesday Tess had no coverage but herself, and it was a busy day, full of nuisance calls. Tess remembered times in Long Beach when she worked a patrol car, going from call to call. At certain times, when she worked the late shift, she'd log on to a page full of calls holding on the computer. Usually music complaints and disputes, she'd cover her beat and handle one after the other. Here, there were disputes, but also reports about a possible body in the river—turned out a kayaker got dumped, but he'd made it safely to shore—and another call of a broken fence and livestock on the roadway. These were all issues that had to be handled, but ultimately no big deal. When it quieted down, she used the time to look for Dustin but came up empty. She also made an appointment with the coroner for Thursday. She'd received the hard copy of the postmortem and wanted to go over it in person, make sure she wasn't missing anything.

Ever since the snow stopped, Tess, Casey Reno, and acting Mayor Addie Getz tried to have lunch together once a week, on Thursday. After the death of Anna Macpherson, Tess's first good friend in Rogue's Hollow, Casey and Addie became her closest confidantes. This week Addie was too busy for lunch, and Tess almost canceled because of her scheduled visit with the coroner. But Casey had a good idea. She had some shopping to do at the mall in town and said she could do that while Tess was with the coroner. So they decided to have lunch in Medford after the visit to the coroner.

Tess went over every aspect of the report and asked if it was possible to determine how the head injury occurred. The coroner could not tell her with any certainty but thought perhaps Tim had fallen from his bike, or maybe he was hit by a car and knocked off his bike. He also went over the scrapes he'd found, wounds Tess couldn't see very well when she did her brief visual exam.

After the meeting, Tess picked Casey up, and Casey treated her to lunch at Jasper's, a local favorite hamburger joint.

"It breaks my heart. Tim was a good kid." Casey Reno wiped her eyes and worked to compose herself while Tess waited patiently. That was the thing about living in a small town—everyone knew everyone else, and when something like what happened to Tim occurred, it touched a nerve in everyone.

"It's mind-boggling, really. Tim was the sweetest boy. I'm not sure Eva and Drake will ever recover."

Tess felt that pinch her heart. She remembered thinking she would never recover when her father died. She did because she knew that's what her father would have wanted.

"They have each other. I can only hope they find it in themselves to recover together."

"You must be looking at the Hang Ten. Honestly, everyone who works at that pot farm is shady, except Bryce. But the big man, the one with the tattoos—" she shivered—"he's scary."

"They are obvious suspects, aren't they? I just have no evidence right now." Tess went back to her burger.

But Casey wasn't finished. "So you've considered them."

Tess swallowed, drank some iced tea. "I have. Carr doesn't have a record, and everyone knows that Don Cherry is an ex-con. But he's off parole; there are no restrictions on him any longer. He's not even one of the Hang Ten employees who carries a gun. As much as I'd like to drag them in and question them, I have no reason. Carr was at the party, but Cherry wasn't." Tess probably spoke more sharply than she meant to.

"I'm sorry, Tess. I know you're doing your job. But this hits so close to home. After what happened to Kayla last summer . . ."

She choked up and Tess understood. Her fourteen-year-old daughter, Kayla, had been kidnapped by Roger Marshall when he tried to flee. Though unhurt, Kayla and her family were certain to have lasting scars from the incident. She could have easily been the kid the town was mourning last summer.

Casey blew her nose. "All of this comes back to drugs. They are everywhere nowadays, and for a parent it's terrifying."

"I'm working on making them scarce, I promise."

"I get that you understand; that makes me feel better. It will only help everyone involved to be certain that the killer is off the streets."

They went back to their lunch, but Tess couldn't stop her mind from working, thinking about the people at the Hang Ten.

Carr was annoying for sure, but Tess felt he was all bluster. It was Don Cherry who bothered her the most. He could kill; he had once already. Research told her he'd done five years in prison in California for assault with GBI, or great bodily injury, and manslaughter. And not just any prison, but Corcoran, one of the toughest in the state. Tess had made a call to his prior PO in California.

"Don kept his nose clean in jail, but he does have tenuous ties to La Eme. With me he checked in when he was supposed to, but you know the workload down here."

Tess did. According to the PO, officially Cherry was clean, but no one with "ties to La Eme" ever really broke those connections. And the drug ring in Yreka was affiliated with the same gang, the Mexican mafia. The man she arrested had been covered with La Eme tats. She hadn't seen any indication of mafia influence in Rogue's Hollow, and even in Medford, officers said they rarely had hard-core issues like that. If there was any evidence Cherry had been at that party, she'd be all over it.

As for Eddie Carr, he had no record. Shaved head, he was thin and wiry, and the way he walked, sneakily, reminded Tess of a cat. He had a rep for being hot tempered and a fighter, despite the absence of a record. Both men had hardened, ex-prison looks about them.

The third man, Bryce Evergreen, the guy Casey would vouch for, was the only one who didn't cause concern on Tess's part. Oliver had given Tess the lowdown on Evergreen. Bryce had grown up in Shady Cove, just up the road, and at one time had been part of the church youth group. But he fell away. He joined a group of druggies who made their mark on Shady Cove and Rogue's Hollow long before Tess's time. Back then he was tight with Tilly Dover and the now-deceased Glen Elders.

Today, Evergreen was a down-on-your-luck story. He'd left the state a few years ago and, by all appearances, cleaned up his life. He got off drugs and started working as a handyman, a kind of jack-of-all-trades, in Washington. But he tended to follow work from place to place. While heading to a job in Portland, he'd been stopped for a traffic violation, and police discovered that he had a very old outstanding warrant in Medford.

Arrested and shipped back to Medford on the warrant in February, as a nonviolent offender Bryce was immediately given a court date and kicked out of jail with a schedule of fines to pay off. But then he had no car and no money and he was far from his home base in Washington. He spent some time at the Medford Gospel Mission after his initial release and before his first court date. Oliver had run into him at the mission and gotten the word out that Bryce needed work. Oddly, it was Gaston Haywood who hired him, something that caused Tess to raise an eyebrow.

"I know. It bothered me as well," Oliver said. *"But Bryce isn't working with pot; he's working as a handyman. And from what*

he tells me, Haywood is so paranoid about theft, there is no way Bryce could get near any pot if he wanted to."

Yet Tess wondered about the temptation there. She had talked to Bryce herself and he appeared committed to staying clean. Like Tilly Dover, the other ex-druggie Tess was familiar with, he wanted that life to stay in the rearview mirror.

Casey interrupted Tess's musings, almost reading her mind. "I wish I could find other work for Bryce. If only for his parents' memory. I hate to see him working at that pot farm." Born and raised in the Hollow, she remembered babysitting Bryce when he was a kid.

"I talked to him," Tess said. "He just wants to make enough money to pay his legal fees, get back to Portland, get his truck out of impound, and leave the state. You know there aren't many places in the valley where he could find a job to pay him quickly enough to do that."

"I know. But I'm afraid being around the element will cause him to stumble."

Tess shook her head. "He seemed pretty committed to staying clean. And he hopes to be gone before October, the next pot harvest." She'd been impressed by his resolve.

"I'll try to find a way to help him," Casey said as they finished their coffee and got up to leave the shop.

"Why don't you help me understand this Oregon weather?" Tess asked as they stepped outside the shop. The early summer weather had been going great, but last night the temperature had dropped somewhat and clouds had appeared. There was the promise of rain and a thunderstorm in the air.

Casey laughed. "This is unusual, but we need the water. Consider it a blessing."

"I consider this whole area a blessing." Tess smiled and meant it. She loved being chief in Rogue's Hollow, a realization that still surprised her. Coming from Long Beach PD, a department with over eight hundred officers, to Rogue's Hollow, Oregon, with eight sworn officers and three civilian employees, had been a shock, but every day was coming easier and there was a smoothness to the routine now. She was even starting to feel a part of the community. Even after seventeen years in Long Beach, while she'd felt a part of the police department, the community at large had always felt separate. Not many officers even lived in the city limits in Long Beach. Here in Rogue's Hollow, they all did. When she thought of Casey and Oliver, it was truly community policing here in the Hollow and she was glad to be a part of it.

18

A few days after being bailed out, Hector met his benefactor.

"What kind of arrangement?" Hector asked. The man before him was short but carried himself like a tall man. He had an impressive number of tattoos and a nasty scar on his face that made Hector intensely curious about how it had happened. But it was obvious the man had not come to chat about himself.

"I want her distracted, harassed. Don't give her a reason to arrest you. Walk up to the line but don't cross it. You do that, and the money will keep flowing."

"Sure thing. Where am I staying?"

"Pot farm called the Hang Ten. Gaston Haywood is expecting you. One thing you must never do is mention me. At. All." He paused for emphasis. "I am a silent partner. You do, and the deal is off." The guy turned downright *Walking Dead* scary at this point. "Tess O'Rourke has gotten in my way too many times. Now I want you to get in her way."

Hector nodded. "I'm cool, man. I live to hassle the Red Menace."

It took some time to untangle his affairs and to pay off some angry creditors, but Hector happily accepted his new sponsor's proposal and prepared to leave the town he'd been born and raised in, the place where he'd generated his first taste of fame. He packed two bags of belongings, just the basics—his computer and printer, a few clothes. He planned on leaving everything else. Let the stupid landlord who left the eviction notice empty the apartment of all the other stuff. It surprised him how much the promise of this new venture had lifted his spirits, given him purpose, made him giddy even. He'd thought of nothing else since he got the offer. He never would have thought of leaving California for a state like Oregon—New York maybe, but not Oregon. But his newfound benefactor made him such an attractive offer, there was no way he could refuse.

And the perks! He'd be able to harass Tess O'Rourke again. He'd have almost done that for free. Almost. Now he had an income. The benefactor gave him a bunch of cash up front with the promise of more to come. Hector had nothing to lose. Everything here in California had slipped through his fingers: His blog had faded from people's minds. He spent his savings losing an election. He was broke. At least now he had a pocket full of green and a full tank of gas.

He didn't look back after he loaded his car and started the engine. In a few minutes, he was headed north on the 405, mind whirring with strategies to make O'Rourke's life miserable.

19

Tess rarely made traffic stops, and when she did, it was usually to issue a warning. People generally saw her blue-and-white police vehicle and stopped whatever infraction they were engaged in. Though she was in Bender's pickup, it was still a marked police vehicle with a light bar. On her way home from lunch, after she'd dropped Casey off in Shady Cove to meet her husband, an egregious infraction happened right in front of her and she couldn't avoid the stop. A gray panel van blew a stop sign going at least ten miles over the speed limit.

She'd just turned off Highway 62 and was driving over the bridge toward River Drive, in a good mood after the great lunch with Casey. The van was heading into downtown Rogue's Hollow on River Drive. The vehicle's speed was enough to catch her attention since the limit in town was 20 mph. The stop sign was the capper. And the van belonged to the Hang Ten; she knew that much because it was written on the side. She made her turn onto River Drive and activated her light bar.

Brake lights came on immediately. She could only imagine the driver's thoughts. It was obvious he hadn't seen her before running the stop. He pulled over right away and ended up stopped in front of Wild Automotive. Tess radioed in the stop, asked for a 28/29 on the license plate and waited for the dispatcher to acknowledge her. Once that happened, she got out of the truck and approached the vehicle.

She could see the driver fumbling around and placed a hand on her weapon out of habit. Walking up on a stopped vehicle like this was way more dangerous than anyone who'd never done it could imagine. Why was the driver speeding? He could be running from a crime for all she knew. She could tell it wasn't Haywood driving; she hadn't seen his blond hair. But it could be any of his employees.

Since he'd pulled over so quickly, Tess was inclined to let him off with a warning . . . if he passed the attitude test. She reached the driver's window. The driver turned her way— Eddie Carr.

"Good afternoon, Mr. Carr. Do you know why I pulled you over?"

"Uh, probably because you got nothing better to do in this dinky little town than harass people."

First test, *fail*.

"On the contrary, I have a lot to do in this 'dinky town.' License, registration, and proof of insurance, please."

"It's not my van."

"You're driving it. And that wasn't what I asked. I need the requested documents."

He glared at her and Tess was about to pull him out of the van.

"All right, all right." He reached to his right and Tess stiffened. But he handed her the truck's registration and an insurance card.

"Your driver's license?"

"I don't have it."

"You don't have one, or you just don't have it on you?"

"Ain't got one. Look, I'm sorry. I'm having a bad day. I promise to slow down."

Tess didn't believe his contrition and grabbed the door handle and pulled it open. "Step out of the van."

"Why?"

"I need to verify your identity, and if you don't have a license, you won't be driving this van anywhere now."

A muscle in his jaw jumped, and she saw the anger spark in his eyes. This guy was bad news—every instinct in her body was telling her that. She stepped back, held his smoldering gaze.

He relented, threw his hands up, and smiled a smile that never reached his eyes. "Okay, okay. Sorry, *Chief*."

He climbed out of the vehicle and Tess followed him as he slowly made his way back to the front of her truck. She had him stand between the two vehicles while she filled out a field interview card with all the information he gave her.

"Spell your full name."

"*E-d-d-i-e.*"

"Middle name?"

He shook his head. "*C-a-r-r.*"

To get an answer to every basic question was like pulling teeth. There were no wants or warrants on the name and date of birth he supplied, but there was a close hit on a suspended California driver's license. She looked at him as she heard the dispatcher ask if she wanted the CDL number. He looked away. If he had a CDL, his name and date of birth should have given her an exact match, not a close hit. That he was lying was clear. Technically, she could arrest him to confirm his identity. But he wasn't a tourist she didn't know; he was a member of the community, and she knew where to find him. He wouldn't be kept in custody for the misdemeanor arrest, that was for sure. There was no room in the jail for nonviolent offenders. Tess was willing to give him a small bit of leeway, in the hopes her grace would get him to open up. People lied about a lot of things, and Tess needed to know what Eddie Carr was hiding. But then, if it had to do with Tim Harper's murder, could she get a hard case like him to make an admission?

In the interest of fairness and of trying to get on his good side, Tess gave him one last chance. "Mr. Carr, do you have any paperwork at all that can confirm your identity?"

"Like what?"

"To get hired, did you give Haywood something to prove that you are who you say you are? Something he can bring to vouch for you?"

He muttered something that was probably a curse. "This

is harassment, lady. I ain't a wetback. I'm an American. I've got rights."

Tess's already-murmuring spidey sense went off like a fire alarm. Evasive, angry, dangerous body language. She was about to call for backup when Curtis Pounder pulled up and parked behind her truck. He got out and walked over to see if she needed help. Tess made her decision. She nodded to Curtis and tapped her wrist, indicating that Carr was under arrest.

She moved to one side of Carr and Pounder took the other. "Mr. Carr."

"What?" He turned his head to look at her and tensed visibly. He knew he was being arrested.

"I'm placing you under arrest to verify your identity."

"I'm not going to jail." For about two seconds, he didn't move.

She watched him as carefully as she'd ever watched anyone. He was like a coiled spring, the tension dripping off him like rainwater.

Timing is everything.

She reached for his right arm at the same time he pivoted and swung around with a closed left fist.

Reflex and instinct saved her from a punch in the face. She felt the fist whiz by as she ducked and then stepped forward, catching his left arm in the crook of her arm and locking it there as her momentum pushed them both into Curtis. Sergeant Pounder wasn't tall, but he was broad and he was already moving to contain the man. He grunted as they smashed together but held his ground.

Curtis grabbed for Carr's other arm. Carr struggled to punch and fight.

Tess and Pounder each had an arm and shoved him toward the hood of her truck, wanting to restrict his movement as much as possible. Together they forced him into the front grille. But the fight wasn't over. They had to turn him over and cuff him.

He was a wiry, flexible guy. As Tess fought to keep ahold of his arm, Curtis managed to shove him around, but neither could get their respective arms behind his back to be cuffed. It was warm, and Tess felt the sweat forming on her face as Carr's arm became slippery.

"Stop resisting," Tess huffed, breath coming hard as she struggled with the man, who had every muscle in his body tensed. His hands were balled into fists. There was no using a twist lock, and fighting to straighten his arms from a full curl was impossible. Keeping her two-handed grip from slipping took all her strength.

She jammed her knee into the back of his thigh. He couldn't move to effectively fight, but he wasn't giving any ground either.

As they struggled, she was vaguely aware of people gathering. But she couldn't move, couldn't let a bit of her hold loosen or let anything interrupt her concentration.

Beside her, Curtis was breathing just as hard, but he was able to bring his left hand up and employ a pressure point, pinching the mandibular nerve behind Carr's ear with his thumb. That caused Carr to flinch, giving Tess the opportunity to force his left arm behind his back.

Curtis pushed again and then forced the right arm back. The fight was not over. It took several more minutes to firmly apply the cuffs. Carr did not want to quit.

"You're gonna regret this," he hissed through gritted teeth. "I'll own this town, own it!"

They searched him, removed a pocketknife and a little cash, but it was a fight every step of the way. It was only when he realized, finally, there was no escape that he stopped, sweat glistening on his bald head.

Since he would now be charged with resisting arrest, Tess and Curtis walked him back to Curtis's patrol car.

"You all saw that," Carr yelled to the people who'd been watching. Mostly tourists—Tess didn't recognize but a couple of faces. "Po-lice brutality, po-lice brutality," he chanted, even after he was securely belted in the car and the door was closed.

Curtis stepped back, wiping sweat from his brow and blowing out a relieved breath. "Wow, that's my workout for the week. What was his major malfunction?"

Tess wiped sweaty palms on her thighs, noticed that Damien, the local paper publisher, was there and he had his camera out. How would what just happened look in a photo?

"He has no ID. I wanted to get him identified."

"He doesn't want to be identified if he put up that much of a fight."

"Yeah, be careful, will you?"

He nodded, then left to take Carr to Medford, where he'd be positively identified by fingerprints and booked into jail.

"You okay, Chief?" Damien asked.

Tess sucked in a breath. "He was under arrest for a traffic misdemeanor and didn't want to be."

"All that for a traffic misdemeanor?"

"Unfortunately, yes." It took Tess a few minutes to get her

breathing to slow and her heart rate to calm. Overcoming the resistance of a person who just refuses to cooperate was harder than fighting someone.

The incident was on rewind in her thoughts, and she realized that Curtis's presence there had prevented a punch fight. Carr had been cornered in every way. If Carr was even his real name. They'd know soon enough.

The crowd dispersed, and she walked back to the van and took the keys from the ignition, then locked the vehicle up. She'd call Haywood and tell him where his van and his employee were and to come get his keys.

— — —

"He told me he cleared that up." Haywood arrived at the station about an hour later. Don Cherry stood behind him but said nothing.

"Apparently not," Tess said, dropping the keys in his hand.

"And you arrested him for *that*?"

"Do you have an ID or something that proves who he is?"

"Hey, he's not illegal. He's an American citizen. This is nonsense. You'll be hearing from my lawyers."

Tess watched him go and checked the clock. Curtis should have booked Carr in by now. She had just picked up her phone to call him when it rang with a call from him.

"Okay, what happened?" she asked.

"He's refusing to be printed. They have him in a holding cell. You know the drill. He won't be processed until he's printed."

"What is he hiding?" she said half to herself, then, "Are you headed back?"

"Yeah, be back to the barn shortly."

The suspense was killing her, but she didn't have much time to think about Haywood or Carr; she had a city council meeting to attend. The council in Rogue's Hollow met twice a month. The first meeting was closed, council members only, with space for Tess. Once in a while Oliver would show up; he was always welcome because Addie liked his constructive input. The second monthly meeting was open to the public, comment was allowed, and complaints were taken. The public meeting was usually the topic of discussion at the closed meeting. Tonight's meeting would focus on the upcoming election and its aftermath. Tess knew that Addie feared what might happen no matter which side won the pot sale initiative, pro or con.

"Tess, are you all right?" Oliver came into her office, face lined with worry. "I just heard what happened."

His concern touched Tess. But how fast information spread around town was always a wonder. She noticed, for some reason, everyone wanted to talk to the pastor and tell him every little happening.

"I'm good, Oliver, thanks." She had been through many a stressful law enforcement moment over the years. This one was over and now was the time to settle back into routine. But Tess knew and would deal with the fact that she came very close to being hit in the face and seriously hurt.

"Any idea why he put up such a fight?"

"He's refusing to be fingerprinted, so my guess is he's not who he says he is." She stood. "Ready for the council meeting?"

Oliver nodded. They walked to the council chambers together.

"I recognize you have a dangerous job," Oliver said, "but something like this happening in downtown Rogue's Hollow is disturbing."

"I'm fine, really." Tess adjusted her vest, wishing she'd thought to change her sweaty undershirt and trying to deflect Oliver's concern. The stop was over. She was fine.

But once inside the chambers, she was peppered with questions about what happened in front of Wild Automotive before she could sit down.

"You created a spectacle on Main Street. Couldn't you handle that any other way?" Cole Markarov asked. He'd been against Tess's hire from the very beginning, so his attitude didn't surprise her at all. "Not to mention all the money you cost the city when you wrecked your police car last week."

"Really, Cole, she did her job. Law enforcement isn't always please and thank you." Casey stood up for Tess before Oliver could.

Addie moved that they start council business and Tess relaxed. It was all about pot now.

"We can't let our personal prejudices color how we decide issues for the community." Cole's attention was redirected, and since he was one of two people running for mayor, once the meeting was under way, he put on his political face. He was generally an abrasive, rude man, but since declaring his run for mayor, he'd become quite the political animal.

"If the pot initiative wins, we'll just have to live with it," he said, acting more magnanimous than she knew he was.

"No one is saying that we won't accept the results of the election," Casey said. "We just have to realize that no matter who wins, half the town is going to be unhappy."

"Of course we'll accept whatever the votes say," Addie said. "All I want to do is make sure we are prepared if the initiative is successful. If cannabis goes on sale on Main Street, how should it be handled?"

For a second, everyone began to talk at once. Tess just leaned back and listened, trying to picture a pot shop in downtown Rogue's Hollow.

"I agree with preparation," Oliver said. "My fear is that the impact of pot on River Drive could be worse than we anticipate."

"What do you think, Tess?" Addie asked.

"I understand Oliver's fear. And to be honest, I'm not for legalized pot sale in town. But I haven't seen any serious impact in Shady Cove."

"But Shady Cove is more spread out; there's more space in their downtown, so to speak. That makes a difference," Casey pointed out.

"True," Tess said. "It would be close quarters here in the Hollow."

"And maybe a whole new Pandora's box of problems," Oliver added.

20

Oliver waited for Tess after the meeting ended, still concerned for her because of the fight with Carr. Together, they walked slowly out of the council chambers toward the PD.

"What will the sheriff do with Carr refusing to be finger-printed?" Oliver asked.

"They have him in a holding cell. Until he's booked, there's no phone call, no bail, nothing. He'll come around eventually if he wants to be processed and be able to call someone."

She looked tired and stressed. His heart went out to her. She was strong, he knew that, but the incident with Carr had shaken her.

"Do you think he killed Tim?" They paused at the front of the station. It was eight o'clock and light was fading.

"I honestly don't know. He makes sense as a suspect. It's everything else that makes no sense. And somehow I doubt he'll confess to me or anyone else. Thanks for walking me out." She reached out and touched his forearm. "I'm fine, Oliver, just fine."

He put his hand over hers. "You can tell me not to worry, you can tell me not to pray—I'll do both. You're my friend."

She smiled and the stress melted away from her features. Oliver decided that he liked making her smile.

"Let me know when you find out about Carr. And call me if you need to talk about anything, okay? I'm a good listener."

"I appreciate that."

He crossed the street to go home. Oliver thought about Don Cherry and wondered if he knew what was up with Carr. Oliver would certainly ask when he had the chance. He recalled the conversation he'd had with Cherry about what he'd begun calling the pot problem. Since that first strange evening when he'd shown up out of the blue on Oliver's porch, Cherry had been back again a few times, unannounced, appearing out of the shadows. That first night, Oliver felt he was being tested, as if Cherry wanted to see if he'd flinch.

"I killed a man," he said.

"Is that what sent you to prison?"

He tilted his head and did not give a direct answer. "It wasn't on purpose. He picked a fight with me. Wanted to show off for his girlfriend. I only hit him once, and he died." He paused, pensive. "Can't say I cared. But I hated prison."

"You joined a gang in prison." Oliver pointed to the tattoos all over Cherry's arms.

"Had to. You don't belong to something in prison, you get eaten alive."

"Even a guy your size?"

"Always someone trying to prove themselves. Last thing I wanted to do was fight my way through prison. That only adds time to your sentence. And it's dangerous. My dad was killed in a prison fight a month before I was born."

"That must have been rough for you, growing up without him."

"Life is rough, padre," he said easily, but Oliver thought the nonchalance was feigned.

Cherry told Oliver a little about the prison chaplain he'd met, a man he seemed to have a lot of respect for.

"He didn't take any guff, told it like it was."

"What did he tell you?"

Cherry chuckled, but coming from him, it did not sound mirthful. "He told me a lot of Bible stories, said I reminded him of Samson." His chuckle became a belly laugh as if that were a tremendous joke. "Imagine that, padre. Me a Bible character?"

He settled down and went on. "'Everyone needs a Savior, Cherry.'" He wagged a finger in the air. "Lots of other stuff."

He then went quiet and Oliver got the impression that he didn't want to specify, so Oliver changed the subject.

"What do you do at the Hang Ten?"

"Whatever needs doing."

"Like threatening old ladies into changing their minds

about recreational pot?" For a second, Oliver thought he'd stepped over some unknown line.

Cherry glared. But then he broke out in laughter. "Aw, I don't want to scare anyone—I just do."

"I'd appreciate it if you didn't. Scare anyone, I mean. Rogue's Hollow is my town, and I like it peaceful."

"Pot is a peacemaker, padre. People who get high don't fight; they get the munchies. Maybe you need to consider the other side of the fence. The Bible don't say, 'Thou shall not smoke pot,' does it?"

"Not specifically, but no good comes out of a drug that alters your thought process. Good life decisions require clear thinking."

Cherry considered this. "Fair enough, padre. A lot of people in prison sure made bad life decisions."

On a subsequent visit, Cherry seemed to want Oliver to know that he didn't ever want to go back to prison, so he would toe the line, obey laws and such. While he didn't want to hear about God and religion, he didn't mind stories about characters in the Bible.

"A good story is a good story. The rest is not real to me, padre. Let's stay with what we can see."

"That's a cop-out. You're talking to me; my business is the spiritual health of my congregation. My guess is that you have questions about spiritual things."

"I got lots of questions, but let's keep our feet on the ground."

Oliver felt there was something underneath all the banter and small talk. One thing being a pastor for so many years had taught him was patience. He'd keep praying and hoping Cherry would open up with what was really on his mind.

For a second, Oliver sucked in a breath. This was something he would have loved to mull over and discuss with his wife, Anna. She would have seen through Cherry, known what game the man was playing. And she would have known how to bring peace back to the Hollow. Generally, though he still felt the loss viciously, he did feel stronger with the passing of time. But issues like this one brought everything home again and stirred up the pain anew.

The ache was back, like a throbbing tooth. He missed Anna.

Sighing, he started up his porch steps, peering into the shadows, but there was no Don Cherry. He opened his door, thinking perhaps he'd bring up Don to Tess. The chief was a clear thinker like Anna. She'd look at Cherry's visit from a law enforcement perspective. Oliver realized why he so enjoyed talking to Tess. She was the law, a perspective so different from Anna, who was grace. Oliver considered himself to be walking the line between the two. He missed Anna's pure grace, but Tess's pure law helped him almost as much.

21

By the time Tess opened her office for the day Friday morning, there was still no news about Carr. Drake Harper knocked on her door before her coffee finished brewing, asking her about the incident.

"Is he the one who killed my son?"

"Mr. Harper, that's not why I arrested him. I don't have any evidence that he killed your son."

"He's a troublemaker—I've heard that from more than one person. And he was at the party."

"I've talked to him, and he denies hurting Tim."

"Of course he'll deny. It just doesn't seem like anything is happening. My son is in his grave, for heaven's sake." He paced like a caged animal. "I want justice for Tim."

"I promise you I'm doing everything in my power to find your son's murderer."

"Maybe you need to ask the sheriff for help."

Tess worked to keep her face neutral. This request stung. *You're not doing your job.*

"If it gets to a point where I think I need their help, I will ask."

He looked at her, and she could tell he didn't like her answer. "Sooner rather than later, I hope." He turned and left her office.

Tess sat at her desk, frustrated. She had faith in herself and patience, but she understood Drake Harper's impatience. Tess knew that the person who killed her father received instant justice—he was shot and killed by her father's partner. It would have been unbearable if the perpetrator had escaped justice.

The phone rang. It was Steve. She answered.

"Wow, Tess, you sure can pick 'em."

"What do you mean?"

"Eddie Carr, aka Edward Carrington. He's got a no-bail warrant out of California for explosives and a no-bail federal warrant for murder and attempted murder of a DEA agent. No wonder he didn't want to be fingerprinted."

Tess leaned back in her chair and closed her eyes, tension and disappointment dissipating. When her gut was right on, it was right on.

"When did they finally print him?"

"About twenty minutes ago. He wanted a phone call, and the only way he was going to get one was after we processed him. Don't know who he called. But now he's quiet. I think the Feds are going to come get him. They might even want to visit the Hang Ten."

"I'd like to get in there."

"Do you think Carr killed Harper?"

"Everyone is asking me that, and I don't know. He's not the only questionable character at the Hang Ten. Don Cherry did time for manslaughter. And I still haven't figured out who the older guy at the party is."

"Was Cherry at the party?"

"No."

"Need any help with this case?"

Hearing that question again irritated her. "If I do, I'll ask."

Gratified by being right about Carr, feeling as if it was one win in her column, she went back to her board, thinking about the fact that Cherry wasn't at the party. Tess was beginning to believe that Tim's murder had nothing to do with the party. His mother was certain she'd heard his voice, that he made it home alive from the party. And because it was hard to imagine someone killed him at the party and then brought his dead body home and put him to bed, she felt it was safe to conclude he wasn't killed at the party, but in his bedroom. Where was his bike? His clothes? His phone? What was she missing?

Her phone rang and she didn't recognize the number. When she answered, she was pleasantly surprised. It was Phillip Whitman's girlfriend calling back. She verified the coach's alibi, telling Tess that he had arrived around 3 a.m. Tess checked off a box—the only two open ones were for Dustin Pelter and the unidentified man. She and her people had looked everywhere for Dustin with no success.

As for the unidentified man, Tess tried to get ahold of the lieutenant in charge of MADGE but had to leave a message, asking about any progress in identifying the man suspected of selling opioids.

The drugs still had to be the key.

Tess spent the balance of her day up at the Spot and working on Harper's case, reviewing everything, searching culverts and wooded areas for Tim's bike. It was hot, tiring work. On her way back to the station, she got a call from DEA Agent Ledge.

"I owe you one, Chief. Carrington was on my most wanted list. He killed a good agent and seriously hurt a good friend of mine. I had no idea he was still in the country. I'm sending Hemmings up there to interview the guy he worked for. What else can you tell me about that place?"

"Well, it's a legally licensed pot farm." Tess filled Ledge in about the Hang Ten. "Haywood keeps up on all the state requirements for a licensed producer. He has the appropriate signage; his workers were likewise properly licensed. Carrington wasn't a pot worker. He'd hired on as security, so he did not need any state license."

"Our intelligence said he was in the Sinaloa area of Mexico. He's changed his appearance, doesn't look anything like his current wanted poster. Thankfully, he didn't have the discipline or the sense to keep his nose clean. If he had, he'd still be free."

"That's the truth. I saw the wheels turning. I knew he was going to resist," Tess said. "But he waited too long to act, and I had good backup. I'd like to visit the farm with Hemmings when he comes."

"Not a problem. Send me all you have on the pot workers."

After hanging up with Ledge, Tess thought about planning her weekend. She still had to cover for Bender, who was due back Monday or Tuesday. If they were fully staffed, she could use the weekend to poke around for Dustin. It was a loose end she wanted to tie up. She whistled softly to herself as she entered the station and headed for her office. The normal working day would end soon, but Sheila was still at her desk. Her officers worked twelve-hour shifts, seven to seven; Sheila was an eight-hour-a-day worker.

"Hi, Sheila."

"Afternoon, Chief. I'll be heading out in a few. Need anything?"

"Not that I can think of, but thanks."

Tess sat at her desk, found the paperwork Ledge needed, and sent it off. She then shuffled through some papers, wanting to be certain she didn't forget anything that needed to be done. The clock was ticking on Harper, but she had nowhere to go with it until she heard back from the lab on the fingerprints. And there was an outside chance something would come up when she visited the pot farm.

Del Jeffers was the officer on duty today, and listening to the scanner, she'd heard him go out to a dispute at the trailer park.

Unable to resist patting herself on the back for catching Carrington, Tess signed a few requests, noted the training schedule, and hummed to herself. But abruptly the quiet in her office was shattered by a commotion in the lobby. A raised voice, eerily familiar but she couldn't place it.

"I want to see the chief."

"Do you have an appointment?"

"I don't need an appointment; we're old pals."

"I still need to check with her—sir, you can't go back there."

Tess heard Sheila's chair scrape the floor and stood as a man burst into her office, Sheila on his heels.

"Plotting how to deprive people of their rights, *Chief*?" He spit the last word out like a curse.

Tess fought to keep her face neutral. This was the last person in the world she expected to see.

Hector Connor-Ruiz.

22

He was a bit thinner than she remembered, and he sported a few days' growth of beard, so he looked older, somewhat haggard. But the disdain and anger in his dark eyes was the same. The hate was the same.

Tess held a hand up, indicating Sheila could relax and go home. "Mr. Connor-Ruiz, there's no need to walk over my secretary."

"She's trying to keep a taxpaying citizen from the chief, who's supposed to be a public servant."

A sick feeling started to form in Tess's stomach, and the only lame response she could come up with was "You pay taxes in California, not Rogue's Hollow."

He puffed out his chest and grinned, showing yellowed teeth. "As of yesterday, I reside in Rogue's Hollow. I partnered with Gaston at the Hang Ten. I plan to get an Oregon driver's license ASAP." He pointed at her with his phone. "You're on notice. I've heard you brutalized one of Gaston's employees yesterday. That's gonna stop. Maybe you could pull the wool over everyone's eyes in Long Beach, but no more. I'm watching you and everything you do." As if to prove his point, he raised his phone and snapped her picture.

With that, he turned on his heel and stomped out of the office.

- - -

"He ruined my whole day."

"I can tell." Casey had stopped by. She'd stepped into the station mere minutes after Connor-Ruiz made his dramatic exit.

Tess groaned and let her forehead bang down on her desk. "Why?" she said into the desk.

"Why what?"

"Why would he follow me here?"

"If that's the guy I read about, he focused on you and got you run out of Long Beach. Maybe he thinks you're his lucky charm. You can weather this storm, Tess. I know you can."

She sat up. "Thanks. And I'm sorry . . . all worried about me. What can I do for you?"

"I have something fun to suggest. We're starting a classic movie night at church. Tonight is the inaugural potluck. My hubby made his famous mac and cheese. I thought maybe you'd like to take a break, eat some good food, enjoy some fellowship and an entertaining movie. You haven't had dinner yet, have you?"

"No, I haven't." Tess almost declined the offer outright, but what did she have planned? Dinner alone and something on television?

"Do you like classic movies?"

"I love them. But I don't have anything to bring to the potluck."

Casey shrugged. "There's always plenty of food. You can bring something next time."

"What's the movie?"

"*Laura* with Gene Tierney and Dana Andrews. It's a murder mystery." She grinned.

Anything to get my mind off Hector, Tess thought as she stood. "Okay, I'm in. Give me a minute to change."

In the restroom that served as her and Becky Jonkey's locker room, Tess squeezed her eyes closed, wishing she could disappear Hector back to Long Beach. She wanted to enjoy this movie night with Casey, she wanted to enjoy her life, but Connor-Ruiz had done exactly what she bet he wanted to. He'd messed with her head, thrown her off-balance.

Opening her eyes, she vowed to her reflection that she'd ignore all of his attacks and let them roll off her back.

23

Tess loved the movie. It was the first time she'd been in the church fellowship hall. She'd been in the sanctuary for Anna's funeral and then, of course, Tim's. There were about twenty-five people in attendance to eat dinner and watch the movie. Some of them she knew. Besides Casey and John Reno, Addie and Klaus Getz were there and even Officer Bender and his wife. Oliver was there as well. He made popcorn.

Gabe's eyes had gone from black and purple to faded yellow-green as they healed.

"Be back next week," he assured her.

It was a relaxing couple of hours. Tess hadn't realized how much she needed to relax. The pleasant glow from the evening lasted until she got home and was alone with her own thoughts and the specter of Hector Connor-Ruiz returned.

She did not want him living rent free in her head. But he was there, and that raised so many questions about his appearance in her new state: Why now? What did he have planned? And what were the people she worked with going to think?

Saturday morning, Tess worked to forget Hector. She planned on staying home and unpacking moving boxes. But it was supposed to be the hottest day so far this year and her heat pump saw fit to stop working. A morning phone call from Jeannie cheered her up immensely.

"Hey, how are you doing up there in the great northwest?"

"I'm doing fine, except . . ." Tess told her friend about Hector.

"You're kidding me. He moved up there?"

"So he says."

"Wow. I'll ask around. I know his blog has tanked, haven't heard a peep from him in a while."

They talked for a few minutes. Tess told her about Tim Harper's murder, and Jeannie told Tess about the latest in Long Beach.

"Let me tell you some good news. Remember my cousin in Portland? She's getting married next week. I wasn't going to go, but I changed my mind at the last minute."

"That sounds like fun."

"It will be. I decided to put a convoluted twist on it. Suppose I fly into Medford on Friday? I could spend the night, leave early in the morning, make it to the wedding. Get to see your new house."

"I'd love to see you. But my house—" She considered the weather and the fact that she kept having problems with an old, cranky heat pump. "The heat pump is temperamental, so it might be too hot here." She'd forgotten to call the technician and knew she'd probably not get someone out until next week.

"Well, we could stay at the B and B."

"How about the inn?" Since Cole was on his high horse again, Tess didn't want to go to the bed-and-breakfast he and his wife owned. The inn would be safe turf, and as much as she loved her house, she didn't want to worry about cooking or cleaning.

"That would be fine. I'll call you later in the week and firm things up."

Tess hung up, happy she'd be seeing Jeannie, even if it was only for one night.

Tess let her thoughts drift back to movie night. The sense of community she'd felt at the church bolstered her. There was a feeling of safety and camaraderie here, a feeling of peace, and as she began to tackle some boxes, it surprised her to admit that to herself.

Rogue's Hollow was home now. While not overly superstitious, she recognized the importance of gut feelings. And she'd learned that you could have feelings about places, situations that could help you, that could increase your comfort level. That was what made certain parts of town more desirable than others, the gut feeling that a place was safe, that you could let your guard down. There were certain parts of Long Beach that made Tess feel safe and certain parts that made her tense with awareness, preparing for the trouble she knew might lurk around any corner.

She preferred the safe feeling, the places where she could let her guard down.

She made herself a sandwich, and between bites, she opened a couple of boxes she'd stacked in the dining room. They weren't labeled, so the first one contained a big surprise. Inside, Tess found a small, long-forgotten box filled with some of her father's belongings. She hadn't even realized she still had the items. It had been years since she'd seen them. Sifting through the box reminded her of her dad and engulfed her in bittersweet memories.

There was his sweat-stained LA Dodgers hat and well-worn baseball glove—her father had been an awesome shortstop for the department's softball team—and the shoulder patches from his uniform shirt. And there was an index card he'd laminated. It was something he'd carried in his uniform pocket every day at work. There were four Bible verses cited on the card with short paraphrases of their meanings.

Sitting in her new home, facing the picture window that looked out over the river, watching the powerful movement of the water and an occasional rafter, she remembered a moment from a long time ago. Maybe ten years old at the time, she was with her dad in the mountains. They'd just finished a rousing snowball fight, one her father had let her win. They were both a little wet, cold, breathing hard and laughing. He'd just made the card and had it on the kitchen table when they went into the house to make hot chocolate.

"What do those numbers mean, Papa?"

Her father smiled and held the card up. *"This is my courage card, peanut."*

"Courage?"

"Yep. The words and numbers help me to always remember who I'm working for." He read the numbers and the verses.

And now, sitting at her own table, Tess read aloud what was written and imagined she could still hear her father's voice reciting the words that meant so much to him.

> *"Romans 13:4—'I'm God's servant. I don't bear the sword in vain. I am an avenger who carries out God's wrath on the wrongdoer.'"*
>
> *"Joshua 1:9—'Be strong and courageous . . . for the Lord your God is with you wherever you go.'"*
>
> *"Matthew 5:9—'Blessed are the peacemakers.'"*
>
> *"Psalm 82:3-4—'Give justice to the weak and the fatherless, the afflicted and the destitute. Rescue the weak and the needy from wicked people.'"*

Only a few words stood out to her at the time, words she would always associate with her father. *Peacemaker. Strong and courageous.*

"Are you a peacemaker?"

"You bet, peanut. What I love to do is keep the peace for the Lord."

"He's your boss?"

He laughed. *"He sure is."*

"Will he keep you safe?"

"You bet he will."

That conversation haunted Tess when her father was murdered. By that time, she'd been attending church with him for years; she understood about God and Jesus and all those verses her father used to carry in his pocket. But she would never understand why none of it had protected her father.

24

When the day began to heat up, Tess went to the station to work in her office. Del Jeffers was working in the field on overtime. The station would be locked, but a front intercom activated. On weekends when there was no one in the outer office, people could still press the intercom for assistance. If no one was in the station to answer the call, it went to the dispatch center where 911 calls were answered.

Tess planned to go back to the drawing board, reviewing everything she had on Tim's murder. At this point she knew it by heart. Besides finding Dustin, the only thing she was waiting on from the lab was the tox screen and whether any prints were lifted from the syringe. Eddie Carr was not off her list or her radar in relation to the Harper murder, but he was in custody and no threat right now. She was mulling over the other people still on the list when she arrived at the station.

Key in hand, she went to open the door and stopped. The front door and vestibule area were plastered with homemade handbills courtesy of Hector Connor-Ruiz.

Beware the Red Menace! Your chief of police is a murderer!

There was a picture of the boy Tess had shot in Long Beach, an idyllic picture of the kid several years younger than he was when Tess shot him, making him look like an angel. Hector had also typed out a paragraph describing Tess's corruption and even mentioning the arrest of Edward Carrington. That was, of course, suspect and possibly a frame-up.

She sighed, counted to ten, and started tearing all the papers off.

"Looks like you have quite the fan club."

Tess turned to see Agent Hemmings smirking at her.

"Agent Hemmings, are you here to talk to Haywood at the Hang Ten?"

He nodded, spitting seeds all over the gutter. "Ledge said you wanted to come along." He turned. "Let's go."

Tess's hands were filled with torn pieces of paper. Why hadn't he given her warning? "Give me a minute, please?"

"Burning daylight," he said as he climbed into a big black SUV.

Irritated on top of being irritated, Tess tossed everything into the nearest trash can and climbed into her truck as he made a U-turn. Why no notice? She could understand working on a Saturday, but Hemmings was just plain rude.

She caught up to him as he stopped at the security gate at the pot farm.

Her window was down and she heard him announce himself. At first, whoever answered the intercom told him to buzz off; he wasn't getting in.

Hemmings explained that they'd been harboring a fugitive by employing Carrington, and if they didn't want to talk nice to him now, he'd come back with a warrant, an entry team, and they'd tear the place apart.

A few minutes later, the gate swung open.

Tess followed the DEA agent in. The dirt driveway curved down to a parking area. The house was on the right, two travel trailers on the left. The gray van Carr had been driving when she arrested him was there, along with three other cars of various makes and models.

Haywood, Connor-Ruiz, and Don Cherry stood outside the front door. Hector had his phone out, ready to record or possibly recording already.

Hemmings got out of the car with an agent Tess didn't know. She followed them toward the three pot men.

"What's *she* doing here?" Hector called out as they approached.

"She's local law enforcement. This doesn't have to be hard. Just answer some questions."

"We don't want her here," Hector yelled.

"I don't care what you want. I'm here to talk to Gaston Haywood. It looks as if he has a penchant for hiring troublemakers."

"Look—"

"Shut up, Hector. Let's just get this over with." Haywood glared at his new partner.

"Wise man," Hemmings said. "You must be Haywood."

Haywood stepped forward and handed Hemmings a folder. "That's all I have on the guy. I thought he was Eddie Carr. I didn't care about his driver's license because he wasn't doing any official driving for me." He tossed an irritated glance Tess's way. "Unless you have a warrant for the house and grounds, this is all you're getting from me."

Hemmings took the folder, threatening a full-blown warrant, but Tess lost track of their conversation. The hair on the back of her neck stood up, and she turned to see Don Cherry staring at her. She stared back and he didn't look away. His eyes were the eyes of a stone-cold killer. There was no doubt he could have killed Tim Harper with his bare hands; he wouldn't have needed opiates. Yet with all his scariness, there still had to be an answer to "why?"

Tess looked away and tuned back into the conversation Hemmings and Haywood were having. But she began to wonder if it would be prudent to look harder at Cherry. He had a rough background—maybe he was the killer hiding in plain sight. Time for more digging.

25

"I don't see that we have anything to charge Haywood with," Hemmings said after they left the Hang Ten. They returned to the police station, where Hemmings grudgingly let her copy the contents of the file Haywood had given him. There wasn't much: a half-complete application for employment and a referral by someone named Howard Delfin.

"His business paperwork is on the up-and-up. Carrington only worked there for a few months." Hemmings shrugged. "The guy is naive—heck, he's a pothead—but I don't think he's criminal."

While Tess agreed with Hemmings, she remembered the level of investigation that went on after Roger Marshall was discovered to be a fugitive. It wasn't just two guys asking a couple of questions. True, Eddie didn't kidnap anyone like Marshall had, but he was a seriously dangerous person. He'd killed a DEA agent, so she expected a little more fanfare.

She had to acknowledge that she was having difficulty looking at the Hang Ten without a jaundiced eye. Maybe a part of her wanted them to be guilty of something. When she'd told Jeannie about the case, her friend had warned, "Don't let that place be a bogeyman." Was that what she'd done? Turned the Hang Ten into a bogeyman and let the killer get away?

Hemmings left and she continued cleaning up the front door, stomach churning as she considered the other problem: Hector Connor-Ruiz and his crusade to annoy her. How bad could it get?

- - -

After the agents left, Hector began to review the footage he'd taken.

"Why do you have to yank everyone's chain?" Haywood whined.

Hector lowered the phone and faced the surfer. "What? I hate cops. You can't just let them trample your rights."

"I didn't let them do anything. That stupid Carr put me in this pickle. Don't you make it worse." He went back inside the house before Hector could respond.

The big guy stayed outside. He leaned against the side of the house, cleaning his fingernails with a pocketknife. Hector had nothing to say to him and decided he'd head into town.

Halfway to his car the big guy spoke up. "Where're you going?"

Hector jerked around to face the guy, snide comment

dying on his lips. The guy was scary. All Hector managed was "What, you my keeper?"

"Just asking."

"To town. My job is to bug the chief—today and every day." He hurried to his car, relieved when the big guy said nothing more.

– – –

Hector walked up and down the main street of Rogue's Hollow every day of the week. He often wore a T-shirt with a picture of the Red Menace silk-screened on the front with the caption, "This woman is a murderer and she's your chief."

No one asked him about it, but a lot of people read it, he was sure. Toward the end of his first week in town, he was already certain that he had beaten her. She was the chief of Mayberry, for heaven's sake. What a comedown from Long Beach. He already hated this place, he thought as he walked into the pizza place, ordered a pie, and sat down, snickering to himself about what a hick town O'Rourke was stuck in. He was halfway through his pizza when a thought occurred. He could truly ruin the woman here, not just get her fired, but *ruin* her completely.

He smiled and chuckled to himself. He'd redouble his efforts. There was no place lower for her to go; he'd drive her there, stomp her down, then be on his way back to civilization.

– – –

As it happened, it got considerably worse for Tess. On her next walk around town, three people stopped to ask her about the man.

"That guy moved all the way up here to make noise about you?" Pete, the coffee shop owner, asked.

"I guess so."

He held up a pile of paper. "He asked if he could leave these here for people to pick up. Then he threatened to sue me when I said no. Kept yelling about equal access or some such stuff." He shrugged. "He left and I pulled them back here. I'm going to toss them."

"Thanks, Pete. Sorry he's being such a nuisance."

Pete wasn't the only person she apologized to. Connor-Ruiz made his presence known around town with more than just handbills and quickly became the topic of conversation. That he could stir up so much in a short time amazed Tess.

"Wow, that little guy has a lot of fuel in his engine," Gabe said after logging in on his first day back.

"Doesn't he?" Tess was glad Gabe was healed but doubly glad to be in her own car again. Forest had finished fixing it and dropped it by before Gabe arrived.

"Any movement on Tim Harper's case?"

Tess sighed. "No, still waiting on the lab for info on the prints. And the bike and the phone are still outstanding."

Gabe's return set the schedule to even, but Hector's activities promised to keep everyone busy. Tess was asked about him during her Thursday walk by just about every business owner, and he seemed to be everywhere. He kept urging people to attend the upcoming council meeting and voice their concerns over their corrupt police chief. As a result, Thursday's city council meeting was packed, and Tess found herself the topic of conversation, Drake Harper leading the charge.

"This man is making serious allegations against Chief O'Rourke," he said, standing, nodding toward Hector, and then reading from written notes. "I want to know if the council is taking any steps to look into them."

"Drake." Addie Getz addressed him first. "I've heard the allegations, and frankly this gentleman has absolutely no evidence to back up anything he says."

"That doesn't answer my question. My son was murdered four weeks ago and the investigation has gone nowhere. She's done nothing—she didn't even take fingerprints at the house after my wife told her someone had been there with Tim. How do I know that's not because the chief is corrupt and not doing her job?"

"I have full confidence in the chief," Casey Reno said.

A few people, led by Hector, booed.

"Well, I don't," Cole Markarov jumped in. "And I think Mr. Harper has a point. Chief O'Rourke has never had my full confidence. Recently she nearly totaled a practically brand-new patrol vehicle. It's high time we revisit her hire."

With that, the room exploded, as people for and against rose and spoke up to have their opinions heard. Tess had never seen the room so animated. It took several minutes before Addie gained control.

"I will have order here," she said. The normally unflappable woman was visibly shaken at the turmoil. "Drake, your concerns are noted and are on record. I'd like to hear from a few others."

After that, the council gave four people the opportunity to speak for two minutes. Two of them—Tess recognized them as habitual problems from the trailer park—blasted her as well, complaining that she ordered her officers to harass them. Hector goaded and egged them on until Addie cautioned that he would be removed as a disruption.

Two people stood to support Tess, but they both seemed intimidated and their endorsements were lukewarm. Tess wondered where Oliver was. He would have stood up for her as well . . . at least she thought he would.

"Thank you," Addie said. "Thank you for your input. I'm ending debate at this time in order to give the council time to consider this issue. We'll decide on a course of action as soon as possible."

"About time," Cole said, casting a triumphant glance toward Tess.

Addie tossed Tess a sympathetic look. But it didn't help. Tess felt slapped in the face by the entire proceeding.

Hector started a chant. "No cover-up! No cover-up!"

As people filed out, Tess saw Oliver working his way in, against the flow.

"Sorry I missed the fireworks," Oliver said as he made his way to the front of the room.

"It was a doozy," Addie said. She briefly recapped for Oliver.

It stung, almost as much as when she'd been forced to leave Long Beach, to see all that sentiment in the council chambers going against her.

Casey nodded to her. "I believe in you, Tess," she said as she left.

She thought she and Forest Wild, the fourth council member, were on good terms, but he wouldn't even meet her eyes. He and Cole Markarov were in deep conversation. Tess knew where Cole stood. Was Forest against her now as well?

"I'd really like to get a better handle on this fellow," Addie said when she finished recapping for Oliver. "Right now he's kicking up a lot of dust."

Tess felt like roadkill.

What a mark Hector had made in only a week.

"No wonder you look stressed, Chief," Oliver said.

Irritated on one hand for being so transparent, while glad on the other hand to see Oliver, Tess tried to curb a temper that was ready to explode. She knew she had the pastor's support, and right now, that was a lifeline.

"It's been a rough week."

"Time for coffee and a little chat?"

"Sounds great, but I'm beat. I'd kind of like to go home and get to bed. Rain check."

"Certainly. And for what it's worth, that guy—I know the type. He wants you on edge, on the defensive. Don't let him get under your skin."

"I really try not to. But if he's not tacking notices to trees and doorways, he's popping up and snapping pictures everywhere. It's disconcerting. And now he's poisoned Drake Harper . . ."

"Drake is hurting; he's lashing out." Oliver sighed. "I was late because I had a meeting with Eva Harper. She's worried about him. People mourn in different ways, and right now all of his hurt is channeled into anger."

"I can understand his anger, but he's letting his outrage be fueled by Hector's made-up allegations."

"Be patient, Tess."

She looked into Oliver's eyes when he said her name. His ability to steady her with a glance amazed Tess. At that moment, she felt such a strong connection to the man.

He continued. "I believe this will all work itself out in time. And the people in this town are good people. They'll see through Connor-Ruiz—I'm sure of it. You're a good chief. You fit in here. Do your best to let all his antics roll off your back."

His words were calming, soothing even, but Tess couldn't help but wonder, would she have a chance to do that before she got fired? And if she were fired, where would she go? What would be left of her career? It was nearly impossible to tamp down the fear that reached up and grabbed her by the throat when she considered losing her job. It was her life.

Working in a small town was a double-edged sword. Yes, it was nice that everyone knew everyone, but then there was the problem: everyone knew everyone.

26

Tess got home from the council meeting Thursday night frowning and fretting. She'd told Oliver she was beat, and that was the truth, but she knew it would be impossible to sleep right away, so she didn't try. Connor-Ruiz appearing and her heat pump dying doubled up to make her feel as if she were in that hot place no one wanted to go. But the more she fretted, the angrier she got. She was not going to let Hector win.

She went to bed around 1 a.m., tossed and turned, barely sleeping. After a shower and breakfast, she headed into town to face a new day, hoping it would be better than the day before. One bright spot came with a call from Jeannie.

"Hey, girlfriend! I'll be in by dinnertime, okay?"

"Great!" Tess flashed between excitement and dread. There was so much going on. But the excitement won out. She needed to talk to her friend. Jeannie would understand what Hector was putting Tess through better than anyone.

But waiting for her at the station when she got there was Damien Gangly, the owner of the small local newspaper, *Upper Rogue Ramblings*.

"Chief, I hope you can spare me a few minutes. I'd like to discuss the council meeting."

Tess didn't want to spare him a second to recap that fiasco. She was tired and cranky and just wanted to drink her coffee and think. But she erred on the side of diplomacy.

"Sure, Damien, come on in." She nodded to Sheila on the way in. It turned out that the topic of Hector not only dominated her night, it would begin her day.

"That guy truly thinks you're evil. He's stirred up every criminal element and even some not so criminal," Damien said as soon as she closed her office door. "He's been here—what?—seven days, and he's already sent me a couple dozen e-mails he wants to run in the paper. Stories he says prove you're unfit for office."

Tess sighed, remembering rule #1: "Listen. Think. Speak." Connor-Ruiz had done more than send e-mails to Damien.

She swallowed some coffee, not wanting to fan any flames. "He does have a vendetta against me. And he doesn't have much respect for police in general."

"But why is he fixated on you?"

"It has to do with something that happened years ago in Long Beach, I think. At least it's the only thing I can put my finger on. He was a college kid, and he got stuck in traffic when a plane crashed on the freeway, just short of the airport. He tried to photograph the dead pilot—it was pretty gruesome—and in doing so, he interfered with the officers trying to contain the scene and prevent any car accidents. I approved the arrest." She shrugged, remembering the civil suits with Connor-Ruiz claiming his rights had been violated and the ultimate vindication the PD received when he lost every decision.

"He sued and lost, and he's been angry with me in particular and the police in general ever since. I'm surprised he followed me up here, but not surprised he still hates me."

"There's nothing more personal?"

Tess held her hands out. "Not to my knowledge."

Damien shook his head. "Well, his messages to me are hate-filled and one-sided. I've told him to write about something current."

Tess laughed grimly. "I'll try not to give him any relevant fodder."

"Chief—" Damien stood—"I also have to ask . . . what is happening with the Harper investigation? Drake Harper put a bug in my ear about you needing to contact the sheriff for help."

"I simply have no leads." She rubbed her forehead. "I understand Mr. Harper's pain, but I'm working that case from every angle. Right now there is nothing the sheriff could do that I'm not already doing."

"At what point will you ask for their help?"

That question took Tess back a step. She hadn't considered that she needed help. She was a competent investigator;

her people were competent; they'd covered every avenue they could cover. The prints were out of their control—all they could do was wait on that front—but Dustin was in their court. Yet no one seemed to know where he was, so they were at a standstill. Indecision and uncertainty suddenly clouded her thoughts.

"When I'm certain I've exhausted everything," she said, hoping she didn't sound defensive.

He seemed satisfied with the answer and asked a few more questions about Cole and the upcoming election. Tess tried to get back to work, but there was a feeling of foreboding roiling in her gut. Connor-Ruiz coming to Rogue's Hollow was just plain bad karma.

27

"It's not going to work, you know." Oliver looked down at Hector Connor-Ruiz. Friday morning the annoying man was sitting at an outdoor table at the Hollow Grind. He had a large coffee, a plate of sweet pastries, and a newspaper in front of him.

Hector looked up. "What?"

"This effort to smear our chief. We trust her."

Hector grinned. "Ah, pops, you're breaking my heart. I don't trust any cop. Especially not *her*."

"You moved to Oregon just to bother her?"

"I came to save you people. What's your name?"

"Sorry, that was rude. I'm Oliver Macpherson. I pastor the local church here."

"Well, Oliver, I think the chief is corrupt, plain and simple." He touched a hand to his chest. "I'm my own sort of public servant. Pointing out all that is wrong with her is my public service to you." He held his hand out toward Oliver, a smirk on his face.

Oliver felt his anger rising. There was no speaking to this man. "What's your endgame?"

Hector took a bite of a peach pastry, confectioners' sugar dribbling down his chin, and spoke with his mouth full. "I have made it my personal mission to make sure that woman never works as a police officer ever again."

"Then I'll have to make sure you fail at your personal mission."

Hector swallowed and exploded into derisive giggles. "Oh, the preacher goes jihad on me. Just remember, she gets no points for having a holy boyfriend." He laughed like a lunatic, and Oliver had to leave, never considering denying the boyfriend line.

- - -

Later Oliver regretted getting in the man's face. And he wondered at the strong urge he felt to protect Tess. It was disconcerting for Oliver to see her so distracted, wounded really, with all the scurrilous accusations Hector was throwing around. And a side issue was that it felt like he was accusing Anna of being mistaken, and Anna was never mistaken, at least not about the goodness in people. Tess was a good person, a good cop. She was a calm, strong presence when a law enforcement situation required it. After the city council meeting, he'd prayed that this new troublemaker, Hector whatever his name was, would relax. He was off-putting on so many levels.

After confronting Hector, Oliver thought about Don Cherry. He wanted to ask the big man about Hector again. He'd tried once. But Don was rarely forthcoming and often talked in riddles.

Oliver also wondered what Tess would think about the visits he'd been getting from Don, if there was anything she'd want him to ask Cherry. The guy just seemed to materialize out of nowhere. Last night, after the council meeting, Cherry had appeared on his porch. It was the first time Oliver had asked him about the guy at the Hang Ten, the one causing Tess all the trouble, and his response had been strange to say the least.

"What do you know about this new boss of yours, the one who keeps spouting off about the chief?"

"Hector?" He gave a dismissive wave of his large hand. "He's not my boss."

"I thought he was Haywood's partner."

"Haywood's not my boss either."

"Was he Carr's boss?"

Cherry looked at him out of the corner of his eye. "That guy was a moron. All he had to do was drive right—that's all—and he'd have flown under everyone's radar. Couldn't do it. I'll tell you, though, your chief is either very lucky or tougher than I thought."

"What do you mean?"

"Carr would have knocked her down and shot her with her own gun without thinking twice. I'm a little impressed she got the cuffs on."

He talked about shooting Tess in such a matter-of-fact way, Oliver had to take a breath.

"Did you know Carr was a fugitive?"

Cherry smiled a Cheshire cat smile. "What's with the twenty questions, padre? We're supposed to conversate."

Oliver had to laugh. "I'm just curious about the rank structure there at the Hang Ten."

Cherry then abruptly changed the subject. Something he did often, usually with non sequiturs, when he didn't want to talk about something. The conversation left Oliver wondering about the pot farm and whether he should mention Cherry's visits to the chief. The indecision inside surprised him. As far as he knew, Cherry wasn't breaking any laws. He was scary-looking, and he was an ex-con, but it seemed as if he simply needed to talk. He waffled between wanting to talk to Tess about Cherry and then thinking talking about Cherry to Tess would be betraying some unspoken confidence he had with the man. He wondered at the indecision. Was it because after several talks he still didn't know what Cherry wanted?

He thought about Tess's life rules, especially the one she quoted often about trusting your gut. Tess had a gift there. Usually when she had a gut feeling about something, she was correct. Was that it? Oliver wondered. He had a gut feeling that something was off about Cherry, something the chief should know?

But that conflicted with the pastoral part of him. Cherry also had a soul that needed to be saved. Somehow he knew he needed to calm the conflict inside the man. He just didn't know how.

28

Friday morning, not five minutes after Damien left, Tess's phone rang with a call from a reporter for the local news station in Medford. She asked for a five-minute interview with Tess and seemed pleasant enough, but an unexpected question knocked her cold.

"What is this rumor of police corruption we hear concerning Rogue's Hollow PD?"

"Excuse me—what rumor?"

"The station was contacted by an individual who resides in Rogue's Hollow. He informed us that he is urging the FBI to commit to an investigation of your PD. What do you have to say about that?"

Feeling the heat rise and forcing her voice to be calm and modulated, Tess asked, "Who is your source?"

"Does that matter? Is the Rogue's Hollow PD corrupt?"

Tess cleared her throat. "I think I know your source. Mr. Connor-Ruiz is mistaken. He likes to make wild and unsubstantiated claims."

"Have you been contacted by the FBI or the Justice Department?"

"No, I have not."

That ended the interview, and Tess left her office because she needed some air; the walls were closing in on her. But she didn't feel like doing a walk-through. Hector's being here was worse than his being in Long Beach. At least there were more places to blend in, in Long Beach.

But was that really what she wanted—to blend in, to hide? That made her cringe. Cops didn't hide. She grabbed her coffee and intended to sit at an outside table and drink it when her radio squawked with a call for her. A bike had been found out near the Dover place, Gabe Bender told her.

"I'm on my way."

Finally, maybe a lead. Tess felt her spirits lift. She couldn't let Hector Connor-Ruiz distract her so much that a murderer got away.

- - -

The bike was in a tangle of blackberry bushes about a quarter mile from the Dover property. River Drive ended just beyond the Dovers' driveway. On the river there was a parking lot and a small day use area called Smugglers Cove, with five picnic areas, each a little private with a table and a barbecue grill. The place was lightly used, mostly by tourists. Locals said though the tables were shaded, there was no shade over the water and it was shallow, not good for fishing.

"How'd you find it?" Tess asked Gabe when she arrived.

"It was Bart Dover. He saw a portion of the bike sticking out of the bushes and called. He was afraid this area was turning into a dump spot. That's happened before. He just asked that we take a look."

Tess studied the bike. It was the same brand as Tim's, and there was a Dutch Bros. Coffee sticker wrapped around the frame. It hadn't been in the bushes long, but it was banged up. And it was a long way from where the kids partied—and from Tim's home, for that matter.

"It's been hit." She looked at Gabe. "There's some paint transfer."

"That was my thought. A car hit him and . . ."

"The driver kills him to hide the crash?" Tess shook her head. "Why take him home and put him to bed?" She paused for a moment. "I'm glad we found this, but it doesn't answer any questions; it just raises more." She looked at the surroundings. "Let's check out the picnic areas, see if there's anything else. Maybe we'll get really lucky and find his phone."

Bender nodded. He started for the two farthest spots and Tess took the three closest. At the water's edge she looked around and then up. There was a clear view of the sky from here and the warm sun beat down. Was it possible that this was the spot Tim picked to photograph the moon? She could picture the boy lying on his back on the picnic table, pointing his phone skyward.

Thinking of that image, Tess searched the area carefully for any clue. Unfortunately, she came up empty.

She called Drake Harper to tell him the news.

"His bike was way down there? Was he in a car accident?"

"The frame is bent and scratched, so yes, there is a possibility someone hit him."

"Can I have the bike or do you need to hold it?"

"We collected some paint transfer and I'll dust for prints. After that, sure, you can have it back."

He gave a grunt of acknowledgment and disconnected.

Tess pulled her kit out of the car and proceeded to do something she'd been trained years ago to do, and had done hundreds of times—dust for prints. She looked at the bike and imagined where the person who threw it into the bushes would have gripped it. It had been mostly hot and dry since Tim's murder. Thunderstorms had threatened but never materialized. There should be prints, and there were. It was comforting in a way, to do things the tried-and-true old-fashioned way. Tess pulled several partial prints off the frame. Some were certain to be Tim's, but with luck at least one belonged to the killer. She placed the print cards into an evidence envelope with the paint chips and put it in her pocket.

"You can take the bike to the Harpers'. I'll send the evidence to the lab."

Gabe nodded and put the bike in the bed of his truck.

Tess called the lab before she headed back to the station, explaining about the prints and paint scrapings she was sending and asking about the syringe.

"We should have something for you by Monday."

Tess hung up optimistic, feeling like she was finally closing in on a killer. If the prints belonged to Carrington or Cherry, that would bring her one step closer to closing the case for sure.

29

It was past lunchtime when Tess sent the prints off. Jeannie texted; she was still on track to be there at dinnertime.

She and Tess would stay the night at the inn. Tess had reserved a room and ordered a surprise dinner set up for her friend along with a couple of movies they both liked. She reached up and rubbed a shoulder that was tense with stress. She needed to find a way to relax in spite of everything swirling around her even more than she had last week. It would be a good break to eat a tasty meal and then curl up in her jammies and watch movies. Tess wanted to zone out and forget the current nastiness with Hector, Tim's death. She went back to her office, trying to decide what to eat for lunch.

Pastor Mac was waiting for her at the station. "Hey, Tess, I was wondering if I could buy you lunch. Am I too late?"

"Not at all, and I am hungry." It was almost two—no wonder she was hungry. "But something light. I'm having dinner with my friend Jeannie tonight."

"Okay, I can do light or a nice bowl of soup." He smiled. "I know you have a lot to do, and things have been stressful for you lately. We can talk about anything but Hector or the city council meeting. Maybe you'd like to cover something less contentious, like the cannabis issue?"

Despite everything going on, Tess had to give a little grin. "You always know the right thing to say."

"A nonconfrontational snack is just what the pastor ordered."

"You're right about that." Tess sighed. "And today has been a good day." She told him about Tim's bike.

"The prints will identify the last person to touch the bike?"

"Hopefully, and then we'll have a direction to go and maybe even a solid suspect."

"Glad to hear it. How about we eat at the inn?"

"That works for me."

As they walked across the street, she worked to keep fatigue at bay. Oliver's company was a bright spot, an encouragement. She enjoyed discussing town issues with him. She appreciated his perspective and his insight. Oliver was the most even-keeled person she knew.

She remembered her father's laminated Scripture card. She'd put it in her pocket, not because she believed in the sentiments on the card, but because somehow it made her feel closer to her father. Should she show it to Oliver? He might get a kick out of it.

After all her angst about Connor-Ruiz, it was nice to be around someone who, Tess realized, had a handle on life, in the face of great loss. Oliver's faith surprised Tess. His wife's murder had not put a dent in it. Lately, maybe in part due to the discovery of the card among her father's things, Tess found herself thinking more and more about God and faith, without getting ragingly angry. She wasn't sure why, but bits and pieces of things her father had said to her while she was growing up had come back to her. In her mind's eye, she could see him sitting at the kitchen table, sipping coffee and reading the Bible like he did every morning before work.

"Haven't you finished that yet?" she'd teased one morning.

He smiled and said, *"There's wisdom here, Tessa. A man can never have too much wisdom."*

Was it that wisdom that helped Oliver pull it together after Anna's death? Aside from his monthlong sabbatical home to Scotland, Oliver seemed to have weathered the storm and come back stronger. Yes, he'd been devastated by Anna's murder, but Tess had heard talk that his preaching was better than ever. His congregation had even grown a bit. Tess knew that his ability to move forward had helped heal a town and a congregation that also felt the loss of a truly special person.

It made her wonder if she was missing something. After all, she'd never seen her dad's faith waver, no matter what he encountered at work. And she could never know what his last thoughts were that morning, his final day of life, when he took a bullet for an abuse victim. For some reason, after so many years had passed, she asked herself what he would think of his daughter, who had turned her back on something he thought was so important. But when her thoughts went that direction, old anger and hurt did surface. Her father was murdered, shot in the street like a dog. Where was God in that? That was the question that rose like a brick wall when she considered returning to church or to faith.

It surprised Tess that despite her inner struggles with the topic, Oliver's genuine, sincere faith impressed her. In a small way, he reminded her of her father. Daniel O'Rourke had been a faithful churchgoer. Tess went with him, and he'd told her often, *"We get our strength from God, Tess. He is who it is that gives us the ability to live a good and righteous life, and to be fair and firm with the people we serve. We need that touchstone; I need that touchstone."*

At one point, Tess thought she knew what he meant; she thought she shared his faith and embraced the touchstone that faith was. But when he was murdered, she lost her faith and her touchstone.

Now, with Oliver Macpherson and his example, she often found her thoughts drifting to church and the message of faith in God that her father had embraced. But she'd yet to take a step forward and attend a service.

The inn was cool and smelled wonderful as they waited to be seated. Since Tess had lived here for so many months, it was almost like coming home.

They were given a table by the window with a view of the water. The dining room was crowded because a local quilting group was meeting. Several tables had been pushed together and the room resonated with the sound of the ladies' chatter and occasional laughter.

Tess decided on the clam chowder. It was Friday and that was the inn's specialty, but she opted for a cup rather than the house-baked sourdough bowl because that would be too filling.

"Ah, that sounds great. I'll have the same."

They chatted a bit, and after the food was served, Oliver said, "I hope I'm not crossing any line, but I haven't seen Sergeant Logan around lately. I wondered if you're still seeing him."

"We're taking a break. I talked to him the other day." She shrugged, realizing that with all the turmoil in her life right now, she felt more comfortable with Oliver than she ever had with Steve. Was that a good thing?

"Sorry to hear that."

"I'm okay. My divorce still stings. I'm probably not ready for anything serious right now."

"Understandable. Have you met the interim sheriff yet?" The sheriff of Jackson County had resigned two years into his four-year term because of health problems. The county had just picked an interim sheriff to serve out the remaining two years of the term.

Tess shook her head. "I haven't. They picked him so fast, he must be a good guy."

"I'll give him the benefit of the doubt. He's got a big job. There are a lot more pot farms in all of Jackson County. I imagine that the problems we've seen here are multiplied in the whole county."

Tess considered that, feeling truly fortunate that there were only three farms in Rogue's Hollow. "Are you still mediating disputes between pot and non-pot people?"

"Here and there. I've tried to get Don to tell me what they really think they can accomplish by being so pushy—"

"Don? As in Don Cherry?" Tess stiffened, wondering what on earth Oliver and the ex-con would be doing talking.

"Yes. He stops by from time to time to talk to me."

"About what?"

Oliver rubbed his chin. "Everything. And nothing. I'm not really sure what he's after. But it bothers you?"

"It's not that. It's, uh . . . He's a dangerous guy. Has he suddenly gotten religious?"

Oliver shook his head. "We just chat. I've told him that you get more bees with honey than vinegar, and if he and his crew would just be nice to people, they'd make more headway. It always seems as though if there is a problem in town, one of Haywood's crew is behind it."

"True," Tess said, still trying to get past the idea of that monster of a man and Oliver *chatting*. "Cherry is scary standing still."

"He can be. But something else is going on with him; I'm just not sure what it is yet."

Frowning, Tess said, "Has he confessed something to you? Something illegal?" *Did he kill Tim Harper?*

"No, not at all. He just talk—"

Before Oliver could finish his sentence, they were interrupted by someone's presence at the table.

"Asking the priest to absolve you of your sins?" Hector Connor-Ruiz sneered.

Oliver responded calmly and smoothly while Tess was still gathering her thoughts. "I'm not a priest, and this isn't a confessional."

Sitting back, Tess worked hard to be as calm as Oliver. "Mr. Connor-Ruiz, this is really getting old. You're being a nuisance to interrupt not only my meal but Pastor Macpherson's."

"That a menace would call me a nuisance. Ha." He raised his voice, did a 360. "I'm just making sure everyone here knows what a fake you are. What a stealer of human rights. What a menace. It's America. I have the right to free speech."

Tess was acutely aware that the quilting group had gone silent. She felt as if every woman at the large table turned their way. Many were locals, but some were from other parts of the valley and probably had no idea about the conflict raging in the Hollow. It was paralyzing. She turned in her chair, not sure how to handle this, but Hector wasn't finished.

"All of you people, this woman is a criminal. That you pay her to be chief of police is a joke, a farce, a—"

Oliver stood and faced Connor-Ruiz. "Excuse me, but you're not exercising free speech; you're being rude. You're interrupting my meal and the meal of every other diner here using a basic right as an excuse to be abusive."

"Hear, hear," a diner at another table chimed in. Tess turned to see Victor Camus, local hunting guide, watching Oliver and Hector. He was sitting with his sister, Helen. Tess hadn't known that she was back in town. "You need to find another place to be a jerk, friend," he said, tone dangerous.

The defense for her was nearly as paralyzing as the bullying. In Long Beach only Ronnie Riggs had stood up so vocally, but would he have done it in a crowded restaurant?

Connor-Ruiz turned toward Victor, and some of his bluster faded. Victor was an intimidating person. The hunting guide had a Clint Eastwood stare going on.

Stepping back, Hector got chicken-chested. "Look, boy-friend." Hector jammed his index finger into Oliver's chest. "Mark my words! She's a menace, you'll see. Death follows her—innocent death. Come to the council meeting next month. Force your council to take action." With that he turned on his heel and left the restaurant.

Tess brought a hand to her forehead as Oliver sat. The fatigue and frustration of the day came to a head. Her throat clogged, and all she could croak out was "I'm so sorry—"

"Don't." Oliver reached across the table and grasped her hand. Tess squeezed back, needing someone else's strength because it felt as if hers was draining away.

"Don't apologize. That guy is the problem, not you."

Tess sucked in a breath, the awful memories of what drove her from Long Beach suffocating her at the same time the strength and defense Oliver offered bolstered her. It was his stormy gray eyes—they always reminded her of the mighty Rogue River, and she felt strength and comfort that doused the burning embarrassment brought on by Hector's tirade.

It was a minute before she could speak.

"Hector Connor-Ruiz—he has no life other than to attack me. He wants people to hate me, to mistrust me."

Pulling his hand back, Oliver shook his head. "He's mak-ing waves, that's for sure. But he'll fail. No one who knows you will believe him. You've proved to us that you're genuine and good; you've proved your quality." He grinned.

"My quality? That sounds like something from a movie."

"It is. I'm a Tolkien fan. Did you see the movies?"

"Ah, Lord of the Rings. Yes, a long time ago."

"Yeah." He chuckled, a rich, masculine sound. "I guess

I'm a bit dated, but it's a classic. And in *The Two Towers* there's an exchange between Faramir and Samwise. Faramir was always struggling to prove his quality to his father."

"That's right, I remember. And when he let Frodo and Sam go, Sam tells him that he's proved his quality." She smiled, the discomfort from the confrontation with Hector fading away as she and Oliver connected on the bit of movie nostalgia.

"So you are a fan. My point is, we know you here, your integrity and courage. The fact that you are a dragon slayer."

That made Tess laugh, and all the stress was gone.

"So don't worry. That guy is not going to tarnish you in our eyes in the least. I've said it before—don't let him get in your head."

"Thank you, Oliver. I won't."

"Good. Now let's finish our lunch and move on to solve all the world's problems."

30

Hector bounced out of the inn with a smirk on his face. This had been easier than he thought it would be. He was getting to the woman, he was certain. In fact, he laughed when he reached his car because he believed that he'd already won. The Red Menace was stuck here in the third circle of hell— that was what he thought of Rogue's Hollow. It had surprised him when he got here how primitive the place was. Locals called it rustic, code for boring.

Though he'd only been in residence for a little over a week, Hector hated this place as much if not more than he hated Tess O'Rourke. He'd made so much headway in a short amount of time, he had a feeling the city council might remove her from her job before the beginning of next week. But it couldn't balance out how much he hated living in the country.

This town, this backward, boring place, was suffocating. The only thing it had going for it was a good coffee shop. The one bar here sucked, and there wasn't even a McDonald's close by. And there were no other entertainment venues unless you wanted to drive all the way to Medford, and Medford was no Long Beach. Happy but frustrated as well, he slowly made his way to his new home, not wanting to get a ticket like that stupid Carr.

His moron surfer roommate and partner wasn't home, and for that he was glad. The big, scary guy was there watching TV. Hector kind of wished the big guy had been arrested instead of Carr. He didn't know Carr, but nobody could be as scary as Cherry. Hector always gave him a wide berth.

He opened the fridge and grabbed a beer. He thought getting the chief fired would be his big life achievement. He opened his beer and was about to take a drink when a disturbing thought struck. If he got the chief fired, then he'd be stuck here in this dull town and she wouldn't even be around to harass.

What would he do then?

The thought paralyzed him. To be stranded here would be worse than enduring Chinese water torture.

So what if it had only been a week? So what if it was a lot of money? Hector considered quitting, going back to California. As soon as the chief was bounced, he'd leave, get out of Dodge and back to the crowded busyness of California. After downing a six-pack, he called his benefactor.

"Hey, man, I hate this place. It's *Deliverance* here. Banjo players on every corner. I'm quitting, heading back to LB."

"We had an agreement."

"Yeah, well, I delivered. Bet the woman is fired in a week. I fulfilled the bargain. This place sucks."

"If that's true, you stay put until she's gone. You owe me. I bailed you out."

"I didn't ask you to."

"That's not the point. You leave, you pay me back. Every cent."

"When I get back on my feet."

"The minute you leave. I'm not a charitable organization."

"I can't stay here. I'll pay you back when I can."

"I'm warning you—"

Hector disconnected. Drunk, feeling brave, he cursed his benefactor and Tess O'Rourke and went into his room to pack. He'd show them. He'd hit it big with news somehow, in a civilized city with a nightlife and a million people hanging on every word of his blog.

31

After Oliver left, Tess checked the time. Jeannie should be in soon. She contemplated going home; she lived five minutes away. Then she decided against it. While she hadn't picked up her overnight bag, Tess had a change of clothes in the car, a vestige of preparedness left over from her time in Long Beach, when she'd taught disaster preparedness and the worry was earthquakes. She'd considered staying at the inn for the whole weekend, even after Jeannie left, but still hadn't decided.

She drank another glass of iced tea and watched the river out the big picture windows in the dining room, a view she never tired of. A drift boat passed by, followed by a raft filled with people. Summer, the busy season on the river, had barely started, but Tess was ready for winter and cooler weather. She'd never been a beach girl. Her fair skin burned too easily, and she enjoyed the snow more than the sand. The first winter she'd spent in Oregon had been snowy and very cold, but she hadn't minded. She'd found that the four-wheel-drive vehicle the city provided was more than adequate to get her where she needed to go.

Next year she'd be even better prepared.

Thinking about next year gave her pause for a moment. The contentious city council meeting was seared in her mind. She'd been trying to forget all she'd heard from people in the community she served, especially Drake in his grief. It was easy not to like the cop. She remembered what an old training officer used to say: *"If you want to be popular, be a fireman."* For Tess that was never an option.

If Cole won the election for mayor, she wouldn't have a job here next year.

Would she stay in Oregon? Tess thought of Oliver, Casey, Addie, Steve—all people she considered friends. The pain at the thought of leaving friends again so soon took her by surprise. But then, this was home now.

The dining room emptied quickly with the exodus of the quilting group; but now people began to dribble in for dinner. Tess finished her tea and moved to a comfortable chair in the lobby, fighting the urge to pace and finding herself full of restless energy. She wanted to be all in for Jeannie's visit because her friend might not be back for a while, but Tim's case would not leave her thoughts. The lab promised her some results by Monday. A real lead on Tim Harper's murder was something she pinned a lot of hopes on. Closing that case should relax Drake and maybe even shut Hector up.

"Hiya, Chief."

Tess looked up into the smiling face of Tilly Dover. A work in progress, the ex–drug tragedy looked clean and sober and happy. Tess had solved the murder of Tilly's boyfriend last summer, and Tilly had been a mess. A bad accident had sent her to the hospital and circumstances had forced her to get clean. She had one relapse after the first of the year, and for a short while, Tess was afraid that the girl was lost. But she rallied, got clean all over again, and now Tess was happy to see that she seemed to be staying that way.

It was Addie Getz who took a chance and gave Tilly a place to live and a job. Now, though she still walked with a limp, she seemed to enjoy her job and being part of the night cleanup crew.

"Hi, Tilly, how are you and Killer doing?"

Killer the dog had belonged to Tilly's dead boyfriend. Tess had given the dog to Tilly, hoping the responsibility of caring for another life would kindle something in Tilly, and it had. She was devoted to the dog, and Tess knew that played no small part in Tilly's rehabilitation.

Tilly grinned. Her blonde hair hung in soft, short curls. She'd had her head almost shaved in the hospital because of lice, but it had grown back nicely.

"She's great; she's a love. And I changed her name—finally picked one that works for me and suits her better, and I think she likes it. She knows it already."

"Aw, what did you name her?"

"Angel."

Now Tess grinned. "Perfect."

"Can I get you anything?"

Tess shook her head. "No, I'm waiting for a friend."

Tilly nodded and limped off, dusting as she went.

Tess glanced at her phone to check the time, and a small groan escaped when she saw the battery was dead. Suppose Jeannie had tried to call and couldn't? She paced for the next half hour, relaxing only when a car pulled into the parking lot.

Jeannie burst through the door. "I made it!"

Tess smiled and wrapped her friend in a hug. "Great. I've really been looking forward to your visit."

Looking tired, Jeannie flopped down into a chair across from Tess. "Flying just isn't fun anymore. Even that short trip was draining."

"Well, you're here. Now I have a surprise for you after you check in. I hope you're hungry."

"Famished."

"Let's go." Tess glanced at the clock, wishing briefly that time could be suspended and all the ugliness of late would disappear before she had to leave the inn.

— — —

Tilly watched the chief and her friend head upstairs. She liked the chief a lot. She was the first cop who looked at her as if she were a real person and not just a problem. Coming off drugs, getting them out of her system helped Tilly realize that she'd been a problem for a lot of years, but she hoped more than anything to change that, to be respectable and support herself. Maybe if she did, her brother would let her come home and visit her nieces and nephews. After her last lapse, he'd given up on her completely. And Tilly was mad at herself for slipping; she'd almost lost her dog because of that, and Tilly couldn't bear losing Angel.

Now, when the itch got super bad, she would get down on her knees and gaze into Angel's soft-brown eyes. Without fail, Angel would lick her face and that would settle Tilly, help her to fight the urge.

Bryce helped her as well. He was like Glen. He understood the itch, fought it himself. And he encouraged her to move on.

"Tills, you're a smart girl; you could do something with your life. Don't ever sell yourself short because you hit a patch of black ice in your life. You recovered," he'd told her. And his encouragement had bolstered her more than anything else.

It was funny to Tilly, because at first when she heard he'd come back to the Hollow, she'd been afraid of Bryce. Her friend since grade school, he'd been there to console her when her dad died so many years ago. And he was the guy who had introduced her to meth. That habit had nearly killed her.

She certainly didn't want to be enticed into a new cesspool. But he was clean now, fiercely so, and he wanted to be her friend. After the loss of Glen, the trauma of witnessing his murder, it was nice to have a friend. Sometimes she'd meet him on the bridge heading to the B and B. He liked to watch the creek water flow underneath and think about fishing. They watched the water together and talked. Sometimes he'd wait for her by the supermarket and they'd walk together for a bit. On his off days they'd sit and have coffee. Once or twice on his night off, he'd even taken her to dinner.

She checked the clock and caught Addie's eye. "I'll be out back for my break."

Addie nodded and Tilly slipped out through the kitchen to the back of the inn, where the employee smoking area was. Tilly didn't smoke; neither did Bryce. But that was where he would be if he got away to meet her.

He was there, sitting on the table, back to her, soft brown hair curling over the collar of his shirt. Her heart leapt in her chest. He always came when he said he would.

"Hey, Bryce."

He turned and smiled, and she saw he had a pizza box in his lap. She wasn't hungry, but she'd have a slice just to eat with him.

"Hey, Tills, you okay?"

She nodded but noticed he looked frazzled. "What's up with you?"

He sighed and opened the box, offering her a slice. She took a slice and munched while he talked.

"There's a lot of stuff going on at the farm that I don't understand. That new guy, Lance Loud, gives me a headache."

Tilly and Bryce had fun giving everyone Bryce worked with nicknames. Cherry was the Hulk, Haywood was Blondie, and Carr had been the Reptile. Hector Connor-Ruiz was Lance Loud. The only one of the group Tilly had ever had contact with was Blondie. He'd stopped her one day when she was still on crutches to ask if she was registered to vote. She honestly didn't know; she'd been on the fringes of society in a drug-laced stupor for so long, she'd forgotten. He'd offered to drive her to get registered and to give her a supply of pot if she'd sign a petition to get something about pot put on the special election ballot. When she'd declined because she wanted to stay clean and drug-free, he'd mocked her and called her names. She didn't like him. Bryce didn't like him either, but he needed the work and Blondie was the only guy who would hire him knowing that he was only here until he paid his fines, satisfied the court, and could leave.

"He's all talk," Bryce had said about Blondie after Tilly told him how Blondie had gotten in her face and Angel had pressed toward him, growling. Angel was scary when she growled, and Blondie had backed off. So far, he hadn't bothered her since. She didn't think Bryce should be working at the Hang Ten, but until today it never seemed to bother him.

"I don't like the new guy either," Tilly said. "He's always trying to start trouble. Someone told me he was here earlier, giving the chief a bad time."

"Lance Loud never shuts up," he said as he grabbed a piece of pizza.

"Is he taking Carr's place?"

Bryce shook his head, chewing. "I don't know what his job is. Things are so tense since the Reptile got arrested. Lance Loud makes them even worse. Makes me feel like my body is covered with a thousand biting ants. He sure hates the chief. Put a picture of her on the dartboard."

Tilly frowned. "I like the chief."

He looked at her sideways. Tilly knew Bryce didn't like cops at all. Especially since he'd lost his truck to impound and been shipped down to Medford to take care of an old warrant he'd forgotten about.

"She was nice to you, so I can give her a point or two for that."

"I saw on the news that the Reptile had warrants. He killed a drug cop."

"I heard that too. I never liked the guy, but he wasn't the one paying me."

For a few minutes, they sat in companionable silence and ate pizza.

Tilly thought about the people at the Hang Ten. If she were still using, she bet that the farm would be a supplier of more than just pot.

"Do you really think Blondie is only selling pot?" she asked after she finished her one slice of pizza. Bryce was going on his third. "I don't want you to get into trouble for their crimes."

"He's a shady guy, that's for sure. *Sketchy* fits him; that's a surfer term."

Tilly liked that about Bryce; he'd been places, knew things—interesting things.

"I don't like the other guys who work there either, particularly," he said. "But I think I'd know if they were doing anything they shouldn't. Besides, they don't want me to have any part of the pot operation anyway, so I stay busy building sheds, fixing broken stuff, and trying to stay out of everyone's way."

"I've heard talk about people in the valley dying from bad drugs. Some people think Blondie is making them," Tilly said.

Bryce shook his head. "If he is, he's not making any at the farm. They have me everywhere fixing everything. If they were cooking drugs, I'd know it."

He wiped his mouth with a napkin and looked at her,

his green eyes so warm. He smiled and the dimple on the left side of his face deepened, visible even through his beard.

"I'd run if they had meth or horse there, I promise. You and me, we gotta stay clean. I never want to be in the sewer again. Deal?" He reached out his hand and they shook. Tilly loved the feel of the rough strength of his hand.

They had a deal; they would both stay clean.

32

While Hector was always in the back of Tess's mind, she and Jeannie didn't talk about him. He became "he who shall not be named." Tess forced herself to not think about Connor-Ruiz and instead concentrate on catching up with her friend.

Theories about Tim's murder also still simmered, but she knew, being at an impasse as she was, she needed some space, some time away from all of it in order to see everything with fresh eyes in the morning. She didn't eat much of the special dinner she'd ordered because of her late lunch. And the visit from Hector had upset her stomach. But she did indulge in dessert with Jeannie later.

"Who are you backing for mayor?" Jeannie asked between spoonfuls of ice cream. "I see placards and signs everywhere."

"Oh, no-brainer—Pete Horning. I can't imagine Cole Markarov as mayor."

"He does seem a little uptight, or as my mom would say—" she put her spoon down and pinched her nose to imitate her mother—"thinks he's just a little too big for his britches, that one."

Tess laughed and leaned back against the pillows.

They each had a pint of Häagen-Dazs ice cream. Tess had java chip and Jeannie, rocky road. Their favorite chick flick, the classic *While You Were Sleeping*, was cued up on the DVD player.

"So," Tess said, "this is your second trip up here to God's country. Last time you wouldn't commit, but what do you think?" Jeannie had been up over Thanksgiving with Tess's mother and brother.

Jeannie sighed. "It's not really me. I mean, I like a little more night action and a little less open space." She waved off Tess's groan of indignation. "Let me finish. I do like the fact that it feels so safe here. And I think you're happy here, aren't you? That's what's important."

Tess paused with the spoon filled with ice cream on the way to her mouth. "It's funny you should say that. I would say that I'm happy here. At first, I didn't think I could ever be happy in a small town." She grinned ruefully. "In fact, at one time I felt like running away and hiding somewhere. But I do like the PD. It may be small, but it's all mine and I like running it. And I have good people."

"It suits you."

"I don't know if that's a compliment or not."

Jeannie grinned. "I've worked around cops for years, and

often when they promote, it goes to their head. The 'yes, sirs' and the deference—it becomes all about power and not about police work." She waved her arms theatrically as she spoke. "It was never like that for you. It has always been all about police work, and here, there's no static; there's just police work. I repeat, it suits you."

"Well, thanks. And there is work here." She updated Jeannie on Tim Harper.

"How twisted is that? Hit the kid, then take him home and kill him. It has to be someone close to him to take that much care."

"You'd think, but I can find no motives. It seems logical that he saw something he shouldn't or photographed something he shouldn't."

"But wouldn't it have been easier to dump him in the river?"

"Yeah." Tess thought back to where the bike was found. If that's where the accident occurred, it *would* have been easier to toss him in the river. She frowned. Every time she seemed to step forward in the investigation, something threw her backward.

"That one is a mess, for sure. But let me tell you a criminal story with a good ending." She told Jeannie about the robbery at the pot farm and the crook who dropped his ID.

Jeannie laughed. "What a zip. Hey, I bet it's nice to be considered legitimate again and not worry about your reputation. Should help you to ignore all the bluster from he-who-shall-not-be-named."

Tess nodded. "It was until the council meeting."

"This too shall pass. Just do your job."

Tess smiled. That was something her father would say.

She put a spoonful of ice cream in her mouth and hummed with contentment while it melted. It was nice to be with a good friend.

"What about that deputy you were dating—what's happening with him?"

"Steve? We still talk. It's, uh . . . We're in the weird area of being friends. I'm . . . well, just not ready to get serious."

"He wanted to get serious?"

Tess nodded and ate some more ice cream. A stray thought hit her right between the eyes. Hector had called Oliver "boyfriend." What was up with that? Tess didn't think of Oliver that way . . . or did she? He was everything she'd want in a boyfriend: easy to talk to, kind, thoughtful, brave, supportive. She felt a tingle ripple through her, and goose bumps rolled along her arms.

"Earth to Tess . . . yoo-hoo." Jeannie tossed a crumpled-up Kleenex and hit Tess on the chin.

"Aw, sorry. I got distracted."

"With what? You were gone. Another planet."

"Just the case, that's all." Tess looked away, not ready to admit to her best friend that she was romantically attracted to a *pastor*, of all things. They finished their ice cream and started the first movie.

But the spark began to grow, despite all of Tess's efforts to squash it, and she realized she'd come to really care about and depend on Oliver Macpherson.

33

The next morning, Jeannie left early, but Tess stayed in the room to sleep in, a rare indulgence. It was comfortable, and since they hadn't slept much the night before, she wanted the downtime. She slept until about 9 a.m. and felt rested physically, but her mind hadn't shut down and her thinking felt foggy. Oliver lingered in her thoughts, and she tried to replace him by concentrating on her case. Hopefully some coffee would help.

She packed up the bag she'd brought with her, checked out to go home and shower. At least her home plumbing had been updated and the bathroom renovated so she knew the shower would be good.

It was another nice day; the rafting place was already busy with tourists. There was a line at the Hollow Grind, so Tess decided to wait for coffee until she got home. Her house was five minutes from downtown, on the river. She'd purchased an acre and a half of land, but she'd barely had time to finish the inside, much less do anything to the outside. It was mostly oak trees and blackberry bushes.

Tess pulled into her driveway, loving the way it curved off from River Drive and wound down toward the water. The house was hidden from the street by trees, and neighbors on either side disappeared behind their own foliage. In Long Beach, after her divorce, she'd lived in a townhome and felt a bit claustrophobic at times sharing walls. Here, Tess loved the private feel of her new home. Neighbors were there, but far enough away.

She pulled toward the garage and stopped. There was something on her front steps.

Frowning, Tess put the car in park and got out. She wasn't expecting any packages. But as she got closer, she saw it wasn't a package.

It was a body.

She pulled out her phone, preparing to call it in, part of her still thinking it couldn't be what she thought it was. This was Rogue's Hollow, not LA. But her heart rate increased as she got close enough to see that it was, indeed, a body. There was blood, already drying, running down her steps.

But the shock of who it was nearly knocked her off her feet.

Hector Connor-Ruiz.

34

Bender pulled up first. Tess had put her car in the garage, then draped her porch with caution tape. By the time her officer arrived, she was pacing off to the side of her house.

He got out and walked to the porch, kneeling to take a close look at the body. Connor-Ruiz had been shot in the middle of the forehead. When Tess ID'd him, she noted how his eyes, usually so filled with hate, were blank and staring. He was as dead as dead could be.

Bender stood, scratched his head, and walked over to Tess. "What happened?"

"I don't know. I didn't stay here last night. I was at the inn. He was here, like that, when I got home." She shoved her hands in the pockets of her jeans. "I called Steve to notify the sheriff's department . . ." She turned as a vehicle pulled into the driveway. But it wasn't Steve; it was a channel 10 news van.

"Oh, man, who called them?" She'd not called 911, specifically wanting to avoid scanner-listening newspeople from getting the jump on the coroner.

They were out of the van quickly. Tess stepped forward, but she was in jeans and a T-shirt. Bender was in uniform.

"Chief!" The reporter hurried her way while the cameraman set up the shot. "We got a call that you shot a man on your porch. What happened?"

"I didn't shoot anyone."

"But there's a dead man on your porch!"

"You'll have to step back," Gabe said, pointing back to their van. "This is a crime scene."

"It's news!"

Suddenly there was a channel 12 news van, and she and Gabe were in danger of losing control completely. It was only when two sheriff cars pulled up and four deputies stepped out that control was eventually regained, and even then, it was not without a fight.

"Are you guys just going to cover this up? Cops protecting cops?" one of the newspeople called out. "We've heard a lot of allegations of misconduct in Rogue's Hollow."

"There will be no cover-up." A tall deputy Tess vaguely recognized spoke, holding up his hands. "But you all need to let us do our jobs." Tess saw the stars on his collar and realized that he was the man selected as interim sheriff. Belcher was his name.

Steve and another deputy moved the perimeter back, off Tess's property, and forced the newspeople out of the driveway. Things began to calm down until another car screamed onto the scene.

The blond head of Gaston Haywood was discernible as he came running up the drive, pushing past the deputy Steve had placed at the perimeter.

"Is he *dead*?" He looked around at all the officers, gaze ultimately fixing on Tess. "She murdered him, didn't she? He told me she would," he howled, voice echoing in the warming late-morning sun. His pointed accusation cut Tess like sharp, cold shards of glass.

35

"She murdered him."

Everything tilted sideways in the next few minutes for Tess. The thorn in her side, the one person she'd contacted through work by whom she'd been personally damaged, a man she could say she hated, was the victim of a homicide on her porch.

She watched as Logan, Bender, and Belcher dealt with Haywood. The surfer was hysterical. Tess wondered if he was high on something because his behavior was over-the-top. Even from a distance, she could see the news crews were eating it up. Suddenly Tess felt like no one was on her side. It was a jolt of fear, insecurity, self-doubt, reminiscent of what she felt after her shooting in Long Beach.

But I didn't shoot anyone today.

Steve walked her way after they'd calmed Haywood down and sent him back to his car. Tess tried to relax. Steve wouldn't think she was guilty, would he?

"What happened here, Tess?" His brows were scrunched together, and his official tone tweaked her ever so much.

She held her hands out. "I have no idea. I came home and found him here."

"Came home? Where were you?"

"My friend Jeannie was here for the night; we stayed at the inn. My heat pump is dead. I've considered staying at the inn for a couple of days."

His thumbs hooked in his gun belt, he looked down, nodding as Tess spoke. Belcher was bent over, peering at the body of Hector Connor-Ruiz. He spoke to Bender as he did so, but Tess couldn't hear what he was saying.

"This looks bad, Tess, real bad."

"Looks bad? You think I killed him?"

He shook his head. "No, but other people will. You've made no secret of how you felt about the guy."

"Yeah, and everyone knew how he felt about me. But there's no way I would kill him."

"Why was he here, on your property?"

"I don't know."

"Have you had any contact with him recently?"

Tess sighed in frustration. It was hard not to think about all the contact she'd had with the pest. "He was in the inn yesterday, when I was having lunch with Oliver."

"Was there a confrontation?"

Something in his question made Tess cringe, like hearing

fingernails on a chalkboard. "Is this an interrogation? Should I be read my rights?"

"You know any competent investigator would ask that question."

"I'd think a *friend* would give me the benefit of the doubt."

He started to respond but stopped when Sheriff Belcher walked up.

"Chief O'Rourke. Like I just told your officer, this is awkward." The man was tall and pale and soft. He looked uncoordinated and uncomfortable in uniform.

"Why would you say awkward?" Tess asked, feeling her confidence surge back with a healthy portion of anger and indignation. "Are you insinuating I had something to do with this?"

Belcher shook his head, jowls jiggling as he did. "Chief, you would be the first to agree that an investigation needs to be impartial, that we, as law enforcement officers, need to follow the evidence where it leads us. You called us, after all. All I meant was that this scene looks bad. Officer Bender tells me this is the fellow I've heard scuttlebutt about. He and his relationship to you—"

"I had no relationship with him. He had a sick obsession with me."

"Nonetheless, it compromises your ability to conduct an impartial investigation, wouldn't you say?"

"I agree it would be unseemly for me to investigate a crime that occurred on my property. But I won't agree that I should be treated as a suspect. Like you said, I did call you in, didn't I?"

"You did," Steve said, then turned to Belcher. "How about

a compromise?" Belcher frowned but nodded for Steve to continue. He turned back to Tess. "Maybe you shouldn't be here while we conduct our investigation."

As a cop, she could agree that he was right, but because of their prior relationship, his body language cut. He was treating her like a suspect, and Tess felt her face flush as a hot poker of betrayal sliced through her.

36

Oliver was technically off on Saturday, but seeing as how he lived on the church grounds, interruptions happened. Since Anna died, he was more amenable to stopping whatever he was doing and dealing with any and all interruptions. This Saturday he was out early to beat the heat, cutting back some bushes in front of the house when he heard footsteps. He turned to see Eva Harper walking his way.

"Pastor Mac, I know I don't have an appointment, but I needed to speak with you. Do you have a minute?"

"Of course." He set his clippers aside, gratified that she looked much better than she had the night of the city council meeting. That night she'd been in pieces, hurting for Tim and worried sick about her husband. It had been an emotional emergency. Oliver knew that losing a child often broke up a marriage, and he prayed he'd have the wisdom to help the Harpers and that they would survive.

"I'm in a healthier place today."

"I can see that. Let's sit on the porch." He pointed to the two chairs on his porch, and they each took a seat.

"I'm so worried about Drake. I can't talk to him. He's obsessed with finding Tim's killer, and it's eating him up."

"I heard about what he did at the council meeting."

"He's furious with Chief O'Rourke. It's been building with each day that passes. He thinks she passed judgment that first night and doesn't care about Tim. I'm afraid . . ." Her voice broke.

Oliver reached out and gripped her arm. "Take your time."

After a minute, she continued. "He can't accept Tim's death and move on. I barely can."

She paused and Oliver waited. When she spoke, her words came out in fits and spurts.

"I fear he'll do something crazy. But what this is doing to him hurts almost more than I can bear. It's as if there is a thin line holding him together and any minute it will snap. I know that catching his killer will not bring my son back. I've lost Tim; I don't want to lose my husband as well." She looked at Oliver. "Can you talk to him, please?"

"I'll talk to him, sure, but he may not be ready to talk to me."

She blew her nose. "He's on the edge. Maybe you can keep him from doing something stupid if he doesn't realize that nothing, nothing at all, will ever bring our son back." Her composure crumbled.

Oliver held her hand while she cried softly. He understood their anguish and pain. Could even see himself exploding with anger like Drake. But Tess had caught Roger Marshall, Anna's killer, right away. *Did that defuse my anger?* Oliver wondered for a moment.

No, it wasn't that. It was faith that God would deal with Marshall better and more thoroughly than I ever could. And he had years and years of his own messages to remind him to practice what he preached.

Could he get that across to Drake?

After Eva left, Oliver went inside and cleaned up. His plan was to go find Drake and see if he would talk. Everyone grieved differently; Oliver knew that well. Anger was perfectly normal, but in general, healthy people eventually moved to other stages, but always at their own pace. Drake might not be at a stage where he would want a conversation, but Oliver had to try.

His phone rang as he was leaving. Surprised that the caller ID said Rogue's Hollow Inn and Suites, he almost let it go to voice mail.

But it could be an emergency.

"Pastor Macpherson," he announced after picking up the phone.

"Oliver, we have a problem." He recognized the voice of Addie Getz. That she'd wasted no time on pleasantries had him on edge immediately.

"Addie, what's up?"

"There's been a murder, and our chief of police is the prime suspect."

— — —

Tess didn't leave her property, but she got out of the way of the deputies and out of the view of the news cameras. There was a small decaying dock at the water's edge on her property, and she'd dragged a camp chair down there. She sat, watching the water, the occasional drift boat, Tahiti, or raft, and simmered, wondering how long before the news guys thought to hop in a boat and catch a pic of her here.

For some reason, she thought about her father's courage card. She had it with her, something she couldn't fathom. The words meant nothing to her, but it was something that her father had carried, held, and read often, and that gave her a modicum of comfort. But what in those words could help lift the cloud of suspicion that was dropping like an anvil on her head?

Part of her wanted to rip the card up and throw it in the river. Trusting in God did nothing for her father; why should she expect that it would do anything for her? She pulled the card out, didn't look at it, but turned it over and over in her hands as she stewed.

Though she understood being excluded, it chafed, like shoes three sizes too small, that she was being kept on the wrong side of the tape. But the image of Hector dead on her steps was seared in her mind.

Without touching the body, she'd done a cursory exam when she made the phone call to Bender and then to the sheriff. Hector had been shot in the head with a large-caliber bullet; the mess told her that. It looked as though he was coming off the porch when he was shot by someone coming toward him from the driveway. He wasn't armed as far as she could see, but there was always a possibility he had a weapon under him. Or the shooter had removed it if one existed.

Did he come looking for her, discover she wasn't home, try to leave, and get shot?

If so, who killed him, and why were they trying to frame her for it?

37

Oliver and Addie waded through a crowd of news reporters once they reached Tess's home. He was astounded by the collection of news media. It was out of the ordinary for a town as small as Rogue's Hollow.

"Mayor Getz, did Rogue's Hollow hire a rogue police chief?"

"We heard that the dead man is the man who was accusing the chief of malfeasance—is that why she killed him?"

Addie waved them all away, saying only, "No comment."

Oliver was thankful that Addie took her duties very seriously and was not inclined to pop off about anything until she had all the facts. In the back of his mind, he considered the contentious city council meeting he'd not been able to attend. He'd heard that people were calling for Tess's badge. *What will this incident do to those who've already lost confidence in her ability to lead?*

There were a few questions tossed Oliver's way, but he barely heard them. His concern was only for Tess. What on earth had happened?

The deputy who met them at the perimeter lifted the tape so they could duck under.

Oliver saw Gabe Bender standing with two Jackson County sheriff's deputies. He recognized one as Steve Logan, the other as the interim sheriff, Belcher. Tess had expressed confidence in him when he'd asked her about it; he prayed that her confidence was well-placed.

Bender approached them. "Pastor Mac, Mayor Getz, glad you guys are here."

"What happened, Gabe?" Addie asked.

He blew out a breath. "It's a mess." A faint outline of two black eyes was still visible on Gabe's face.

Oliver listened to him explain everything that he knew had happened up to that point.

"Gaston Haywood claims to have a letter Hector wrote documenting when and where the chief threatened him. Sheriff Belcher sent a deputy to the Hang Ten to retrieve it."

"They can't—you can't—possibly believe Tess killed this man?" Oliver stared at Gabe, trying to read him. "She's not capable of cold-blooded murder."

"Anyone, at any given time, is capable of anything."

They turned as Belcher walked up. Gabe made introductions.

"Officer Bender explained to me that it is department policy you be notified, Mayor Getz, when shootings occur involving your officers."

"That's correct."

Belcher glanced from Addie to Oliver and back. "I'm not sure what place a pastor has here."

"I trust Pastor Mac. I want him here."

Belcher pursed his lips. "As you wish. We have a dicey situation here. Chief O'Rourke claims to have found the body and to have had nothing to do with his death."

"I'm inclined to believe her," Addie said, and Oliver wanted to hug her. He did not care for all the grim law enforcement faces surrounding him.

"Well, be that as it may, we have to go where the evidence takes us. Right now, I'm hearing that Chief O'Rourke might have had a pretty strong motive to kill this man."

"If you think that, you're wrong," Oliver said. "I've known Tess as long as she's been here, and I'm certain she couldn't be a murderer."

"Pastor, I appreciate your observations, but as a law enforcement officer, I have to follow evidence."

"Are you placing her under arrest?" Addie asked.

"No, *not yet.*"

Oliver thought he heard a boom in the distance and realized it was the pounding of his heart. This man truly thought Tess was a killer.

"I do think it's best that we handle the investigation. It would shield us from accusations of a cover-up. And we have the resources to conduct a proper investigation." His tone was condescending and it rubbed Oliver the wrong way. When Addie responded, he had to suppress a smile because the man had obviously irritated her as well.

"I have no problem with you heading up the investigation,

with Officer Bender's help. I want him to keep me in the loop regarding all developments—is that understood?"

"I have plenty of deputies—"

"I wasn't asking. This is my town. I want Officer Bender part of the investigation, period."

For a minute, they stared at one another.

Belcher blinked. "Of course, that makes sense. However, I have a recommendation."

"I'm listening."

"For the time being, it might be wise if Chief O'Rourke were relieved of her duties."

"What?" Oliver couldn't help himself.

"In the interest of appearances, I think it would be best for now, until the investigation is concluded or she, at least, is cleared of all involvement."

"I'll have to put that before the council." Addie gave a wave of her hand. "Where is Tess now?"

"Sitting down at the dock," Steve Logan told them.

Oliver looked at him. He'd been so quiet, Oliver wondered where he stood in all of this. He remembered asking Tess about the man yesterday. Logan had dated Tess for quite a while. Surely he didn't believe Tess could murder anyone. But there was nothing he could read in the man's face that gave him any comfort.

— — —

Oliver left Addie with Belcher so the sheriff could tell her about all they had observed so far. He wanted to talk to Tess, so he walked down to the dock where she sat. He thought about the claim Gaston Haywood had made. A letter Connor-Ruiz left, documenting threats Tess had made? Oliver knew in his heart that was impossible. Tess was not the type to threaten, and she was certainly not a killer. He reflected over the last year. He'd only seen evidence that she was a brave, compassionate, sometimes stubborn, maybe a little reckless, dedicated law enforcement professional.

She turned as he approached, and he believed he saw relief cross her face before she tensed up and shut down.

"How are you doing, Tess?" he asked.

"I'm peachy."

Oliver knelt on one knee next to her, following her gaze to the river. "The truth will come out, Tess; it always does."

"I'm not exactly batting a thousand on discovering the truth lately. Half the town thinks I'm incompetent because I can't solve Tim Harper's murder, and now the other half will probably decide I'm a homicidal maniac because of this. Somebody sure wanted to make it look like I killed Hector."

"That doesn't sound like the Tess O'Rourke I know. She doesn't wallow in self-pity. Where is the dragon slayer?"

For a second Oliver was afraid he'd made a bad situation worse. But then she closed her eyes and smiled. "Careful, Oliver. Call me a dragon slayer, and Belcher may take that to mean I slew Hector."

"He may be on the wrong path right now, but if he runs an unbiased investigation like he said, I have faith he'll find the evidence to point him to the true killer."

"Faith that God will help that to happen?"

"Well, ultimately, faith that God is in control of all outcomes, yes."

"Humph." She reached into her pocket and pulled out a laminated three-by-five card. She held it up, showing it to him, but not close enough that he could read it.

"I found this card in a box of my father's things. He called it his courage card. It has Bible verses on it, verses he considered important to him as a cop. Out of nostalgia, I've been carrying it around, looking at it from time to time, thinking of my father." She shrugged. "I even thought about showing it to you, chatting about the meaning of the verses."

"Why didn't you?"

"Because it's all so useless!"

Her vehemence surprised him and he waited until she continued.

"When I was a kid, going to church with my father, I always thought God would keep bad things from happening to him. After all, he had such *faith*. But God didn't keep him safe. And now I haven't darkened the doorway of a church for so long, why in the world would God do anything for me?"

"That's not the way it works. It's not quid pro quo with God."

"But what is it with him? When I think about what could happen if Belcher charges me with murder like it appears he wants to, I feel like I'm being closed in a vise. I need cold, hard facts on my side, something solid."

Oliver nodded, praying for the right words. "Faith is something solid—it's a confident assurance. You are innocent; believe that the truth will prove that fact."

They were interrupted when Steve Logan walked up. He cleared his throat. "Tess, we need your duty weapon for comparison purposes."

She nodded and shot Oliver a look that broke Oliver's heart. It said, *Your God betrayed me again. How can I ever believe?*

38

Faith.

Tess pondered that word for a while as Saturday played out and she found herself the number one suspect in a murder. It mystified her why Oliver hung on to his faith, even after the loss of Anna. How could he? And if her father had known that the God he trusted was going to let him be murdered in the street, would that have changed his faith? Her dad and Oliver both believed an all-powerful God ran the show. Tess couldn't. After her father's death, she believed *she* was solely in control of her destiny, not a capricious God.

She thought back to the shooting controversy that had forced her out of Long Beach. In that situation, everything was known except why the kid she shot hadn't complied with her instructions. She could fight the accusations then. She knew what she did and why, and that knowledge kept her strong.

Here and now, she knew nothing except there was a dead man on her porch. How could she fight with so much unknown? It always seemed to circle back to faith. She had to have faith in the justice system. But her faith in that system was sorely tested when Belcher requested she go with them to the county offices to be interviewed. And besides her firearm, they confiscated her personal laptop. Jeannie was the first person she called when she got home after a long day of being grilled.

"I'm not gone twenty hours and already you're in trouble?"

Tess's spirits were buoyed by the sound of her friend's voice. It was good to talk to Jeannie, but she wished her friend was in front of her and not on the phone. Jeannie had given a statement over the phone Saturday afternoon. Tess knew Belcher had called her, catching her not long after the wedding had ended. He'd told her that she might be subpoenaed for a deposition.

"It's a nightmare, Jeannie," Tess said.

Belcher had decided to run the investigation himself, with assistance from another deputy. He pulled Logan from the case because of his relationship to Tess. No matter; Tess didn't want to speak to Steve Logan at all.

The interrogation was harrowing because she'd learned some of what had been recovered at the scene. Hector had a copy of an e-mail in his pocket, from Tess's personal account, asking him to meet her to discuss their differences.

From her personal account.

That was why they'd wanted her laptop. Thrown off-balance, Tess had no explanation for this development.

"I did not send him an e-mail," she'd stuttered when Belcher held the evidence bag up for her to see. "I don't even know his e-mail address."

"Can you explain how he received this message, asking him to come to your house?"

"No. No, I can't. But if you think I lured him to my home, killed him, then called the police to report the body, you really think I'm stupid."

Tess wasn't that up on technology. She knew how to do the basic minimum and had been happy Rogue's Hollow PD did not have as many tech toys as Long Beach. But she did think she took all the needed precautions to keep her account secure.

"So are you saying you were hacked?"

"I must have been. I never sent Hector an e-mail," she repeated.

Belcher didn't seem satisfied with that answer, but he moved on, bringing up the altercation at the inn, trying to make Tess mad, or at least get her to admit she'd been furious with Hector.

"I wasn't the one who stood up to him. Pastor Macpherson and Victor Camus spoke to him directly and told him to back off."

"How did that make you feel?"

"What?"

"Were you angry that these men had to stand up for you? Were you angry that Connor-Ruiz was questioning your ethics in a very public way?"

"I was irritated that he was rude enough to interrupt everyone's meal. I was not mad, nor was I homicidal."

They'd gone back and forth for a few minutes, but Tess recovered her composure quickly. Empowered by the firm knowledge that she was innocent, she pushed back, asking Belcher to charge her or let her go. He let her go with an admonition not to leave the state.

Other than the e-mail discovery, she was told little else about the murder scene and headed home, still reeling over the fact that this had happened in her quiet, safe-feeling enclave. She was also worried about Addie. Her friend was a competent small-town city councilwoman, but she'd not liked the job of interim mayor.

"Too much gobbledygook," she'd said. *"The election can't take place soon enough for me."* Certainly at this point, she had way more gobbledygook on her plate than anyone could have bargained for.

"Tess, I believe you, but this is a lot bigger than anything I've ever contended with. I hate to agree with Belcher, but it does look bad."

"Are you removing me from duty?"

"I, um . . . Not today. I do have to bring the council together. But maybe you should consider taking some vacation days. You've almost been here a year; you deserve some time off."

"Can I think about it?"

"I can't guarantee you'll have a lot of time, but I won't push it today."

Tess was grateful for Addie's support, as tenuous as it was. She had a little breathing room. The only other thing she

learned about the investigation was that Haywood had produced a note he claimed Connor-Ruiz had written. She told
Jeannie about that.

"This letter supposedly documents how many times I
threatened to kill him."

"I knew that guy was cracked when he was in LB, but
that's delusional even for him. What's in the water up there?"

"I wish I knew. The only person I can think of who would
want to frame me for a crime is Connor-Ruiz, and he's dead."

"Maybe he *is* trying to frame you. Maybe he committed
suicide and did everything possible to make it look as if you
murdered him."

"I don't think even Connor-Ruiz was that cracked."

After she hung up, Tess debated calling an attorney
acquaintance in Long Beach. While she knew she had had
nothing to do with the murder, she also knew that if someone was trying to frame her, it would be for her own good to
retain legal representation.

It was a warm night. She'd not yet cleaned up the mess
of blood on her porch. Tess stepped out of her house and
walked back down to the dock. It was dark enough now that
boaters were nonexistent.

She looked out over the powerful rolling river, wishing
she could believe, wishing she had the faith that Oliver had
and there was someone she could cry out to.

What would her dad do? He'd pray, she knew that.

But Tess felt a drowning helplessness. Prayer and faith
weren't avenues she traveled on.

39

Haywood wanted a beer after the deputy left. He opened the fridge, but there was none left. Slamming the door, he opted for option two and went to roll some of his product. Don Cherry was sitting in a recliner, feet up, watching him.

"What? Don't you have some work to do?"

"You don't want to start a fight with me, that's for sure."

Gaston found some courage. "Where'd you blink off to when the cops were here?"

"None of your business. Boss says everyone is to lay low because of Hector, stay on-site for a bit."

"He didn't tell me that."

In an instant, Cherry lowered the footrest and leaped up,

getting right in Gaston's face. He moved fast for a big man. Since Gaston barely made six feet and Cherry stood at least six foot five, it was beyond intimidating to have him so close.

Gaston backed up and hit the wall.

"I'm telling you now. Everyone lays low. Everyone. You tell the kid. Got anything smart left to say?"

Gaston swallowed and tried to stand to his full height, pretend he wasn't frightened. All he could manage was "Will do."

Cherry backed off and went back to the recliner, clicking the TV on. Gaston stomped through the kitchen and then outside into the yard to look for Bryce.

Haywood hated Cherry—and the jerk Carr, for that matter. Both guys scared him. Haywood didn't care for Hector, either. He was annoying and whiny, but he'd had no say in the matter. He'd been relieved when Carr was arrested, but then the boss showed up suddenly and Gaston realized how little control he had over anything.

Bryce was the only one Haywood liked. The kid was a solid worker. He only wanted to earn enough money to pay his fines and get home. Haywood understood needing money. He'd inherited a little money but had needed much more to get his farm up and running. He'd found an investor easily enough, but what was the saying? You lie down with dogs and you get up with fleas. Cherry, Carr, and Hector were fleas. The biting kind.

As usual, Bryce was working. He was digging up some water lines, looking for a leak.

"Hey, Bryce."

The guy looked up. "Yeah?"

"Got some bad news."

Bryce straightened up and faced Gaston. "Pump's working. I saw to it first thing."

"It's not the pump. It's Hector. He's dead."

"Dead?" He didn't look too surprised. "I figured something was up when I saw the sheriff's car. What happened?"

Gaston shoved his hands in his pockets. "We think the police chief killed him."

Bryce said nothing.

"Anyway, until it's cleared up, the boss wants everyone to stay put here, no going off-site."

Bryce frowned. "Not at all, not even for coffee?"

"We got plenty of coffee here. It's just temporary, okay? The chief must have a vendetta. First she jacks Carr; now she kills Hector."

He didn't look happy, but Bryce nodded.

Gaston turned and walked back to the house. That's what he liked about Bryce—guy just did what he was told, no drama.

He took his time as he walked, gaze sweeping the plot of land he'd thought would be his golden ticket. He'd thought he'd make enough money his first year to pay off his investor, but that hadn't panned out. There were so many expenses related to starting a business he'd never considered. Then he got beaten up and robbed. True, he got the loss back, but he wasn't doing as well as he wanted everyone to think. He'd tried to pay back a little of his debt, get the hooks out at least a bit. His investor sank the hooks in deeper and sent him Carr, then Cherry, telling him the extra bodies would be good security. But it wasn't like either of them did a boatload of work. Then came Hector, and Haywood had no idea what his job was.

The boss wanted to expand. He wanted that old man Arthur's place in a bad way. Why he didn't just buy it bugged Haywood. When Hector first arrived, Gaston thought the boss had sent him to work on the old guy, get him to sell. But Hector was only interested in bugging the chief. And Haywood didn't get that. Why poke the chief in the eye if you wanted to run a business and not be bothered?

Gaston had come home on Friday to find Hector packed, ready to head back to California. But he was drunk, and Gaston was sure he'd sleep it off. Then his investor appeared at the Hang Ten, up for a visit. And he was scary. Haywood had never even seen him until now. All their business to this point had been handled through intermediaries. Out of the blue he showed up at the gate. He wasn't alone either, but whoever he'd traveled with did not come in the house.

A few hours later, Hector was dead.

Gaston hated to face the pickle he was in. The boss had known about Hector awfully quick. This morning he'd told Gaston what to say to the cops and later gave him the note to hand over to the sheriff. Gaston didn't ask any questions. He did like any good Borg would do on *Star Trek*—he complied.

At the moment he didn't know where the boss was. He'd disappeared with the other guy before the deputy arrived. Gaston got that the boss wanted all fingers pointed at the chief for the crime. He didn't really care one way or another about her. The only thing he'd had in common with Hector was a hatred of cops.

But Haywood disliked violence. He only carried a gun

for show. He would curse and scream with the best of them, but when it came right down to blows, he didn't like pain or the sight of blood, especially his own. He'd only glimpsed Hector's body, and that was enough to make him physically sick. Worse still was the fact that he knew the chief did not kill the guy. Haywood figured Cherry had done the deed.

Cherry seemed to have a better relationship with the boss than he did. They had an unspoken understanding; Gaston could see that. They were gone last night, and that left Haywood with the most troubling questions of all: Why did his investor have Hector killed? And was he now in danger as well?

40

Casey Reno was the first council member, besides Addie, to contact Tess after the murder. She stopped by Sunday morning. Tess had just finished cleaning up the blood from the porch. She welcomed the distraction when Casey showed up.

"What happened?"

"I don't know, Casey. I found the guy dead and I have no idea why he was there or what he was doing. I was just going in to have some coffee. Join me?"

Casey nodded and followed Tess inside. She sat at the kitchen counter while Tess busied herself in the kitchen making a pot of coffee.

"The only thing Addie told me was that it looked as

though he'd been executed. Who would do that?" Horror was palpable in Casey's voice.

"I'm not in charge of the investigation. But I will admit the first place I'd go is to the Hang Ten. I'd talk to Haywood, but by producing the letter, he preempted the deputies."

Casey nodded. "You know my thoughts about that place."

That Casey trusted Tess and seemed certain someone else was responsible for Hector's death relaxed her somewhat. But Casey would be the easy one. Tess had saved her daughter from a pedophile. She would probably never think ill of Tess.

What would all the other council members think? Addie so far had said that Tess could stay on the job. Would that stick?

- - -

Word spread fast about the murder. By Sunday, Oliver had already answered many inquiries when people found out that he had been on the scene. Everyone wanted to know if Oliver thought the chief was a killer.

"Absolutely not" was his standard reply.

Sunday morning the church secretary, who should have been in the sanctuary and not at her desk, handed him a pad of paper with several names on it. "They all called leaving messages asking about the chief. Just wanted you to know that after the service, people aren't likely to be asking you about the message."

The phone rang again. "Should I answer it?"

"No, come on. It's time for service. If it's an emergency, people have my cell number."

He preached the message he'd planned, on always remembering that God could be trusted with all of your burdens. And as his secretary predicted, a lot of people came forward to ask him about the chief and the murder. He tried to pin down where all the rumors were coming from that the chief had been arrested, but he couldn't. All he could do was tell people the truth as he knew it.

One surprising face greeted him after service—Drake Harper. He hadn't been in the service that Oliver had seen, but he walked up to Oliver as he was closing the sanctuary doors.

"Eva wants me to talk to you."

Oliver nodded, working to hide his shock at the man's appearance. He was unshaven, it looked as if he'd slept in his clothes, and there were dark circles under his eyes. This was a departure from the proud, squared-away serviceman Oliver had come to know.

"Eva is worried about you. I only want to help."

"How can you help? By defending that police chief? She doesn't care about Tim. She's nothing but a killer herself."

"Drake, I understand your pain. I still miss Anna. I—"

"Don't you preach to me!" He waved a finger in Oliver's face. "You know why Anna was killed and where her killer is. Whoever hurt Tim is still out there, enjoying life, getting away with murder because no one wants to find him. Well, I do. And I will, and he is going to pay for what he did to my son. Stay away from me. I don't need your help."

He stormed away, across the parking lot. Oliver wanted to go after him, convince him that he was wrong, but he knew Drake wouldn't listen. He prayed for the man, fearing the direction his grief would take him.

41

Monday morning, Tess still hadn't heard from Addie but guessed she wouldn't until Addie had talked to the entire council and weighed the situation carefully. After a sleepless Sunday night, she took her time at home with coffee and a light breakfast. She normally dressed at the station but knew that this morning her duty weapon would be conspicuously absent. Her 9mm was at the state crime lab and might be there a couple of days. Sighing, she went into her closet, opened her small gun safe, and considered her old duty weapon, her .45. Tess had carried the .45 for the first couple of months as chief but then decided to switch to a 9mm.

There was no earthshaking reason for the switch. She'd

seesawed back and forth while in Long Beach about the best weapon to carry. With the .45 she carried four extra magazines; with the nine she only had to carry two because each mag contained fifteen rounds compared to the six in the .45 magazine. Here in the Hollow, all her officers carried nines, so for the sake of easy ordering for qualification ammunition, Tess switched shortly after the apprehension of Roger Marshall. She did have to be mindful of the budget.

She considered carrying her .45 now, then placed it back in the safe for the time being. Belcher had assured her that her gun would be returned as quickly as possible, so until then, she wouldn't carry a weapon.

I'm innocent and my gun will be back soon, she told herself.

She left for the station, the remnants of her morning coffee in a travel mug. The weekend's events turned over and over in her mind. She'd hated having Hector here, but he was irritating and obnoxious, not physically dangerous. She'd never wished him dead.

Tess nodded to Sheila and entered the locker room to change. Not having her weapon didn't worry her as much as it just felt odd. She'd not fired a gun since her hire here except for qualification and the apprehension of Roger Marshall. And that situation had been a rare and dangerous one. Most law enforcement in Rogue's Hollow was routine and handled with words, not weapons. Plus, she had the option of delegating work to her officers, which she'd do until her duty weapon was returned.

She'd been in the office only a short time when her phone rang. It was the state lab in Salem with news about her prints.

"There was only one print on the syringe, on the plunger,

LETHAL TARGET

a partial thumbprint. It matches one you took off the bike. But there's no hit in the system. A written report is headed your way."

Talk about good news, bad news. Clear enough prints to run through the system, but no match. That meant her probable killer had never been arrested. It wasn't Don Cherry or Eddie Carr.

No hit in the system . . .

Tess sat back and pondered this development. If not Cherry or Carr, was Haywood a possible suspect? He hadn't been at the party, and there were really no other red flags where he was concerned. She'd made a mistake concentrating on the Hang Ten—she could see that now. But when she looked at her other possible suspects, aside from the man they'd yet to identify, she saw a list of generally clean-cut high school graduates and one high school baseball coach. Was one of them a killer?

She pulled out the interviews and reviewed them all. There was a colossal lack of motive if everyone was telling her the truth.

Coroner put the time of death at between 2:30 and 3 a.m.

Coach Whitman was only at the party for a few minutes early, around 11 p.m.—that was corroborated by everyone. His girlfriend in Salem verified he arrived at her home about 3 a.m.

Dustin Pelter was still missing. They'd been looking for him for nearly three weeks. That was suspicious, but she had a hard time seeing the drug addict as a killer who could plan.

So with no lead on the unidentified man, all that remained for Tess to do was to concentrate on the boys, one by one.

Duncan claimed to have headed out early. His parents confirmed that he got home a little after midnight.

Josh Heller left next. Greg Nguyen said he took off with Trace Danner a little after one and Tim was the only partier left.

Tim said he was leaving as well but planning to find a good location for some moon photos.

They'd never identified the older man who'd been at the party. MADGE said they might have a lead on him, but she'd heard nothing further.

Tess phoned the lieutenant in MADGE, got his voice mail again, and left him another message.

She needed to speak to the boys again. But time was ticking; she feared Addie would soon relieve her of duty or force her to take vacation time. She picked up the phone to call Duncan first.

Delia Peabody answered the phone.

"I'm looking for Duncan."

"He's not home. Uh, Chief, what happened? I mean, I read about that man; I saw news reports—murdered on your porch?"

Tess hated the tone of Delia's voice, the indecision. The woman had lost faith in the chief of police.

"Delia, I don't know what happened. But I'm certain that the Jackson County sheriff will figure it out."

"Well, Duncan is fishing with his friends. Greg will be leaving soon; he's going to visit his school, so the boys wanted to get in some time together on the river before he left."

"Where do they usually go?"

"Their favorite spot is below the fish hatchery. What's this about?"

"I need to clear something up. It's a question that has come up regarding Tim. Procedure more than anything."

Delia accepted that explanation and Tess disconnected. She knew where the boys were likely to be. There was a fish hatchery below the dam at Lost Creek Lake. She'd heard from others that it was a good place to fish. It wasn't in the Hollow, but it was close.

Tess looked at the time. A little after nine. It would be a piece of luck to catch the boys. She grabbed her portable radio and headed out to find them.

42

Lost Creek Lake was off Highway 62, east of Rogue's Hollow. It took Tess about fifteen minutes to get there, and she found the boys right where Delia had said, on a rocky bank below the dam and across from the boat ramp. Because it was Monday, the boys basically had the area to themselves. Trace and Josh had lines in the water, and Greg and Duncan were munching on chips and talking. She was trying not to be paranoid, but a sinking feeling hit that the boys were not happy to see her.

"Chief, you looking for us?" Duncan asked.

"I was," Tess answered as she picked her way carefully across the rocky retaining material to reach the guys.

"Something up with Tim's case?"

"In a way. I wanted to go over everything again. You heard that we found Tim's bike?"

They nodded.

"It was the guys at the Hang Ten, wasn't it?" Greg asked.

"No, it wasn't. I have evidence that cleared them." Tess didn't miss the looks that passed between the boys, and all her instincts went to code red.

"So we're missing something. It's really a shame that we couldn't recover his phone and look at the pictures. I believe it all comes down to the photos he took. Are you certain he didn't say anything to you about where he was going to take his pictures?"

"We—" Duncan started to say something, but Greg cut him off.

"We've told you everything we know. He was our friend. If we knew where he went, we would have said."

Duncan suddenly became interested in his shoes, and Josh and Trace went back to their fishing poles.

The boys were hiding something. Why hadn't she seen it before? She'd have no luck with them as a group, but Tess knew she'd revisit this, one boy at a time.

— — —

Tilly rarely read the newspaper and only saw the news when she was cleaning in the bar area of the inn and the TV was tuned to a local channel. She'd been brooding because Bryce hadn't been around to see her all weekend. Monday night she glanced at the TV and saw the chief's name, which caught her attention. She had to pause in her cleaning and read the closed-captioning. She felt her jaw drop when she saw that Chief O'Rourke was considered a person of interest in a murder.

A picture of the victim flashed across the screen. She knew that guy.

Lance Loud was found dead on the chief's porch! Tilly felt dizzy for a moment, and she had to sit down. She liked Chief O'Rourke, looked up to her. Was it possible?

After a minute she shook her head. "No."

"You okay, Tilly?" the bartender asked.

"What? Yeah, sorry." She stood.

"I don't think the chief did it either," he said. Then he changed the channel.

Nodding, Tilly hurried to finish her work, considering the last words she read: *"Evidence is being collected and analyzed while Tess O'Rourke remains on active duty. 'I see nothing that indicates Chief O'Rourke is guilty of anything except the misfortune of having a murder occur on her porch' was the only comment acting Mayor Getz would give."*

Good for Addie, Tilly thought. *Chief O'Rourke is a good person, a kind person.* Someone else killed Lance Loud. She needed to talk to Bryce more than ever.

43

By Tuesday morning, news of the murder had hit every nook and cranny of the Upper Rogue. Tess heard a lot of rumors mixed in with facts and determined not to be distracted or angered by the murder or the rumors. She was still waiting to hear from Addie and felt that news would come sooner than later.

Her contact with the boys the day before was foremost in her mind. She didn't want to think the young men had anything to do with the murder. But as she laid out the facts, her stomach began to rumble with discomfort.

At first, she'd concentrated on the drugs; after all, that was the problem of the day everywhere. But Tim's autopsy told a different story—the head injury, the damage to the bike . . . The drugs were an afterthought.

If some stranger had hit Tim on his bike, if they weren't going to call 911, they would have left him where he lay.

Instead, he was taken home and put to bed. A profiler would say this indicated knowledge of, friendship with, a certain fondness for. And the missing clothes could be someone removing or destroying evidence.

Since the coroner said the head injury wasn't fatal, if one of the boys did hit Tim, what would keep them from calling 911? Why take him home and kill him with drugs? But then, she thought, what if one of them accidentally hit him? That caused a head shake. It didn't make any sense.

It wasn't that she didn't think the kids were capable of murder; she'd arrested too many teen murderers in her career. But what possible motive could there be? Still, they were hiding something, and until she discovered what that was, they'd be listed as suspects.

Then she came back to Dustin. Tess tapped her chin with an index finger. He was what an old partner would have called a drug tragedy. Months ago she'd seen him with "the nods," something that happens with heroin users after they shoot up. The inability to keep their eyes open made them nod off, then catch themselves, then nod again. In that condition, he would not have had the ability to stage Tim's murder like it was. Several people claimed Dustin was clean now, off heroin and simply a pot addict. She did know he'd gotten his driver's license back, so he'd stayed clean long enough to do that. But he'd certainly done a Houdini, and she really wanted to talk to him, if only to set her mind at ease.

He might not seem like a calculating killer, but none of her suspects were in that category.

Tess blew out a frustrated breath and pulled out the entire file. She was again impressed by the work Jonkey had done on her report. The computer-generated diagram of the party area was detailed, a good, clear drawing. She'd noted the debris on the ground and listed the description of the guy Duncan didn't recognize, the party crasher, drawing her own composite. The woman had talent.

Unknown crashers were unusual here in this small town, where everyone knew everyone. In Long Beach a party crasher and violence were not unusual, and sometimes the crashers got away with it because when they fled, they fled miles away and had no real connections to Long Beach.

Here in the Upper Rogue, Tess had been quick to talk to and get everyone identified, except for the old guy. People she talked to thought he looked familiar, but no one had a name. But everyone seemed certain that he didn't live in Rogue's Hollow. For Tess that shifted her suspicion away from Haywood and his crew. Tess went back to the beginning.

The older guy was described as a male white in his forties, with bushy gray hair, wearing a brown leather jacket. He was taller than Duncan, who was five-ten, and he was pudgy with a pockmarked face. He drank beer. Duncan didn't see him smoke any pot.

The ringing phone interrupted her musings, and she picked it up without even looking at who was calling.

"Chief O'Rourke."

"Hello, Tess."

She pulled the phone away from her head, tempted to hang up, but decided that would be childish. Bringing the phone back to her face, she answered. "Steve."

"That's all I get? Not even a 'Hi, how are you?'"

"What can I do for you, Sergeant?"

"Okay, if you want to play it like that. Do you still have the .45 you carried on duty when you first came here?"

"Yes, why?"

"Where is the gun now?"

Tess pinched the bridge of her nose and tried to keep the snarkiness out of her voice. "At home in my safe."

"You sure?"

"Yes—wait, Connor-Ruiz must have been killed with a .45. My nine doesn't fit, does it?"

"Tess, believe it or not, I'm trying to help you. Belcher will need the .45."

"Come and get it. And bring me back my nine while you're at it."

"Connor-Ruiz was a thorn in your side, wasn't he?"

"Yes, he was. Oliver told me once or twice to calm down and ignore him."

"Did you do that?"

"Yes, I did that—what do you want from me?" A light went on in her thoughts. Logan wasn't on the investigative team. Tess stiffened. "What are you doing, trying to trick me into a confession? Are you recording this call?"

He cleared his throat and Tess felt her heart drop. A guess, a shot in the dark, just shattered whatever feelings she had left for this man. Oregon was a one-party state, meaning a conversation could be taped if at least one party knew it. It wouldn't be admissible in court, but it could still be done. That Steve would do it broke her already-brittle heart.

"Well, for posterity and the recording, I didn't kill Hector Connor-Ruiz. Like I said, I was at the inn for part of the afternoon with Pastor Mac. We had soup. I stayed there to wait for my friend Jeannie, and then for the rest of the night we were in room 330. Good luck finding the real killer. Come and get the .45. I haven't fired it in at least three months."

She hung up the phone and fell back into her chair. She was holding her head in her hands when Sheila popped her head in the office to tell her that Pastor Macpherson was there to see her.

"You okay?" Sheila asked, face scrunched in worry.

Tess managed a smile, feeling weak and worn-out though it was still early. She and Oliver hadn't parted on the best of terms on Saturday. She wasn't mad at him, but considering all he represented, she'd taken out a little of her frustration on him. She'd try to be more cordial today. Oliver might be a pastor and preach everything she couldn't believe, but he was also a friend who was unwavering in his support for her.

"Yeah, just not enough coffee yet this morning. Send the pastor in."

All her angst about their last meeting faded when he popped into her office with two cups of coffee from the Hollow Grind and a bag that suggested sweet stuff from the Rogue's Hollow bakery.

"Morning, Chief. Thought I'd drop in with some fuel for your day."

"Are pastors mind readers? You sure read mine." She leaned forward as he set the goodies down. The coffee she sipped immediately while Oliver placed a plastic container holding a cinnamon roll on her desk. He handed her a fork and a napkin, then sat back with his own plastic container and fork.

Tess inhaled the warm, sugary smell before she took a bite. Her stomach tingled as she looked at Oliver for the first time with a different perspective. *Boyfriend.*

"I love these," she said, mouth full. She swallowed. "But I really must get back to running, or I'll need a new uniform. Having coffee with you is a fattening proposition."

Oliver smiled and swallowed. "These really are special, one of life's simple pleasures. I only indulge occasionally."

Tess took another bite and washed it down with coffee. "Did you come here this morning wondering if I was still standing, still chief?"

He shook his head, a wry smile on his face. "I know you're still standing and you will stay that way. You're made of sterner stuff, and this attempt to make it look as if you've done something you're not capable of will all be for naught. I would have come by yesterday, but it was a busy day."

Emotions welled up and Tess swallowed a lump in her throat with another sip of coffee. "After Saturday, your confidence is heartening. I thought being subjected to a grand jury grilling was bad. I've never been on the receiving end of a criminal interview."

"Like I said before, the truth will show itself. It always does." He fiddled with his cinnamon roll, and Tess felt he had something on his mind.

"What is it?"

A smile played on his lips. "You're a trained observer. Hate to add to your plate, but I'm worried about Drake Harper.

He's in a bad place, and he's convinced you've missed something, that Tim's murderer will get away with it."

Tess sighed, disappointment in herself pinching hard. "I have missed something, and I'm trying to rectify it." She told him about the prints. "All this time I would have bet money Carr or Cherry had something to do with it. I violated my own rule #8: 'Never assume.'"

"But that was logical at the time. The only other suspects . . ." His eyes widened and Tess could tell that the thought hit him right between the eyes. "You don't think that the boys . . ." He shook his head. "No."

"I don't know what to think." She told him about her conversation with the guys.

"Do you want me to talk to them? They all go to my church except Duncan. It might be something harmless that they don't want you to know. Boys will be boys."

"I'll have to think on that." She stood and paced to her whiteboard. "If only I had the last photos Tim took. My gut is telling me the answer is there. He took a photo that gave someone a reason to kill him."

"Did you already explore Tim's cloud account?"

She turned to face him. "His parents said they didn't know one way or the other about a cloud account. Do you know something different?"

"He had a cloud account at the church, I'm sure of it. Travis, my youth pastor, had the ability to access it when Tim had pictures that he wanted Travis to see."

"Is Travis around? Can you check?"

"Sure." Oliver bent down and punched out a text. "Not sure when he'll answer."

Now Tess was amped; she felt as if she were mainlining the caffeine. The answer could be in Tim's photos.

There was a knock at the door. She turned and saw Addie and Casey in the doorway. They almost didn't have to say it; she could see it in their faces.

"Can we speak to you a minute, Chief?" Addie asked.

Oliver got up to leave, but Tess stopped him. "You can stay, Oliver."

He nodded and returned to his seat.

Addie took a deep breath. "I've talked to all the council members. If we voted today on whether or not to leave you on duty, the vote would be tied, two to two." Addie sighed and looked pained. "I had to lay out all the information and decide not only what I think is best for the town but what is best for you as well. I don't believe you killed that man, Tess, but I can't look at this as a friend. I have to be the mayor. So I'm asking you to take some vacation. As of now you're off duty. I'm afraid with all the dust that's being kicked up and all the ammo this has given Cole, things will get rough for you. I know I've taken more calls than I can field. There's even a national cable news crew in Medford on their way up here to cover this story. I'm sorry. This is a mess."

"We both hope everything will be cleared up soon," Casey added.

Tess could only nod and sit back down with her cooling coffee and half-eaten cinnamon roll.

44

Tilly found Bryce Tuesday morning. She'd done something she'd never done before, taken a walk she'd never wanted to take. She went to the pot farm.

It took her and Angel forty minutes to walk there, and when they arrived, Tilly's weak leg ached. She circled around through Arthur's property because she'd heard he was out of town for a while. She followed the outer fence until she was sure no one in Blondie's house could see her, then squeezed in through a hole. The outer fence encircling the entire property was cheap metal netting strung along wood posts. The fence around the product grow was redwood, and Tilly couldn't climb or squeeze through that. Fixing the hole in the outer fence was on Bryce's to-do list, and she was glad he hadn't gotten to it yet. This was a dangerous move, but she needed to see her friend.

She was careful to keep an eye focused in the direction of the house and stay out of the line of sight. When she did have to be in the open, she moved quickly and watched for any sign that she'd been spotted. Blondie lived in the house. The Reptile used to live there too, but he was in jail now. The Hulk and Bryce lived in separate RV trailers that Blondie had on the property. On her side was the time of year. The bulk of the pot workers wouldn't be needed for a few months.

The last time she and Bryce had talked, he'd told her he was working in the pump house. It needed a new roof and the pump itself needed work, so she headed there first. She could hear him humming as she approached and she relaxed a bit. But she waited a few minutes to make certain no one was with him before she said anything. The cold weather had caused a lot of problems with the farm well and pump system. Bryce had been working on it almost every day. Bryce had told Blondie that they needed a new system, but Blondie wouldn't spring for one.

His head was down and his back to Tilly when she and Angel walked up. Tilly smiled. She liked the way his soft brown hair fell. He wore it to his shoulders, and it always reminded her of the way ancient rock stars like the Beatles wore their hair. She thought it was cute.

After a minute, she cleared her throat and he jumped.

"Tilly! You scared me! What are you doing here?"

He was jumpy and mad, and Tilly stepped back.

"I hadn't seen you and I missed you. I was worried."

His features softened, and he set down the part he was working with and grabbed a dirty rag to wipe grease off his hands. "Sorry, but things are weird around here right now. I don't want Blondie or the Hulk to see you. They get mad if people trespass."

"The pot is small right now. What's he worried about?"

Bryce shook his head. "I don't know, but Blondie's jumpy and the Hulk is downright scary. That's why I haven't been down to see you. Ever since Lance Loud got killed, they don't want me going anywhere."

"You're a prisoner?"

"Just about." He looked toward the house and then took her elbow, directing her back to the farm boundary. "The Hulk gives me the creeps. He's always watching."

"You're okay, though?"

"Yeah, yeah." He smiled. "I'm getting paid because there's a lot of work to do here. They're all just paranoid drug people—you know how that goes."

She returned his smile. She did indeed remember the paranoia. "Yeah, I do. I just missed you and wanted to be sure you're okay."

"I'm good." He squeezed her hand and gave Angel a pet.

"I wanted to talk to you about Lance Loud. They think the chief killed him."

"I know. Blondie told me. And I heard him and the Hulk talking. You know her better than I do."

Tilly held his gaze. She knew Bryce felt like the cops were always hassling him for no reason since he got off drugs. And being arrested in Portland had cost him his truck. He feared it would be impossible for him to make enough money to get his truck out of impound once his court date was out of the way. That was one reason he put up with so much stuff that Blondie dished out.

"She wouldn't, Bryce. She's a good person."

He cupped the side of her face softly with his hand. "I know she's been good to you. That earns her some points. But she can deal with it. You just worry about you and Angel, okay?"

She tilted her head, relishing the feel of his hand against her skin. "Okay."

"I'll do the best I can to convince Blondie to let me go for coffee in the morning. I'll tell him I need to get away from here for a bit. I'll explain that to him as soon as I get a chance, all right?" They'd reached the fence line. He faced her and his warm smile made Tilly's toes tingle.

"Thanks, Bryce. I'd like that a lot."

He helped her through the hole, and Tilly and Angel trekked across Arthur's property back toward the road. She glanced back once, but Bryce was gone and she tried to fight the worry. She'd lost Glen and saw Bryce as a godsend, a guy who understood her just like Glen had. She prayed fiercely, *Please, God, please don't let anything happen to Bryce.*

— — —

Bryce went back to work, worry for Tilly straining his concentration. Then he thought of his own predicament, working at a job where he was currently being kept a virtual prisoner. Blondie had said it was because of the Reptile's arrest and Lance Loud's murder, that everyone who worked on the farm was in danger.

"It's for your own safety to stay on the down low, at least until the murderer is in jail," he'd said.

He believed the chief had some sort of odd vendetta against all pot growers and had killed Lance to send a message. She would kill everyone affiliated with the farm if given the chance. Bryce had told Tilly it was simply paranoia speaking, but he didn't really believe that. And he couldn't afford to say out loud what he did believe. Something was going on. The Hulk and some new guy, a short Mexican dude, had brought some boxes of stuff, put them in the two sheds Bryce used for storing tools. They filled both sheds, double padlocked them, and told him to find another place for his tools.

And Blondie's demeanor made him wonder if, in spite of all Bryce had seen that was aboveboard, everything going on here was *legal*. He'd escaped the drug life and was living on the straight and narrow until that stupid warrant tripped him up. Had he made a huge mistake taking this job?

He pondered that question until Tilly came to mind. He'd had a crush on Tilly when they were kids in second grade. It had ebbed and flowed over the years, and he thought it had died out when drugs fried his brain. But when he saw her again a few months ago, that smile, the eyes so blue they put the sky to shame, he knew he'd never gotten over her. Haywood called her "that broken chick." And yeah, she was broken, but so was he. Maybe together they could make one whole person. She was why he stayed at this job. It paid well, and his one goal was to make what he thought was enough money to get him and Tilly out of here. He hadn't told her yet, but that was his plan.

He was finishing up in the pump house when the Hulk

came and stood in the doorway. Bryce didn't hear him walk up. He looked up because it suddenly got darker.

"Where were you earlier?" the Hulk asked, cigarette bobbing in the corner of his mouth.

"Huh? I've been in here all day."

"No. You walked down to the fence line—I saw you."

Then he must have seen Tilly. Bryce swallowed, trying to think fast. He didn't want to get in trouble, but then neither did he want to get Tilly in trouble. He remembered something the friend who helped him get clean once said: *"The truth is always the best way to keep from getting tripped up; you can always remember the truth."*

He said, "Look, Don, I'm sorry. You know I like that girl from town, and she's sweet on me. She found her way up here, worried because I haven't been to see her lately."

"What, does she think we'll hurt you or something?"

"No, no, it's not that. She just missed me, is all." Bryce braced himself, unable to tell if the Hulk was fighting mad or just curious.

"She shouldn't be coming up here like that."

"I know. I told her it was a no-no and walked her off the property—that's it. You won't tell Haywood, will you?"

Cherry's eyes narrowed. "At least you're an honest stupid sap. No, I won't say nothing. But don't let it happen again. And seal up that hole in the fence, now. Haywood ain't going to want any strangers mucking things up. I've got some errands to run. This place needs to be secure. Understand?"

"Yep."

He tossed his cigarette down and mashed it out with his boot before leaving.

In spite of the early morning cool, Bryce wiped sweat from his forehead. Carr had been the one with the rep for being hot-tempered, but Cherry was the scary one. His eyes were dead black holes that looked right through a person. Bryce knew he was a man who could kill without a second thought, if it suited him. He had to get out of here. He was due a big paycheck the day after tomorrow; maybe he'd leave then and find other work somewhere. All the money in the world would do him no good if he were dead.

45

Work was her *life*.

Work was her *identity*.

Tess swallowed some cinnamon roll with her coffee, steadying herself as the news from Addie sank in. On one hand, she didn't blame Addie. She knew that once a furor got started, it was practically impossible to quell it. On the other hand, she felt as if her world was just rocked by a 9.0 earthquake. And she was without a disaster preparedness kit for this.

Call it vacation or something else, she was, essentially, relieved of duty. Unless the real murderer was arrested immediately, she was going to have to find some way to occupy her time.

"Looks like I'll have to leave it to someone else to find Tim's killer," she said to Oliver, trying to smile and fight the hurt and fear that threatened to swallow her. Any strength she had in that moment she used to keep breathing. But when she looked into Oliver's clear gaze, she felt an infusion of strength return because she knew he believed in her. It was a lifeline.

"Addie hasn't lost faith in you," he said. "This is just politics."

"*Politics* is a four-letter word. I just got a useful lead in Tim's case and I'm sidelined." Furiously, she worked to concentrate on Tim and not what was happening to her. But the question burdening her heart blurted out before she could stop it. "I did nothing wrong. Why is this happening to me again?"

"This is far from the same thing as your prior shooting. This is a misunderstanding that needs to be cleared up."

"I wish I could be so sure. It's like your God is out to get me." She tried to sound like she was making a joke but wasn't sure she succeeded.

Oliver shook his head. "Saturday at your home, you mentioned a card of your father's, one with Bible verses."

"Yes." She pulled the card out of her pocket. "Here it is."

"May I see it?"

"Sure." She handed it to him.

Oliver scanned the card, reading each verse out loud. When he finished, he looked up and smiled. "Great verses. All great encouragement for people in uniform. None of them warning that God would be out to get anyone."

"Maybe. At any rate, all I remember from so long ago is

that the words *strong* and *courageous* stood out to me. That was my dad."

"You take after him."

"I wish that were true. My father would have answers for all this; he had answers for everything. What if I can't be a cop anymore?" Fists clenched, Tess fought to keep her composure.

"It won't come to that. But if it did, is that the worst thing that can happen?"

"What do you mean? This is my life—it's all I've ever wanted to do. Losing my career would be failing my dad." She stared at him—surely he understood that much about her.

"Tess, I'm not a father and I didn't know your dad, but there is nothing in you that anyone could call a failure."

She heard his words, but everything was cutting too close for Tess now.

"Can we have this discussion another time?" She stood. "I need to get Curtis in here and let him know he'll be in charge. We just got Bender back and were full strength. Now this . . ."

"Sure, sure." Oliver got up to leave but turned at the door. "You're a good, smart cop. Fight the urge to lose your confidence. And I'm always available if you need someone to talk to."

She nodded thanks and he left.

Tess tried some deep breathing to steady herself before she called her sergeant. The more she thought about the situation and the more steadying breaths she took, the more her confidence returned. She couldn't quit or let herself get bogged down by worry—she was on vacation and she'd make the best of it.

She glanced at the courage card, not seeing the words, but seeing her dad. *"It's always too soon to quit."*

I must make the best out of what I have left.

She was about to call Curtis when Sheila knocked on the door.

"Sorry, Chief, but Damien is here, and he wants a word."

Tess thought for a minute. She could beg off—she was, after all, on vacation—but that would be cowardly. She would handle the media inquiries. "Send him in."

Damien walked in, looking grim. "Hello again, Chief."

"Hi, Damien."

"Do you have a statement about the body on your porch?"

"No beating around the bush with you. All I'll say is that I had nothing to do with the murder of Hector Connor-Ruiz, and I'm confident the Jackson County Sheriff's Department will find the killer."

"That guy made quite a splash here in a very short time."

"Yes, he did."

Damien looked down at his phone. "I wanted to give you a heads-up. This is becoming a campaign issue."

"Figures." Addie had mentioned as much.

"Cole Markarov is placing ads." Damien read from the phone. "'I never wanted to hire this person for chief, and now I'm proven right.'" He looked up. "He then goes on to call you a suspect in a murder, and he berates Addie for expressing any confidence in you at all."

Tess bit her bottom lip and forced herself to follow rule #1: "Listen. Think. Speak."

"Cole didn't waste any time. Damien, I had nothing to do with this homicide, but for some reason, the man was murdered on my porch. Anyway, the investigation is only two and a half days old."

"The rumor is you killed him, Chief."

Tess clenched one fist behind her back and held the reporter's gaze. "You should know better than to believe rumors, Damien. I can't comment further because this office is not handling the investigation."

"He wasn't a very likable guy."

"No, I don't guess that he was. But I'm sworn to serve all the people, not just the ones I like. Hector was a member of this community. I want his killer apprehended."

"Does it say anything that you've been removed from the investigation?"

And from duty.

"All I can do is repeat that I have every confidence in the Jackson County sheriff."

Damien studied her for a moment, then gave a nod and left. Tess slowly released her fist, wondering where the rumor had started and just how far it had spread.

46

Oliver had wanted to tell Addie she was wrong to bow to the pressure but knew it wasn't his place to do such a thing. As he walked across the street to the church, he prayed for Tess and for a quick resolution to the murder of Hector Connor-Ruiz. He could tell Tess was shaken by the request she take time off. Addie might not believe in the charge, but putting Tess on vacation was a huge vote of no confidence.

It was more and more apparent to him that while Tess had come far in life, she was still being held back by the anger she felt over the loss of her father. He was not only reminded of Drake, Oliver also thought of a woman in the fellowship he knew well. Years ago, Nan had climbed behind the wheel of her car impaired by alcohol. Driving too fast on a curvy road, she'd lost control and rolled the car, injuring herself and killing her boyfriend and their young child. Nan served several months in jail after she was released from the hospital.

Why was a word that had Nan stuck even years later. Oliver had spoken to her many times, prayed for her often. She said she knew God had forgiven her, but she couldn't stop asking why. *"Why did I get behind the wheel that night when I knew better?"* She couldn't move forward, couldn't put one foot in front of the other. Oliver knew that could have just as easily been him. His "why" question about Anna would never be answered either. Nan was stuck, and Drake was stuck; their issues were obvious because they wore the pain on their sleeve.

Tess was just as stuck, but she'd buried her pain deep, covered it over with a mission to honor her father by being a good cop. Oliver knew that things people buried had a nasty habit of surfacing at the most inopportune moments. He prayed for the strength and wisdom to help both Tess and Drake.

Drake had to grieve in a healthy way. And he had the support of a loving wife. Oliver prayed that Eva could bring him around. Tess was more of a challenge. Oliver had to figure out how to show her that there was no betrayal where God was concerned. He'd heard enough about her father's death to know that the man had made a choice, a heroic choice, to lay down his life for a citizen he served. And he understood enough about Tess to realize she'd do the same thing if the situation presented itself.

She still hurt over her father's loss. How to get the message across that it was okay to still hurt, that it was okay to hate how he left her so young, that his loss was not the result of a betrayal by God? Her father wouldn't have wanted her to walk away from her faith—Oliver was certain about that.

As he reached the church, he wondered about the murder of Hector Connor-Ruiz and who could be trying to frame the chief. He never for an instant doubted that she was innocent. She was not a killer; she was strong and fearless and relentless in the pursuit of justice. It wasn't in her to kill someone in cold blood. He'd learned a lot last summer when the two of them had raced to Diamond Lake to save Kayla Reno from Roger Marshall, the pedophile.

He'd seen the Connor-Ruiz homicide report; Addie had shared it with him because it so disturbed her. It was cold-blooded. Connor-Ruiz had been shot execution-style by someone with a very dark heart. That wasn't Tess.

He knew this town, this area in the Upper Rogue, and the question she'd asked troubled him, rocked him to his toes. Who here was coldhearted enough to murder Connor-Ruiz and then try to make it look like Tess had done it, and why?

Oliver recognized that the pot laws had brought a lot of strangers to town. He hated to look at every newcomer with skepticism, but unless there was another Roger Marshall in their midst, Connor-Ruiz was likely killed by a newcomer. But who?

He decided it wouldn't hurt to ask around and maybe help the investigation a bit. Don Cherry might have answers.

- - -

After Damien left, Tess closed her office door, needing quiet to think. It made sense that the shooting would become election fodder. Cole Markarov had hated her from the beginning of her employment. The news really didn't change anything.

Sheila stepped in to tell her that two news organizations were on the phone, wanting interviews. After taking the calls and being as brief as possible, Tess began to see wisdom in Addie's decision, though it hurt. As long as she was on duty and a murder suspect, the inquiries would keep coming and get more pointed. But taking a vacation was so cowardly. It was hiding. Her father had never hidden from anything in his life.

It was crystal clear to her that she had only two options: give up, go home, and hibernate until she was arrested or the real killer was caught; or forge ahead, vacation or no, and try to find Tim's killer. Of those two options, there was only one she could pick.

She would find a way to use her forced vacation to her advantage. She could concentrate on one thing—finding Tim's killer—and not have to deal with anything else if she didn't want to.

Satisfied with her plan, she texted the officer on duty, Gabe Bender, and told him she was officially on vacation, and Curtis was in charge. She called Curtis Pounder and told him the same thing. She changed into civilian clothes and perused her office, considering Rogue's Hollow PD. The department she'd inherited was a good one; she knew it would run smoothly even if she was forced to step away. And after a year of working with these guys, she knew they rarely stood on rank. They would all do their jobs and ask each other for help when they needed it.

A glance at the clock told her that Steve would be there soon to pick up her .45. That in and of itself might clear her once and for all, but she wasn't going to lean on a maybe. Then she remembered that Oliver thought there might be a cloud account with Tim's photos. She sent him a text, asking if he'd heard anything from Travis yet. Satisfied she'd done all she could in the chief's uniform, she locked her desk and grabbed her things. Her mind turned Tim's case repeatedly as she climbed into her SUV and drove home.

— — —

Tess got home and made herself a sandwich. She wasn't hungry, but she needed something to do while she waited for Steve. Before she sat down to eat, she retrieved her .45 from her small gun safe. She released the clip, ejected a round from the chamber, left the chamber open, and set it in the living room.

Then she had too much nervous energy to sit and eat. She took a bite of her sandwich, set it down, and paced, only stopping when she heard car tires crunching on the gravel in her driveway. She peeked out the window. Steve climbed out of his patrol car. In seconds, he was at her door.

"Morning, Tess," he said as he stood in the doorway, the evidence bag with her duty weapon in his hand.

Tess felt stiff. Not too long ago his appearance at her door would have brought a smile, but right now she didn't know where they stood.

"Or maybe I should say afternoon." He stepped into the living room when Tess stepped back. "Why are you in civvies?"

"I'm officially on vacation. A first for me."

Something like concern crossed his face—he knew exactly what she was saying. But then it was gone and his cop face was back in place.

"Here's your nine. Do you have the .45?"

"No problem." She held her hand out for her 9mm and he gave it to her. She set it down in the bag and picked up the .45, holding it by the trigger guard and handing it to Steve. "Here you go. Any chance you can tell me when I'll get my laptop back?"

"Techs are still working on it."

Tess nodded but could tell that Steve had more to say.

"Can we take a minute to clear the air, please?"

"What, since you couldn't match my nine to the murder, suddenly you're conflicted?"

"I never thought you killed that guy. Look, Belcher is breathing down my neck. He's in charge and he wants to stay there. I think he believes solving this murder with a high-profile arrest will enhance his résumé, give him a leg up on the competition."

"What about impartial investigation?"

"Aw, it's politics!" He threw his hands up. "You know better than anyone else how politics mucks things up. I care about you, Tess. I'm doing my job the best I can under the circumstances."

Taken aback because this certainly was not the Steve at the crime scene or on the phone, Tess blinked and thought carefully before responding.

"Steve, you're a good cop; I know that. But you betrayed my trust. I wasn't asking for special treatment; all I was asking for was the benefit of the doubt. And then you called me on a taped line, for heaven's sake. I just can't forgive that right now." She held her hand out toward the door.

"That was Belcher. I don't know how to show you that I'm on your side in this. Someone is trying to frame you; that became clear to me right away. So be careful." He turned on his heel and left the house.

Tess stood for a long time after he left, with the door open, until she could no longer hear his tires on the gravel drive.

— — —

Tess picked at the rest of her sandwich. Her phone dinged with a text from Oliver. **Sorry, no recent pics from Tim on the cloud.**

Disappointment bit. She wanted to call and talk to Oliver, but the phone rang before she could punch in his number.

Surprise raised her eyebrows. It was her old friend, DEA Agent Ledge.

"Agent Ledge. What a surprise."

"I hear a lot has been happening for you lately."

"You could say that." She wondered what he'd heard, if rumors that she was a cold-blooded killer had reached his ears. She didn't offer the information.

"I've been meaning to call. But . . ." She could hear his phone being slid around as if he were talking and walking at the same time and a lot of voices in the background.

A terse "Hang on" was all she got. After a few minutes with Tess frowning, wondering what was going on, he came back on the line.

"Look," he said, "it's going to be all over the news shortly.

We just had a pair of agents ambushed and shot. One is dead, the other hanging on."

Tess froze.

Ledge continued. "It was a targeted ambush. They were lying in wait for the agents. But the good guys returned fire. One of the cowards is dead, the other in custody. O'Rourke, you might be next."

47

Bryce's small RV trailer behind the main house at the Hang Ten was old and got stuffy with the slightest rise in outside temperature, but it was home while he worked on the farm. Sometimes he wished he had stayed at the Gospel Mission, but without a car to get him back and forth from Medford, he had to be close. And it was quiet most of the time, unless Haywood was playing music to bug the neighbor, or he was arguing with Hector. But the neighbor was gone right now and Hector was dead. Yet loud, angry words rang from the house. It was lunchtime, and getting hot, so all of Bryce's windows were open while he toasted a grilled cheese sandwich.

He could make out Haywood's voice. It got high and

reedy when he was upset. The other voice was lower, more measured, and Bryce couldn't understand what the man was saying.

He frowned and turned off the burner. It didn't sound like Cherry, but it might be the new Mexican guy. Haywood just kept saying that it wasn't his fault, that he didn't know anything about guns, he wasn't into gun violence.

He wasn't making much sense and he had diarrhea of the mouth, the kind that comes on when you messed up and you were afraid of the person calling you on it. Bryce knew what that felt like. He'd been in that position with his father more times than he cared to remember. But who was Haywood afraid of?

Bryce stretched, realizing his nosy bone was tweaking him. He scratched his beard, wanting to peek and listen, wanting to know what the fight was about. He peered out the small, open window at the end of the trailer. Bryce saw a car in the driveway he wasn't familiar with. When did that get here? He hadn't heard it pull up.

Bryce noticed so many things that were off lately. The Hulk and the Mexican had filled the Reptile's old room with plastic tubs. They'd been coming and going—this after Haywood had said everyone was supposed to stay put. The Hulk had been riding around on a sharp little ATV, heading up the canyon lately. He'd begun to fear that Tilly was right, that Haywood was up to illegal things, and he wanted to leave. But he knew they'd never let him, so he would bide his time and wait.

The voices in the house lowered, and Bryce pulled his T-shirt on. It was probably in the seventies outside, maybe fifteen degrees warmer inside the trailer. He could always say he was just out for fresh air if anyone asked him what he was doing. A little bit of fear roiled his stomach. What was that old saying? "Curiosity killed the cat"? *I'm smarter than a cat,* he thought.

As quietly as he could, he opened the door to the trailer and stepped out into the noon sunshine. Looking from side to side, he tiptoed to the window. He peered into the house and saw the short Mexican dude he'd seen once before standing beside someone he'd never seen before, a tall guy who looked like a cop. Haywood was pacing. He looked nervous. Bryce didn't see the Hulk. They were talking about damage control and somebody named Howard.

Bryce frowned, wondering what was going on. He was about to turn around and go back to his trailer when he felt the cold steel of a gun press into the back of his warm neck.

48

Leaving Tess hanging with a promise he'd call back, Ledge disconnected. Since she didn't have her laptop, Tess hit the browser on her phone. She checked a news site and found the breaking news story.

"DEA Agents Ambushed outside Supermarket." It happened a few hours ago. The agents were not named yet, and Tess wondered if she knew them. Most of the guys she'd worked with on the search warrant were great guys, family men, and it broke her heart to think one had just been killed. The surviving agent was said to be in the hospital in critical condition. And Tess read that there was speculation this was connected to an incident a couple of days earlier where a pipe bomb was found underneath a DEA vehicle.

Tess hadn't heard anything about the first incident and wondered what this was all about. Was it related to the raid in Yreka? What did Ledge mean that she might be next? Thankfully, she didn't have to stay on pins and needles for very long.

"Sorry about that. Life is off the scale right now." He sounded harried and more on edge than he'd ever been during the short time Tess had worked with him and Agent Hemmings.

"What did you mean I might be next?"

"Didn't Hemmings call you, warn you about the threats?"

"No, I haven't heard from Agent Hemmings since he came up here to ask about Carrington. Is he back here in Oregon?"

Ledge said something inaudible. "No, he should have called. Chief, I just saw a news report about you. It said they found a dead guy on your porch?"

"Yes."

"What's up with that?"

"I don't know. I'm not handling the investigation. Not sure why he was there or what he wanted." She held her breath, wondering where Ledge was going with all of this.

"Hmm. Well, I have something for you to chew on. We got a lot of threats after that raid in Yreka. Hemmings was supposed to give you a heads-up. I'll be all over why he didn't. Seems like the kid who died in the raid, the one who fired at the entry team—he was the Ghost's little brother. The Mexican mafia put a hit out on all cops and agents associated with the raid."

"Threats? A hit?" The words were surreal to Tess.

"At first, we figured most of the chatter was normal stuff,

blowhards angry that we shut their operation down, venting. Vowing to kill agents, cops; threatening to blow us up, yada yada yada. But two things happened: We got a positive ID on the Ghost, José Gonzalez Garcia. The dead kid was Geraldo Herrera Garcia. His mom came in to claim his body and she filled in some blanks. José Garcia is his half brother: same father, different mothers. That made us take the threats more seriously. And Garcia has more of a rep than we thought. He's wanted for several homicides in Mexico and is a possible suspect in a dozen this side of the border. Because we had this information, our agents were prepared. That's a big reason why we didn't lose both guys." He paused.

"The second thing is, you arrested Carrington. The guy's a bomb maker; his fingerprints are all over a lot of explosives we've recovered. It's obvious now that he was busy before you arrested him. We need to tear his place of employment apart. And it's possible that the dead guy on your porch surprised a hit man and took a bullet for you. Just a thought."

Tess digested this information, mind whirring. After finding Hector dead on her porch and becoming a suspect in the murder, Tess didn't think anything could cause her jaw to drop, but this info did. She knew Hemmings should have taken a harder line on the Hang Ten.

Ledge was still talking. "The shooter in custody isn't talking; neither is Carrington. But I don't need to tell you everyone in law enforcement will be after Garcia, high priority. I'll send you everything we have on him that's been confirmed. If he did miss you and get that other guy, I don't doubt he'll try again. There's an urgency to his moves right now. Scuttlebutt says he's tying up loose ends to disappear over the border."

"But why mess with me all the way up here?"

"It's an image thing with him. Even though you only assisted in Yreka, you became high profile because you ran down Alexander; you made the mafia hit parade. Watch your back."

"I will," Tess said as she tried to digest the fact that she might have been the target of an assassin and not Hector. Was that what happened? Did he come to her house for his own reasons and interrupt a killer? Did she owe Hector her life?

"Should I be concerned about the Hang Ten?"

"We're concerned with what's happening here, now. I'll have to get back to you on that place."

"Can you send the threat information to the Jackson County sheriff, and to me at my private e-mail?"

"I will. I'm on my way to the hospital. I'll keep you updated."

This new information put Tess on edge.

She thought for a long time about the assassination attempt on the two agents. In a crowded city, there was a certain amount of cover provided for people who wanted to blend in. This was the advantage of living in a place as small as Rogue's Hollow. Strangers stuck out, though they were usually tourists. If the Ghost was after her and he came himself, or sent one of his men, she would know. Unless . . . one of his men was already here. Like Roger Marshall, this person could be fitting in.

Carrington had fit in for a few months. Was he up here making bombs? Was that why Haywood was so afraid Arthur was spying on him?

Did Hector die for her? Or was killing Hector and framing her the plan?

Tess shot out an e-mail to Bender, telling him what Ledge had said, admonishing him to be careful and to let her know if they came across anyone suspicious from out of town.

After finishing the e-mail, Tess called Oliver and asked about the cloud account.

"Sorry, Tess. Travis checked the account. There's nothing new there from Tim. The last photo on the cloud Travis received from Tim was on Easter Sunday."

Crushed by this news, Tess put her phone down, at a loss as to where to go next.

What am I supposed to do? she wondered. *Twiddle my thumbs, wait for something bad to happen?* She paced.

The safe thing to do was to sit and let the DEA do their thing, obey Addie, be on vacation. Tess couldn't play it safe; it wasn't in her nature. She knew, first thing in the morning, she'd be off doing something.

49

Oliver arrived home a little early Tuesday night, and as luck would have it, he had a visitor. He smelled cigarette smoke before he saw the source. Don Cherry was back, standing off to the side of the house, in the shadows as usual.

"Evening, padre."

"Don. I thought you quit smoking."

"I've quit a million times," he said as he crushed the butt out on the ground and walked over to where Oliver stood, blowing smoke out of his nose and mouth as he approached.

"You've not been around for a while. I wondered what happened to you." Oliver stepped up on the porch and took a seat in his rocking chair, expecting Cherry to join him and sit in Anna's chair, but the man remained at the bottom of the steps.

"Life happens."

Oliver waited. Something was weighing on the usually talkative, sometimes even glib, man. His posture was tense and it made Oliver nervous.

"Padre, what do you think happens to people who do things they know they shouldn't?"

"What kind of things?"

"Bad things. Stuff you'd probably call sin." His gaze settled on Oliver and it was disconcerting. Cherry had brown eyes, but in the evening light they looked black.

"Is someone making you do things you don't want to do?"

He glared at Oliver and punched his own chest with a meaty fist. "Do you think anyone could make me do what I didn't want to do?"

In all the times they'd spoken, this was the first time Oliver fully realized how dangerous Don Cherry was. The last thing he wanted was to start a fight with the man, but he felt he needed to be bold. It was time to get to the bottom of Don Cherry.

He leaned forward in the rocking chair. "Don, everyone is a sinner. Unrepentant sinners will ultimately face the wrath of God. He's a holy God who will not tolerate bad things, stuff we call sin. Like your friend the jail chaplain told you, everyone needs a savior. Is that what you want to know?"

"You guys are good at saying stuff like that. What I want is proof of this God!" he roared and leaped up on the porch, towering over Oliver. "The chaplain in prison couldn't prove it any more than you can. You got that same smug look.

You're so sure of this God, prove it to me." Spittle flew from his mouth.

"Why do I have to prove something you already know?"

Cherry rocked back on his heels. "What? You're crazy. Why would I ask for proof if I knew?"

Oliver stood and Cherry backed up a step. "Don, after speaking with you several times, I know you do believe in God. And you know there is much in your past, and perhaps in your present, that you need to confess and repent of. But you don't want to humble yourself. You're operating under the delusion that God is your equal, someone you can manipulate like you manipulate people, and not an all-powerful deity. Stop fighting. He wins in the end."

Oliver watched the anger drain from Cherry's face. The big man went pale and backed up into the porch post.

"You're crazy," he repeated before he turned, jumped down off the porch, and disappeared into the night.

50

Wednesday morning Tess woke up even more determined to do something than she had been the night before. She ripped the evidence bag and pulled out her 9mm. The gun was empty and she loaded it, making sure to rack a round into the chamber. She grabbed her off-duty holster and belt and strapped the gun on.

She'd go back to the basics—for Tim's case, that was back to the Spot—and see if anything at all would jump-start her murder investigation. She pulled her personal car out of the garage. It wasn't a low-profile car; it was a bright-red Mercedes two-door coupe. She could count on the fingers of one hand the number of times she'd driven it since she moved to the state. The patrol SUV was the more practical vehicle. But right now she was on vacation and it was her only choice.

The Spot was empty. It even looked as if someone had cleaned the place up. Tess wandered around the rocks and tree stumps, natural seating that made the place an attractive area to party. She thought she was alone but heard a cough. Placing a hand on her gun, she called out, "Who's there?"

"Huh?" A head popped up from behind a rock. It was Duncan Peabody.

"Chief." He stood and brushed off his shorts. It looked to Tess as if he'd been crying, but she didn't mention it.

"Are you by yourself, Duncan?"

He nodded. There was an energy drink in his hand. "All my buds are getting ready to leave for college." He ran an arm under his nose. "Guess I'll have to get used to rolling solo."

Tess had heard from Casey that because Duncan had been a troublemaker in his early high school years, he'd barely graduated and did not have the grades to go to college. This meeting was fortuitous. She'd wanted to talk to him away from his friends, hoping he'd be more forthcoming, but she'd also dealt with group loyalty before. Duncan wasn't a two-bit thug trying to avoid being a snitch; he was a kid with one foot in the adult world. What would work to get him to talk?

She stepped toward him. "What do you plan to do with yourself now that you're out of high school?"

"I dunno." He swigged the drink. He wouldn't meet her eyes. His friends were a big part of his life.

Tess tried to think back to how it was with her friends in high school, but that didn't help. Her high school years were dominated by the death of her father and the drive to become a cop like he was. She didn't remember much of high school cliques or misguided loyalty. She fell back to what usually worked, a direct approach.

"Duncan, what are you guys hiding about the night Tim died?"

"Huh?" He looked at her, eyes wide. "We told you everything."

"I don't think you did."

"Don't you think I want to find Tim's killer more than anyone?"

"Certainly not more than Mr. Harper. It's just that every time we talk, I get the distinct impression there's more than what you're telling me. I'm not trying to get anyone in trouble except the person who killed Tim." Her gaze bored into him until he looked away.

"We told you everything."

"I think you're holding back. I don't know why, but that's what I think. Every day you hold back, Tim's killer stays free."

He rubbed the back of his neck but wouldn't look her way.

Rigid with frustration, Tess didn't want to give up, but what would be the key to open this kid's mouth? She started to leave, then stopped.

"I thought you'd changed. You saw Glen and Anna murdered, and that made you want to stop being a delinquent and become a productive member of the community. Withholding information is not consistent with that change." She thought she saw him flinch, but still he said nothing. After a few minutes, there was nothing to do but go home.

- - -

Tess arrived home frustrated and cranky. Nothing she said got Duncan to spill the beans. Greg was gone, visiting his new school, and while she wanted to talk to the other boys, she knew that would be pushing it. She'd spent the day driving everywhere in the valley hoping to find Dustin loitering around somewhere and came up empty there as well. A call from the Medford PD lieutenant in MADGE interrupted her frustrated pacing.

"Chief, wanted to let you know we've got a line on our fentanyl dealer, fellow by the name of Howard Delfin. Got a positive ID. He was arrested once in California for a DUI. He rents a house in Shady Cove." He rattled off the address, but Tess barely heard him.

Howard Delfin. That was the name on the letter of reference for Eddie Carr.

"Outstanding news." So the party crasher had a name. But he also had a record, so his prints weren't the ones on the syringe or the bike. But he still might lead her to the killer.

"We expect a warrant soon but are taking it slow," the lieutenant continued. "Fentanyl is such a dangerous commodity, we need to be certain no officers are in danger from contact with the substance."

"I understand. I'd like to be there when you serve the warrant."

"I'm not sure that would be appropriate."

"Why not?"

"Chief, you're the subject of a murder investigation. I can't in good conscience invite you along on a warrant service."

"I had nothing to do with that murder."

"I might even say I believe you. But I'd be in trouble with my superiors if I ignored the investigation and asked you along. Sorry."

He hung up, leaving Tess fuming.

She'd not even had the chance to tell him about the Delfin connection.

At least I have that lead, she thought. Working to stay positive, Tess set about making dinner. She needed to go grocery shopping; all she had were eggs and some bacon. Breakfast would have to do for dinner. Just as she cracked the eggs into a bowl, she heard what sounded like several vehicles pulling into her driveway.

Checking, she found a state police car, a couple sheriff cars pulling up. Were they coming to arrest her for murder?

51

Oliver was an early riser; therefore, he was also in bed early. But when Steve Logan came to tell him that Drake Harper was missing and so were his guns, all thoughts of an early bedtime fled.

"Have you told Tess?"

"That was our first stop."

Something in the deputy's response bothered Oliver. "Is she in danger? Did Drake threaten her?"

"Not directly, but he was angry. Actually, according to his wife, he was seething. Tess declined our offer to have a deputy stay nearby."

Of course she would. Oliver wanted to go to Tess but

decided he could best help by talking to Eva and looking for Drake.

That was what he'd been doing and now, after a fruitless search that lasted until after midnight, he was finally heading for bed. He climbed the steps of his house, certain he'd done everything he could do to assist in the search.

He nearly jumped out of his skin when he saw someone curled up in a ball on his doorstep. Briefly he wondered if he'd be in the same position as Tess. But the person wasn't dead. When she moved, he saw it was Tilly, and then he spotted her dog off to the right.

"What's the matter, Tilly?"

"Pastor Mac, please, can you help me? I'm so scared." She stood up, and from the redness on her face he could tell she'd been crying. The dog sat quietly while she grasped Oliver's hands.

"Come in. Tell me what's wrong." He gently pulled his hands free and opened his front door, motioning her to go inside.

Oliver switched on a floor lamp. He pointed to the couch, but Tilly ignored him to pace, throwing her hands in the air as she talked.

"It's Bryce. He promised to meet me for coffee, but now he's disappeared. He always does what he says. I'm so scared something has happened to him. He should have come to coffee. I'm afraid Blondie has hurt—"

Oliver grabbed her by the shoulders as gently as he could. "Whoa, whoa, you need to calm down. You're talking about Bryce Evergreen?"

"Yes, we're friends. I meet him for coffee sometimes. But

he hasn't come. I've texted, but he's not answering. They keep him prisoner. They closed the fence. I can't find him. I haven't seen him . . ." She began to sob.

Oliver pulled her close. "Tilly, I want to help, but you're not making much sense. Please, have a seat, let me get you some water, and then you can tell me what's going on."

She began the kind of sob breathing that people do when they're about to hyperventilate, but she sat on the couch. Oliver offered her the Kleenex box and then went into the kitchen and filled a glass of water. By the time he got back, she'd calmed noticeably. He gave her the water and she took a sip.

Oliver sat next to her. "Okay, now tell me about Bryce." Oliver remembered the young man who'd been troubled with drugs before he left the valley. And he was happy to see that he'd returned clean and was trying to make his life work. Bryce had been to church a couple of times. Oliver remembered him sitting with Tilly. But it had been a while.

She sniffled. "He's disappeared. I saw him on Tuesday morning and now he's gone. I tried to see him up at Blondie's place, but I can't get in anymore. I'm scared that Blondie hurt him."

"By Blondie, you mean his boss, Haywood?"

She nodded and grabbed some Kleenex to blow her nose. "They treat him like a slave up there, and now I think they hurt him."

She started to cry again, softly this time, and Oliver sat back, wondering. Tilly had so many of her own issues, but she was genuinely frightened. Did she have good reason to be afraid?

Oliver knew that Bryce needed the work at the pot farm to pay off his legal issues and get his car back. But he also had a bad feeling about Haywood and his operation. And he had a problem with pot growing in general. It wouldn't hurt to take a drive up to the pot ranch and ask to see Bryce.

"It's me, isn't it?"

"What?"

"Me. I'm a jinx. Glen is dead and now Bryce . . ."

"Stop that, Tilly. No such thing as a jinx. You're a child of God. And we'll get to the bottom of where Bryce is. I'll go up there myself and talk to him, first thing in the morning, okay?"

She looked up at him, so much pain and loss in her eyes, Oliver felt it hit him in the center of his chest like a fiery dart.

52

Thursday morning, Tess got up early after barely sleeping. The police who'd paid her a visit the night before hadn't come to arrest her; they'd come to warn her and to do a search of her property.

"Drake Harper is missing, and so are two of his guns." Steve had looked grim and professional as he delivered the news. "His wife is afraid he might want to do you harm."

"I haven't seen him."

"These guys are here to look around, if that's okay with you. And Belcher wants to leave a deputy here in case he comes around. Drake is a career Army officer; he's served three combat tours."

Impressive though that sounded to Tess, she declined the offer. "They can search, but I don't need a babysitter. I'll be fine."

"He's not thinking clearly."

"He's hurting. I understand him. And I can take care of myself."

Steve and the others left, but she could tell he wasn't happy about it.

Now, as she set up her coffeemaker and pushed Brew, she checked the clock and wondered where Drake could be.

She showered and dressed for the day, floundering over where to start. After all, time was ticking away. Steve had suggested she stay close to home until Drake was accounted for. But dressed, hair wet, Tess poured her coffee into a travel mug. She'd just secured the top when she heard a car on her drive. Setting the coffee down, she picked up her handgun and walked toward the door.

It was another sheriff's car. With news about Drake? Then she saw who climbed out of the driver's seat.

"It's rush hour around here," she muttered to herself as she walked out to meet the man.

Belcher met her at the porch. In his hand, she saw her .45.

"The ballistics were inconclusive," he said, stepping toward her and handing her the evidence bag holding the gun. "We can't say that this was the gun, but we can't say it wasn't."

"Yet you're returning it, so someone in the lab must have told you that it was highly improbable." Tess met his gaze and stifled a snarky comment. Belcher had a soft face, with an expression that always seemed to be mocking. It was no different today.

"All I'll say is that the investigation is open and ongoing. And you're the only person in the area with any motive to kill Hector Connor-Ruiz. No one else knew him as well as you did."

"What about the information the DEA sent? The threats agents are facing? Did you read any of that?"

He scrunched his nose as if smelling something bad. "That type of targeting would never happen here in our small community. The Feds will get their guy. As far as Connor-Ruiz, after all the evidence is collected and analyzed, it will likely go to a grand jury."

Tess felt her pulse rise. In a measured tone she said, "He said mean things about me. In my book, that is not a very strong motive for murder. Any grand jury will understand that. Besides the fact that I have an alibi."

"A good friend who would cover for you."

"Keep reaching."

"We'll see. Mind your manners, Chief. Don't leave the area." He looked down his nose at her and then got back in his car.

She waited until he was long gone before picking up her gun belt. Before putting it on, she changed her mind. The less threatening she was today, the better. Tess grabbed her coffee mug, headed for her car, and pondered the visit by the sheriff. Why was Belcher so fixated on her? Was it really because he thought a high-profile arrest would help him?

Tess couldn't see any scenario where there was enough evidence to convict her of a murder she didn't commit. She and Jeannie were in all night; time of death wouldn't help. And both her guns had been cleared.

All the evidence right now appeared to be in her favor. Still, she had a strong feeling inside that told her she needed to watch her step.

With that thought, a heavy feeling of foreboding settled on her, and Tess wondered if she'd already become damaged goods as far as the town was concerned. With Cole using her as a campaign issue and even Forest Wild turning against her, did she have any chance of remaining chief?

Politics could blind people. Was that what had happened to Belcher? Would all the people of Rogue's Hollow decide she was a bad egg?

She couldn't entertain the thought. If she did, she'd fall apart. There was only one thing to do—charge full speed ahead.

53

Tess had the address for Howard Delfin and considered what the MADGE lieutenant had said. They were working on getting a warrant, but they were being careful, not rushing the process. She might have a window of opportunity to talk to Delfin, ask him about Eddie Carr. She didn't want to mess up MADGE's invest, but her time was running short. And she wouldn't push; she just wanted to get a feel for the guy. Was he Tim's killer?

In her little roadster, she drove out to Shady Cove. The address was about ten minutes away. Tess turned from Highway 62 onto Old Ferry Road and wound up the road for a bit until she reached Delfin's street, a quiet cul-de-sac.

The lots were large here and the area was what Tess liked to call semirural—no sidewalks, no picture-perfect square lawns here; rougher-edged landscaping dominated. Delfin's address was straight ahead at the end of the street.

Tess pulled to the side of the street two houses down and parked in the shade of an oak tree. Right away she saw some problems to serving a search warrant. There was no way to sneak up on Howard's home. The structure backed up to trees and a wild, dry hillside. The neighbors were far enough away, but with the windows and view, Tess would hate to be the one walking up the driveway's steep incline to the front door with a warrant.

She wondered if MADGE had the house under surveillance and studied each car she saw parked on the street. None of them were occupied and none looked like plain cars. But police agencies here were peopled with a lot of officers who were experienced hunters and hikers. Someone could be positioned in the forest to watch the house if MADGE was certain Delfin was making opiates.

It was possible her visit would make waves.

Oh, well.

Tess carried a small .380 caliber backup weapon in her car. Steve knew she had the small gun, but neither he nor Belcher had asked for it. And Tess saw no reason to offer it up to Belcher. She'd had nothing to do with Hector's murder—with a 9mm or a .45 caliber or a .380.

Wanting to look as nonthreatening as possible—she was already in jeans and a T-shirt—she'd not worn her belt holster, but she still wanted to be safe. So, in the interest of being prepared, she slipped the handgun into the small of her back and climbed out of the car. Tess stayed close to the edge of the street. It was warm but not yet the forecast ninety degrees. Still, sweat started on her brow. It was quiet—pleasantly or eerily, depending on your perspective.

She passed one car, noted it was empty, touched the hood. Also cool. Then she began the trek up the steep driveway. At the top of the drive there was a small pickup parked in front of the garage door with bricks behind the rear tires. It didn't look as if it still ran.

The front door was up a few stairs and across what looked like a large wraparound porch. Tess reached the bottom step at the same time she heard a car coming up the street. Before she could turn and check out the vehicle, a man came running around the corner of the porch to her right.

Dustin Pelter.

"Hey!" Tess called.

He saw her and screeched to a stop like a cartoon, eyes like saucers, reeking of fear.

"I didn't do it!" He turned to run back the way he came, slipping but catching his balance enough to disappear around the corner of the house as Tess hit the top step. She accelerated after him, reaching the corner, pausing briefly in case he'd set a trap. He hadn't. He was sprinting along the side of the house.

Glad she'd put on her trail runners, Tess went after him, getting good traction as she raced up the dusty path. Dustin didn't turn when he reached the back of the house; he kept running up the hillside behind the house and Tess continued after him.

Arms pumping, adrenaline fueling her, Tess closed the

distance. Dustin was a junkie, after all. She doubted he'd be able to run far.

He was grabbing trees, bushes, trying to pull himself up the hill.

Breath coming hard, sweat stinging her eyes, Tess yelled, "Stop, Dustin! You've nowhere to go." The trail was hard packed, and she bounded up as Dustin slipped to his knees. She could hear him crying.

"It wasn't me." He whined breathlessly as he pulled himself up, went another couple feet, and fell again.

"I just want to talk to you." Tess was close enough to smell him, and she slowed, wanting her breathing to steady. "Stop. There's nowhere to run."

He was crawling now, and in three long strides, Tess reached him.

Quivering and breathing hard, Dustin kept repeating, "It wasn't me."

"All right." Tess placed her right hand on an oak tree, leaning in, and wiped sweat from her brow with her left hand. "It wasn't you. Turn around and talk to me."

He started to cough and Tess feared soon he'd be dry heaving. He coughed and squirmed into the dust. She waited, taking stock of their location. She had a view of Shady Cove and the house below.

After a moment, Dustin calmed and sat up. His face was streaked with sweat, dirt, and tears. He wiped his hands on his knees and leaned forward, now hiccuping. "I just found him like that, that's all."

Tess frowned. She'd initially thought he was talking about Tim. "Who?"

He looked up, thin body quivering as hiccups ripped through him. "He—" His voice died in his throat, silenced by the crack of a rifle shot.

Tess ducked instinctively and slipped, falling facedown as two more shots rang out and bark exploded from the tree next to her.

Cover.

The word screamed in her brain—she had to find cover. Staying as flat as possible, Tess scrambled up the hill as two more shots hit the tree. She felt bits of bark cut her face. Dragging herself behind the tree, she pulled her gun from behind her, feeling like she'd brought a cap gun to a firefight.

"Dustin," she hissed and got no response.

Tess stuck her hand around the tree, pointing the gun toward the house below and violating training that told her not to fire until she knew what her target was. She just wanted whoever was shooting at her to know she was not unarmed.

She fired twice and waited. The day returned to the quiet she'd noted before the shooting started—now definitely eerie. Then she heard a car door slam and a car burn rubber out of the cul-de-sac. Pushing herself to her feet, she stood, trying to get a glimpse of the car.

She saw it turn right onto Old Ferry Road, heading toward Highway 62. She couldn't tell the make, just that it was a dark sedan. Frustrated, she shoved the gun behind her and pulled out her phone. Only to stop in shock when she looked down at Dustin. He'd been hit, blood blossoming across his dirty white T-shirt.

54

Oliver drove up to the Hang Ten. He'd had to convince Tilly to stay behind, but it hadn't been easy. She was really frightened.

The pot farm gate was locked, and from his spot in front of it, Oliver could see no movement at the Hang Ten. It was 9 a.m. on Thursday; he expected someone would be awake. The tight security didn't surprise him. He knew about the robbery here, and of many others at different farms. Back in October during the pot harvest several farms had been the victims of invasion-style robberies. The farmers took precautions now. But Oliver did wonder if things were more secure because of Hector's murder.

He punched the button on the intercom several times before someone answered with an angry "What?"

"It's Oliver Macpherson. I'd like to talk to Bryce."

There was a long pause. Then a different voice answered—Oliver was certain—and it wasn't Haywood. "Bryce isn't here."

"When will he be back?"

"He won't. He left. Went home."

"What? He still had fines to pay and one more court date."

"Hey, pal, not my problem. He's gone." The intercom clicked off.

Oliver hit the button again, hoping to reconnect and ask for Don, but to no avail.

He frowned. He didn't know Bryce well, but the young man he'd talked to was adamant about keeping his court dates and clearing up all his legal problems. Bryce did want to leave the valley, but not before he was in the clear with the justice system. Oliver didn't believe that would have changed.

Was he afraid because Hector had been murdered? That put a whole new light on things. Now he didn't know what he was going to tell Tilly. On top of everything else, Drake Harper still hadn't turned up. Put that together with the odd visit from Cherry after Hector was killed, and fear began to knot in his stomach.

But he did know what he was going to tell Tess. Something was wrong at the Hang Ten. Very wrong.

— — —

"The chief isn't here," Sheila said. "But you look wigged-out. Is it an emergency?"

Oliver hit his head with his palm. "That's right—she's on vacation." He reconsidered Bryce. The thing was, he needed Tess's thinking here. Was he being too suspicious or not suspicious enough? "I'm not certain. I'd just like to speak to her. Who is on duty?"

"We're thin. It's Officer Bender now, but he's been helping Jackson County with their murder investigation. Del is covering on overtime. Do you want me to call him in?"

Oliver shook his head. "No, I'm not sure what's going on. I don't want to interrupt him." Slowly he turned to leave, then turned back. "Has there been any word on Drake?"

"Not a peep. Poor Eva. How's she holding up?"

"Last I heard, she was staying with the Peabodys for a while."

"I hope Drake is okay."

"Me too. I'll leave a message for the chief and, on second thought, go find Del. Thanks, Sheila."

55

Tess had a nasty cut on her cheek from tree bark. Paramedics arrived and gave her a Band-Aid before screaming off to the hospital with Dustin, who was alive, but just barely.

The once-quiet cul-de-sac had filled with sheriff vehicles and state police cars in short order. Tess followed the medics down the hill to face Steve Logan, who was part of the crew of deputies flooding the street. There had been no sign that anyone was in Delfin's house. The gunshots hadn't brought the occupant out, if he was even home.

"You okay?" he asked, gesturing to her cheek.

"I'm fine," Tess said with more force than she meant to.

Anger darkened Steve's brow and Tess knew she needed to

relax. None of this was Steve's fault. "I've got Medford calling, asking what we have here. What happened?"

Tess told him. "I never even knocked at the front door. All I planned to do was size Delfin up."

"MADGE was handling this," he cut her off. "Why were you meddling?"

"I'm not meddling. It's my name I'm trying to clear." Her voice rose, anger that he couldn't see why she needed to do something seeping out.

"You're not the only competent cop in the valley." He folded his arms and shot her an arrogant cop glare.

"I know that. I also know someone is trying to frame me for murder and your boss seems gleeful about it. I'm not under arrest, so I'm out of here." She stomped away.

"Tess, wait."

She stopped. Something in his voice made her turn back.

He sighed and threw his hands up. "Can we start over? I didn't mean to come off like I did." Contrite, he walked to where she stood. "Look, I understand why you're here, but . . . well, you could have been killed. Maybe we're not together anymore, but that doesn't mean I don't still care what happens to you."

The anger and tension in her melted away, and she fought to control a tumble of emotions. She had almost been killed, and the thought still made her knees weak. And in spite of all the bad stuff between them lately, Steve could still be an ally, a friend.

"Thanks, Steve. A do-over is in order." Collecting her thoughts, she gave him the whole story and he listened without interrupting.

"Get a good look at the shooter or the car that peeled out?" he asked when she finished.

She shook her head. "We need to check out the house, determine what Dustin was doing here."

Steve folded his arms. "We? Tess, as I recall, you're on vacation."

Too tired and frazzled to even argue, Tess waved her hand. "Fine, you check. Is Delfin even home?"

"We got two 911 calls from—" he pointed—"that house and a house on Old Ferry Road, but no call from this house."

"Was anyone able to give a description of the shooter so far?"

"Nothing clear. Wait here."

Tess leaned against a sheriff's car while Steve went to talk to a state cop. The car was parked some distance from the driveway and yellow tape was strung across the area. They'd found the shooter's brass. He'd been firing a rifle, and Tess guessed this was where the shooter's car had stopped. He'd shot at her at least once from here. And then he'd run up the side of the house to shoot again.

She looked up the hillside, realizing that the guy knew what he was doing to hit Dustin from this distance. She was lucky he'd missed her. Straightening, she walked to the edge of the tape, noting the yellow evidence markers where the brass was.

There were officers up where she and Dustin had been when they were shot at, collecting evidence, and there were officers canvassing the street, trying to determine if anyone had seen clearly who shot at her. Tess was a bit numb; she recognized a little shock setting in. But even through the cloud of shock, she felt there were answers here, with Delfin. Delfin could be the out-of-place partygoer. But what was his connection to Tim?

Steve and the state cop had an animated conversation before they both walked up the driveway to Delfin's house. They banged on the front door and got no response. After a few minutes, they walked around toward the back of the house.

Tess started to feel life flowing back into her limbs as the shock wore off. She took a swig of water from the bottle the medics had given her. She'd barely put the bottle down when Steve came striding down the steps with purpose toward her.

"Did you go in the house?" he asked.

"No, I told you. I didn't even knock on the door. Why?"

"Back door is open. We went in. There's a male subject inside with a bullet in his head."

— — —

Murder and shooting investigations were the most complex and time-consuming investigations cops engaged in, and it was getting dark when Tess left for Rogue's Hollow after the MADGE lieutenant had spoken to her. He was not a happy camper. If Delfin had been making opioids, all of his stuff was gone. Officers cleared the house, found some drug residue, possible signs of drug manufacture, but that was it. The male subject was positively identified as Howard Delfin, and he'd only been dead for hours.

No one on the cul-de-sac could describe the car that sped away, but they'd all heard the shots. Tess mentally reviewed the incident over and over as she drove home, tired, sore, and hungry. The weight of defeat burdened her. Delfin was the last lead. The only bright spot was that at last report, Dustin was still alive. She could hope that if he lived, he would fill in some gaps. She was so preoccupied, she forgot she was on vacation and drove to the station instead of home.

"Are you okay, Chief?" Sheila, who should have been home an hour ago, was still there. She stood, face white with worry as Tess walked inside. "We've been listening to the shooting on the scanner. Del wanted to go down there, but the state police called him off."

Tess looked at her shirt and arms and realized she was a mess. Dusty, dirty, and a little bloody from Dustin and her own superficial cuts, she felt clammy and sticky.

"I'm okay, just a couple of scratches."

Del had stopped what he was doing and stepped toward her. "Someone took a potshot at you?"

"Not sure if it was me they were shooting at or Dustin Pelter." She told him what had happened.

"Been looking all over for that guy. What a way to find him."

Tess headed for the bathroom, needing a pit stop. She stopped because it looked like Del had more to say. "Is there something else?"

"Yeah, there is." He frowned. "I had a talk with Pastor Mac a couple of hours ago." He told Tess about Bryce being missing and the pastor's visit to the pot farm.

"Pastor Mac went up there looking for Bryce?" Tess grimaced, irritated that Oliver had done something potentially dangerous.

"He didn't make it past the gate."

"Did you go up there and ask about the guy?"

He shook his head. "I got no cause. If they want to slam the door in my face, they could, and I hate it when that happens."

Tess sighed and leaned against the doorframe. He was right; if Haywood didn't want to open the gate, the only thing that would get them through was a warrant, and she hadn't heard anything that would justify a warrant. Even if Bryce skipped out, if his court date wasn't for another week, there wouldn't be a bench warrant until after he didn't show up.

"I'll go talk to Pastor Mac. But I need to clean up first."

Tess rinsed her face off in the bathroom, really wanting a hot shower and meal, then a nap. But first Drake, now Bryce. What was going on? Or did it just bother her that Oliver put himself in an odd position by visiting the pot farm?

56

Oliver answered the knock at his door, surprised to see Chief O'Rourke there so late in the day. He hadn't expected to hear from her until morning. She always looked petite, almost fragile, when out of uniform. He knew it was deceptive. From experience he'd seen that Tess O'Rourke was anything but a fragile woman, at least physically. But tonight he could see she was tired, and there was a nasty cut on her cheek.

"Tess, are you okay?" he asked.

"I'm fine, Oliver. We had a big mess happen earlier. I'm tired, but fine. Del told me a little about your problem."

"I'm glad you're here about that. I am really bothered. Please, come in. Tilly's here."

He motioned for her to follow him into the house. Tilly was seated at the kitchen table finishing a meal Oliver had made for her. He'd succeeded in calming Tilly somewhat, but he couldn't admit to her that he was just as concerned about Bryce as she was.

"Have a seat, Chief. Tilly, tell the chief what you told me."

Tess listened as Tilly told her story and why she was afraid for Bryce.

"And you went up to the pot farm yourself?" Tess asked Oliver when Tilly finished.

"This morning." He thought he saw irritation cross her face and ignored it. "And I agree with Tilly. Bryce wouldn't up and leave without saying something. And he wouldn't skip out on his payments and his final court date."

"Does Bryce have any family here? Anyone we could talk to, anyone he might have talked to about his plans?" Tess asked.

Tilly shook her head. "His parents are dead. When they died, he left the valley to clean up his life and escape the people who were pulling him down. For the last five years, he's moved around from place to place."

"He never mentioned any friends to you?"

"He mentioned a couple of bosses he liked, but they're in Montana and Idaho. And the guy who hired him in Portland fired him as soon as he heard about the warrant."

"Unfortunately, I don't have any probable cause to force Haywood to open up so we can look around."

Tears sprang to Tilly's eyes. "What about Arthur's place? Or up the canyon? Bryce said he thought Cherry was doing something up there. Maybe they took Bryce somewhere . . ." She rambled on, practically hysterical.

Oliver put a hand over hers and spoke softly. "Calm down. We'll figure this out, I promise. We'll keep praying. Something will make it possible for us to get to the bottom of this. Don't lose your faith, Tilly."

Tess said nothing. Oliver, for the first time he could remember, wished he could read her mind.

"What are you thinking, Tess? Maybe I can help."

— — —

Tess knew that Oliver's offer to help was a true one; he wasn't just saying it to be kind. But her thoughts were so tangled at the moment, there was nothing he could do to free the knot. From what she'd just heard, Bryce had disappeared Tuesday, around the same time as Drake. Coincidence? Hector Connor-Ruiz had been murdered on Saturday. Was Bryce Evergreen a cold-blooded murderer? Or should she be looking at Drake? Did Drake kill Hector because he was attached to the Hang Ten? And if he did, where was he now? What was the connection between both men being missing? Or was there no connection?

Oliver was waiting for an answer. Tilly was looking at her expectantly. She had no answers for either of them. Tess was exhausted and she had a headache and she knew she needed some downtime.

"Oliver, I'm at a loss right now." She glanced at Tilly, not wanting to say that she'd have to find Bryce and look at him hard for Tim's murder. He could be the killer hiding in plain sight.

"You need sleep," Oliver said. He pulled Tess outside onto

the porch, out of earshot of Tilly. "I told you I've been visited a few times by Don Cherry."

"Yeah, and I told you I didn't think that was wise. The man is dangerous."

"I agree." He proceeded to tell Tess about the last conversation he'd had with the big man.

"He said that?" she asked. "'Bad things. Stuff you'd probably call sin'?"

"He did, and I don't know what he meant."

"As odd as that is, it's still not enough to get us into the pot farm if they don't want us there." She turned as if to leave, then turned back, irritation bubbling under her skin like hot water. "What made you tell him that you thought he believed in God?"

"I know he does. I believe God speaks to every person on this earth always, every single day. Some listen, some don't. For most of his life Cherry has not listened, but for some reason, he can't tune out what he's hearing now. I think that's why he comes to talk—"

"I thought you said you didn't know why he came to talk to you."

"He's never said in so many words, but something is bugging him, goading him, and it underlies all the banter."

"So you think God is speaking to a two-bit criminal?" Tess stepped back. Fatigue and frustration made her cranky. "What on earth would God say to him?"

"My guess would be 'Turn and repent.' You don't agree?"

Tess looked away for a moment. "Ever since I was sixteen, I wanted to hear from God."

"What makes you think you haven't?"

"Because I still don't know why he took my father from me."

"I think you do know the answer to that question."

"Stop trying to read my mind." Eyes narrowed, Tess felt her anger building.

"You told me once about the inscription on your father's headstone, the Bible verse: 'Greater love has no one than this, that someone lay down his life for his friends.'"

"So?"

"Your father laid his life down; it wasn't taken from him. It was a choice he made because of the profession he chose. Your father's death was tragically heroic; it wasn't a betrayal by God."

Tess stared at Oliver, anger boiling over. All the rage she'd directed at God for most of her life she now directed at him.

"You're saying being murdered was my dad's fault?"

"Not fault. Choice. He—"

"I don't want to hear any more of this. You have overstepped your bounds." She turned on her heel and left.

57

Furious, Tess drove straight home, her feeling of exhaustion chased away by righteous indignation. She felt blindsided by Oliver's "insight." How could he say that about her dad? How could he think he *knew* anything about her dad?

Even her appetite was gone. She sat in her recliner and stared out her window into the dark, reliving the day the chief of police came to tell her that her father was dead. Pieces of her dream resurfaced while she sat there awake. She wasn't there at the time, didn't visit the scene until years later, but somehow her subconscious reconstructed the event and she saw her father get shot and fall.

After several hours of brooding, she got up and retrieved

the box of her father's things. She hadn't decided what to do with it because she knew what was at the very bottom of the box. The day she found it, she'd purposely avoided emptying it. Tonight she did.

There at the bottom was her father's Bible and his journal. The Bible was well-worn because her father had used it for years. And it was taped together because the night he died, Tess had thrown it across the room and it split in two pieces. Her mom had repaired it and placed it in the box.

Tess held the Bible and sat in her chair. She didn't know how long she sat there, but eventually a painful realization hit her hard, like the business end of a baseball bat. Oliver was right. Her father made a choice, a choice she knew he would make again if given the chance.

So if Tess knew that was true, why did it make her so angry to be confronted with the truth?

"We protect people, Tessa. That's what we do. No greater honor than to save someone's life."

Tears fell and she didn't stop them. As an adolescent, she'd been hurt and angry that her dad had chosen a stranger's life over his own. But if he'd made any other choice, he wouldn't have been her father. All these years she realized she'd directed her anger toward God when she was in truth angry at her father. She was angry at him for the same thing that made her immensely proud of him.

"Tragically heroic."

Her father died a hero's death by choice—not because of a capricious deity. As the tears ended, the anger faded and Tess felt as though a huge weight had been lifted from her chest. She fell asleep in the chair clutching the beat-up Bible in her hands.

Tess woke at some point during the night, stiff from sleeping in the chair, and got up and went to bed. When her alarm woke her, she felt rested. After a hot shower and her first cup of coffee for the day, she thought about her conversation with Oliver the day before and knew she'd have to apologize for storming out on him. She also considered the situation with Don Cherry very nearly confessing to being a homicidal maniac, and Bryce and Drake Harper being missing.

Who was the bad guy? Knee-jerk, Tess would say Cherry. But where did Bryce go and why? How did Drake fit in? Oliver and Tilly obviously saw no bad in Bryce; Casey Reno had told Tess she believed Bryce was a good guy. But was all that just wishful thinking? Were they blind to him because they knew him before, when he was a kid?

When Tess took the murder off the table, even though she didn't know Bryce well, she might be inclined to write him off as a flake, not a killer. But she put a lot of weight into what Oliver told her he felt. Bryce wouldn't leave and blow off his court fines and final court date.

A week and a half was a long time to wait and see if the guy truly did leave town. Even longer if he was the killer who could clear her name once and for all.

Then there was a third alternative—Bryce was a victim of foul play. Who would want to hurt a down-on-his-luck guy like Bryce? And why? He seemed to truly be trying to get back on his feet and fix things in his life.

Where did that leave Don Cherry?

And it did not escape Tess that Haywood's pot farm worked its way into nearly every dark plot: Hector's murder, Bryce's disappearance. Even Carr—Howard Delfin had written his letter of recommendation. Did Delfin know Carr was a fugitive, and was he trying to put one over on Haywood? Or was the surfer a criminal mastermind who wanted the cover?

What in the world was going on there at Haywood's farm?

58

"*You have overstepped your bounds.*"

The words stung in Oliver's thoughts as if he'd stepped on a wasp's nest. They kept him up; he barely slept, and when he did get out of bed the next morning, he felt anything but rested. His intention was not to hurt Tess, but to hopefully get to the root of the barrier between Tess and God. All he could do now was pray that the Spirit would work to heal the pain she'd carried with her these many years.

At any rate, by the time he finished breakfast and his devotions, he knew he couldn't push her. He'd done what he thought was right, and he had to wait and see what the result would be. As the sun rose in the sky and he saw that it was going to be a gorgeous day, he decided he couldn't sit around and brood or second-guess himself. And there was still no word on Bryce. He owed it to Tilly to not let that issue fall by the wayside.

It would be a good day to do a thorough check of Arthur Goding's home. Before the man left on vacation, he'd given Oliver a key and asked him to keep an eye on things.

"I'm worried about those pot growers," he'd said. *"Don't want them putting salt in my well, hurting my livestock, or doing any other type of mischief."*

Oliver had driven up to the house a couple of times, walked around, and spoken to the kid feeding the animals, but he didn't look in the house or check out the workshop or really take Arthur's worries seriously until Bryce's disappearance. This was Rogue's Hollow—a person could trust their neighbors, couldn't they?

Pot farms like the Hang Ten had changed all that.

Tilly had mentioned Arthur's place. Bryce had told her that Cherry was riding an ATV up the canyon. He'd almost have to cross Arthur's property to do that. Suppose something was going on at Arthur's? He wasn't due home for two more days.

Since Oliver had nothing on his plate until a midmorning meeting with Travis and some other pastors from the valley, he left a note for his assistant pastor saying that he'd be back shortly. He then drove up to Arthur's place. He decided to walk the whole property, keeping an eye on the pot farm. As he cruised up the driveway, his gaze raked over the next-door neighbor's farm. It looked quiet, but there was a different car in the parking area, one that wasn't familiar to Oliver. He wondered who the visitor was.

The boy tending Arthur's livestock didn't live real close. Arthur's property and the Hang Ten were rather secluded. But he would hike over or ride his bike. Oliver didn't think he was old enough to drive. As a former 4-H kid, he took good care of animals.

Oliver paused at the animal pens in the front of the property, where nothing looked amiss. The goats and chickens looked happy enough. The only structure the boy would have to enter was the small barn, across from and slightly in front of the house.

Oliver then did a 360 and surveyed the area. He knew the history here; originally the two parcels of land had been part of a much bigger parcel owned by the logging baron who'd built the town and the mill, the remnant of which was Oliver's church.

The heirs held on to the acreage for as long as they could, carving off pieces here and there. But logging took a hit all over the state in the eighties, and they eventually subdivided everything. Arthur had built his home and lived there for about fifteen years. His next-door neighbors for most of that time were a retired couple, former schoolteachers. Arthur and the man had been fishing buddies and good friends. But when he died, his widow left for Arizona to live with her kids. The property was vacant for a couple of years until Haywood purchased it.

Redwood fencing was the signature of a pot farm in Oregon, and Oliver couldn't resist a head shake as it came into view. He watched for a few minutes but didn't see any people. No Bryce, no Don Cherry, no Haywood. Oliver had not seen or heard from Cherry since their confrontation on his porch earlier this week. He wondered what the big man was doing. Had Oliver made any headway with the man at all?

Oliver used the key and let himself into Arthur's house. At first glance, everything looked fine. He made his way to the first bedroom, the den, then the kitchen, and that was when he saw something out of place. The door to the pantry was open.

Frowning, Oliver opened it wider and saw empty spaces. There was food missing. He didn't know what was gone, but from what he remembered, the pantry had been well stocked. His gaze moved to the sink, where he saw dirty dishes. Arthur was a neat person; he never would've left a mess in the sink, and the food was not all dried out like it would have been had it been there for more than a month.

The hackles on the back of his neck rose, and he knew he'd be calling Tess about this situation.

He moved to the back door. It was locked securely. He began to check every window in the place. There it was, the back bedroom window. The screen was off and it was unlocked. And the bed in that room had obviously been slept in. The kid taking care of Arthur's animals would not be doing this, Oliver was sure of that, but he'd have to talk to him, see if he had noticed anything odd.

Someone was living in Arthur's home while he was gone.

"Who would break in here to stay?" Oliver mumbled. It made no sense that the pot growers would. And the couple of homeless who came to mind weren't likely to hike all the way up here for a place to stay. He glanced down and saw a muddy footprint on the bedroom floor that banished all doubt that someone had been inside the house.

He reached for his phone and realized he'd left it in the car. Sighing, hands on hips, Oliver knew he'd need to notify the police right away. And explain to Arthur how he'd let this break-in happen during his watch. He turned to exit the house and make the call.

He hadn't heard the man come into the house, but there he was, in the hallway, pointing a gun.

"Sorry you had to come here today, padre," was all he said before he fired.

59

After pouring her second cup of joe, Tess almost picked up the phone to call Oliver but resisted. She'd slept in this morning, rising at six instead of five, and she knew Oliver was an early riser, so she was reasonably sure he would be up. But what to say to him escaped her. After about a minute she put the phone down without pressing the button. Still processing all that he had said to her the night before, she knew she needed to apologize in person, not over the phone. She thought about just showing up on his doorstep but decided no. She wasn't ready yet.

As she sipped her coffee, she wondered about Dustin. Steve had promised to call with an update, so she'd have to wait. Yawning, she walked into the living room to open the blinds. She almost didn't see the envelope on the floor by the front door. It must have been slid under the door. Tess had yet to address the gap there after she'd changed the flooring.

Stiff with apprehension, Tess picked it up. It was addressed to Chief O'Rourke in neat block letters. When she pressed it between her palms, she could tell there was something hard inside. She walked back into the kitchen, opened the envelope, and dumped the object out. It was a thumb drive.

There was also a note, which she unfolded and read.

Chief O'Rourke, I'm sorry I lied. Tim did have a cloud account. I know the password, and I logged in and downloaded all the pictures he took the night of the party. I couldn't tell you before because . . . well, it was Greg. He was smoking pot that night and was afraid if the wrong person saw the photos, he would lose his scholarship.

Anyway, Greg left for school now, and I want you to find Tim's killer. Here are all the pictures, even the ones of Greg. I don't see anything here that would seem to help find Tim's killer, but you are the cop.

Sorry again. Are you going to arrest me?

Duncan Peabody

Tess groaned even though the drive gave her a jolt of hope. She still didn't have her laptop back from the sheriff's office. She put the drive down and hurried to take a shower, leaving her hair to dry in the cool morning air. She stopped for coffee and headed for her computer at the station.

Jonkey was just going off duty. She frowned. "Hey, Chief, are you back?"

Tess held up the drive. "These are the pictures from Tim's phone."

"How?"

"Long story." She told her about the note as she unlocked her office, flipped on the lights, and turned on the computer.

"You really think they'll tell us who the killer is?"

Tess crossed her fingers on both hands. "We can hope." She popped the drive into its slot and watched as the pictures loaded.

There were twenty photos displayed. The first were shots that must have been from before the party, as it was daylight. Tim's mom was in one and there were a couple selfies of Tim. Then there were the nighttime party pictures at the Spot. Tess recognized everyone, even Howard Delfin. He wasn't the subject of any photos, but he was in the background of two with a beer in his hand. Dustin was also in the background once or twice.

And there was Greg, goofing with some pot, rolling a fat joint. Tess had no interest in getting Greg in trouble. She figured drug testing would do that if he had a problem.

Conspicuously missing from the photos was Eddie Carr. The boys had said that the fugitive didn't want to be photographed. Tess went back through the early photos. Coach Whitman wasn't in any of them either.

She kept going. Toward the end was a photo of the moon, surprisingly good considering it was taken with a camera phone. There were two dark photos that appeared to be the picnic area at Smugglers Cove. Tess squinted. She could see the back end of a car in one and in the next a figure beside the car.

"Argh." She sat back in frustration. "It's too dark. I can't make out the person or the car."

"Wait, don't lose hope." Jonkey turned the computer her way. "There's photo software that might help us."

"Really?"

Jonkey nodded. "Yep. Let me take this home and see if I can enhance it. I bet I can at least get you the plate number on the car."

"Oh, bless you. I'll do all I can to get the OT approved."

"I want to do it." She popped the drive out. "I'll call you as soon as I have anything."

"Thanks, Becky."

"No, thank you, Chief. You don't give up, and you set an awesome example to emulate. I'm behind you." Thumb drive gripped in her hand, Jonkey left the office and Tess, speechless.

Tess checked the clock; she hated waiting. And she was still officially off duty. She sat at the computer to check e-mail and considered calling Belcher and asking about her computer. But she didn't have the strength to go toe-to-toe with him right now.

It was still early, yet she felt drained and realized that it was an emotional fatigue. An understanding was beginning to dawn. This wasn't only about the murder investigation; it was about her birthday, her father, and the argument she'd had with Oliver the night before. He'd ripped off a scab covering her most painful wound—the loss of her father—and she'd mourned for him all over again, only now she knew she finally had peace with his loss.

It was time to talk to Oliver. Tess wanted—no, needed—to apologize to him. Probably she should also thank him. Then she'd call her mom. She and her mother had never been terribly close and had only gotten more distant since her father's death. Tess felt like she needed to reach out to her mother with new understanding.

She felt lighter somehow. A lot of anger she hadn't realized she'd been hanging on to was gone.

Oliver was a hard person to stay mad at in any event. She'd grown to appreciate his friendship. If Belcher did seat a grand jury like he threatened, she'd want Oliver in her corner. And she'd love to chew over things with him because he'd give her perspective and maybe a little peace. He had a way of looking at things that helped her clarify her own thoughts. She'd become a little dependent on his counsel and insight. Was that a good thing or a bad thing?

Tess knew that she'd rather focus on just about anything right now than Hector's murder case. Even though all the evidence was circumstantial, there was an adage that a grand jury could indict a ham sandwich. Tess didn't want to be that sandwich.

She punched in Oliver's number, and the call immediately went to voice mail. She left a brief message and expected he'd call her back soon.

She thought about the photos and wondered if Jonkey would get anywhere. The woman was talented, so there was hope. Tess paced, debated going home to wait. After a few minutes, she decided to brew coffee. When it finished, she filled a cup and sat at her desk and turned on the computer. She checked her e-mail again, answering a few necessary queries, then caught up on some news. Time seemed to tick by slowly.

When she finished with the computer, she took a look around the office, pain pinching when she considered that she might never wear her chief stars again. It hurt, but it wasn't smothering like before. Tess knew this wasn't the end of the world. It would be hard, for sure, but it would not defeat her.

Sheila knocked. "Chief, I know you're still on vacation, but Travis is here. He's got a problem and wants to talk to you."

Tess stood and stretched. "I was just about to leave. I'll come out and talk to him." Tess had met Travis once. He was Oliver's youth pastor. She greeted the young man in the lobby. "How can I help you?"

The look on his face was grim and instantly put Tess on edge. Then she realized that Oliver had never called her back. It hadn't been that long, but any delay was highly unusual for the man. He was prompt—even if he was tied up, he'd text. A feeling of uneasiness washed over her. Where was Oliver?

"Chief, I hope it's nothing."

She noticed his rigid body language. He didn't think it was nothing.

"It's Pastor Mac. I can't find him."

"What do you mean you can't find him?"

"Well, he's usually the first one in the office. He texted me earlier today, said he was checking on something, but he'd be in soon." Travis glanced at his watch. "That was two hours ago. He's not answering his cell, and that's not like him at all."

Tess asked, "What was he going to check on?"

"He said he was going up to Arthur Goding's place."

"Why there?"

"Arthur had given him a key. Oliver's gone up there a couple of times just to make certain the pot farmers weren't up to any mischief. But I drove up there and didn't see his car."

"Hmm." Tess folded her arms and leaned against Sheila's desk, pensive and working hard to keep the fear tamped down. A third missing man? What was going on? Oliver wasn't the type to disappear or to ignore his phone. He was probably the most visible figure around town. Besides the church, he was involved in the community; he cared. And it bugged her profusely that he'd gone to Arthur Goding's. It was too close to the Hang Ten.

"Travis, is there any place else he might have gone? Some place that's a dead zone and he's not getting a phone signal?"

"I've driven everywhere around town I can. His car is nowhere that I've looked, and if he said he'd be back soon, then he wasn't planning on going far."

"Okay. Officer Bender is on duty this morning. I'll get ahold of him and explain the situation. We'll need a little more information to call out search and rescue." She straightened. "Travis, we'll find him."

Travis calmed a bit. "I've called Jethro Bishop and a couple of other ushers to help."

Tess nodded and walked around Sheila's desk, placing a hand on his shoulder. "We'll find him," she repeated. Her voice sounded a whole lot more certain than her insides felt.

60

Tess took Travis back to her office. She wanted to be certain that he was put in touch with Gabe and that everything possible was done to find Oliver.

Just then Sheila popped her head inside the office. "Sorry to bother you again, Chief, but there's a cable news crew out here. They want an interview."

Tess sighed. She had no obligation, and she should be gone. She could close the door and hide until they went away. But that just wasn't how she rolled.

"That's okay, Sheila. I'll handle it. Travis, give me a minute." She stepped back into the lobby and saw a well-known cable news anchor holding a microphone in one hand and adjusting his collar with the other. A local news crew was also getting into position.

"Oh, Chief O'Rourke, can we have a few minutes of your time?" The cable guy smiled what Tess was certain was an insincere smile. This man was one of her harshest critics during the turmoil in Long Beach. The urge to say no was overpowering. Instead, Tess steeled herself as if she were preparing for court testimony.

"I can give you a few minutes, but that's it."

He motioned to the cameraman behind him and Tess saw the light go on. This was probably going to be everywhere today. "We've just heard the news that a grand jury will be seated to consider the murder that occurred on your porch—do you have a comment?"

Taken aback, Tess worked hard to keep her face blank. "I hadn't heard that. My comment is I'm innocent."

"The victim was from Long Beach. Did he follow you here?"

"He moved here, I know that, but I can't speak to why he moved here."

"Connor-Ruiz wrote several letters accusing you of corruption, even notified the FBI, asked them to investigate. What do you have to say about that?"

"I welcome any investigation. I've done nothing wrong, and I work with honest and professional cops."

"The Connor-Ruiz murder is now a major campaign issue—can you comment on that?"

"No more than I already have. I'm innocent. Thank you."

There was more commotion on the street. Tess heard a familiar voice, and Cole Markarov burst into the station.

"Just what is going on here?"

The local newspeople turned to him. Like flies to honey, they began peppering him with questions, and he preened for them.

"Councilman Markarov, what do you have to say about the grand jury?" The cable guy spoke loudly, and his cameraman tried to muscle the local people out of the way.

"Why is Chief O'Rourke still working?" The local man was closer, and he had Markarov's attention.

"I'll give you all a statement shortly," Markarov said, smiling for the cameras.

Then he turned to face Tess, smile dying. "What are you doing here, in this office? You were told to cease your law enforcement duties and take vacation days. The only reason it was vacation and not suspension was because Addie was certain that you would be voluntarily hands-off. You haven't been—why, I even heard you were involved in police activity in Shady Cove just yesterday."

"Is that true?" the local guy called out.

All eyes turned to Tess, but Cole didn't let her answer. He began to give one of his campaign speeches. "She's only brought big-city corruption to our small community."

She listened to him drone on and knew it would be a disaster for her if he won. She also believed it would be bad for the town. Cole was all about Cole; he wasn't civic-minded. Currently his whole campaign was centered on Tess and how the first thing he would do was fire a corrupt police chief.

Tess wanted to speak up, but she was given no chance. It was Travis who jumped in.

"I asked the chief to help me. Pastor Oliver Macpherson is missing. She was trying to help me find him."

Cole stopped midsentence and turned to Travis, a mixture of irritation and shock on his face. "Pastor Mac? What's happened?"

"Are you organizing a search?"

Cole held his arms up and stepped in front of Tess and Travis. "It's not up to her." He turned to Sheila. "Who is the officer on duty right now?"

"Gabe Bender."

"Call him in here to assist Travis."

Tess sighed. *"Listen. Think. Speak."* That rule certainly applied now. "Travis, Gabe will get to the bottom of things." She almost told Sheila, "I'll be home if you need me," but thought better of it. She grabbed her car keys and forced her way through the pack and left the station.

- - -

Fear for Bryce made Tilly crazy. Pastor Mac couldn't help her; she doubted Chief O'Rourke could either. She found herself craving a hit of something strong, really strong. She knew she couldn't sit around. Idleness would make the craving worse, and she feared she would cave in.

She had a sweatshirt that belonged to Bryce. He'd given it to her the last time they had dinner, so she wasn't sure how much scent was on it, but she wanted to find out. She put it in her backpack and went to find Pastor Mac and ask him if he thought Angel could track Bryce. Angel had led the chief to Glen's tent back in the summer after he was murdered. Maybe Angel could help her find Bryce.

He had to be alive. Tilly didn't want to consider life without Bryce. And she bet Blondie was hiding him somewhere on the pot farm. Maybe there was a dungeon in the basement. Or maybe they'd made a jail at the old logging camp. She couldn't consider any possibility other than he was being kept somewhere against his will.

She stopped before even getting to the pastor's house. Something was going on. Jethro and a few other men were in a circle praying in front of the house. Fear gripped her heart in a vise and Tilly felt sick. Her first thought was that something bad had happened to the pastor. Heart beating fast and breath coming in a rush though she was standing still, Tilly tried to think. The next person she should go to was the chief.

Hurrying away from Pastor Mac's house, Tilly started to cross the street to the police station, only to see one of her brother's work trucks coming up the street. She waited for it to pass, but it came to a stop in front of her. The window rolled down and she looked up to see her brother, Bart, regarding her.

"Tilly."

"Hey." She wasn't sure what to say. Bart had been there for her when she was in the hospital. He'd helped her struggle through the broken femur and the detox. Then she relapsed and he washed his hands of her. She realized now she'd hurt him that one time more than all the other lapses. He'd banned her from the family business and farm. It had been months since they'd spoken. She didn't blame him; he had small children. Drug addicts shouldn't be around small children.

"Where are you headed?" he asked.

"Uh . . ." She glanced behind her, still wondering about the activity outside the church. If Pastor Mac were okay, he would have told her if something was up about Bryce, wouldn't he? Then she looked at the police station. The chief might think it silly that she wanted the dog to track Bryce.

She said the first thing that came to mind. "I need to get to Chainsaw Ridge. Can you give me a ride?" She held her breath for what seemed like an eternity.

Finally he said, "Sure, hop in."

Tilly pulled the door open and let Angel hop in first. Then she climbed in and closed the door, appreciating what a big move for Bart this was, but mind still churning with worry for Bryce. She had no idea what she would do when she got to Arthur's but was planning on doing something.

"You going to see Bryce?" Bart asked as he drove along River Drive.

Tilly shot him a glance. He smiled.

"Small town, Tilly. Even I've heard that you like the guy. I was worried at first. I remember Bryce got you hooked in the first place. But now . . ."

Tilly swallowed. "But now?"

"I hear things. Like I said, it's a small town. Everyone says Bryce is changed, that it's the real deal. I hope he's good for you."

"I think he is. I . . ." Her throat started to close as emotion overwhelmed.

"What's the matter, Tilly?" Bart slowed.

Tilly worked to keep her voice steady. She poured out the fear she had for Bryce.

Bart pulled over to the side of the road. "So what are you

doing going to Chainsaw? Shouldn't you be talking to the police?"

"They can't help. Bryce is an adult. They think he just left. But he wouldn't just leave. I know it." She dissolved into tears.

"Tilly, I know you're not high. I can see that you are truly terrified. We need to go to the police. I'll drive you there, okay?"

Tilly looked at Bart. He'd been so distant for so long. Now he wanted to help.

"Okay, Bart. Thanks. Let's go." As he drove, Tilly sobbed silently and prayed that Bryce wasn't dead like Glen.

Bart made a U-turn, and Tilly hoped she'd finally find some answers concerning Bryce.

61

Tess felt frustration fill her like cement as she reached her car. Gabe Bender pulled up. She hadn't talked to him since she'd been asked to take vacation. He'd been helping Belcher with Hector's murder investigation.

"You're needed inside," Tess told him.

"What's going on?"

"It's complicated and I have to leave. I heard about the grand jury."

Gabe's expression told her nothing. "Belcher asked us to keep quiet about the investigation. That's all I can say, Chief."

Tess nodded. "You're a good cop, Gabe." She left him on the sidewalk and approached her car, feeling the walls closing in though she was outside.

She drove down the street slowly, not sure what she should do and worried that her home would become a prison if she went there. Tess thought about going to Jonkey's home but knew her officer would call her if she discovered anything.

No, the most important thing right now was Oliver. Where was he?

Tess wanted to swing by Arthur's home and look around herself, but that was probably where Gabe would go, and she certainly didn't want to give him any trouble.

She made the turn for the Stairsteps, a local tourist attraction, and inspiration struck. Tess accelerated. She drove to the end of the road and the utility shed. Glad she'd thrown her gun into the car at the last minute, she strapped the belt on and racked a round in the chamber of the 9mm before securing it in the holster. She unlocked the shed and stepped inside. The Kubota and the single-seat quad were parked next to one another.

Tess unlocked the key drawer and grabbed the key for the single quad. This might be foolish, but it was the only way she knew to come around the pot farm from behind. And something Tilly had said kept repeating in her mind. Don Cherry was riding an ATV up the canyon, maybe fooling around at Arthur's house. A chill went through her as she had the thought that Cherry could be dumping bodies in the canyon.

I won't consider that, she thought. *Oliver can't be dead—he can't be.*

She pushed the single quad out, locked up the shed again, then climbed onto the quad and fired it up. Heading up the trail, Tess drove as fast as she thought safe and hoped she could find the trail above the old logging camp.

--- -

The trail was steep in spots, but it was easily traversed with the quad. Tess passed two sets of hikers and got yelled at for disturbing the peace. After she'd traveled for about half an hour, she stopped, shut the vehicle down, and tried to get her bearings. She stood on the seat of the quad and was gratified when she caught a glimpse of the Rogue River. From the bend in the river, she knew she was close to where the canyon behind Arthur's place would be.

Tess went along for several minutes and then almost rolled past a path heading down. Very carefully she directed the quad down the trail. Brush caught her pant legs and crunched under the quad's wheels. Soon she was below the tree line and then she glimpsed the millpond. The trail got wider, and soon Tess was at the camp. She drove the quad to almost the same place she and Gabe had stopped what seemed like a lifetime ago.

Turning the motor off, Tess took stock of her surroundings. She still had some ways to go to get to Arthur's but wasn't certain about how far she should take the quad. The noise of the motor would give her away if anyone was paying attention. She climbed off and walked to the closest building. Frowning, she studied the ground. The brush was all compacted around the largest structure, the one Gabe had said was the mess hall. Small tire tracks were everywhere.

If these were all from Don Cherry, what was he doing up here?

She walked to the structure and tried to open the door. It wouldn't budge. For something that looked ready to fall down, the door was super secure. New boards were obvious.

Tess stepped back and looked the door over. She saw the problem. There were pieces of wood wedged in the top of the door and along the side. As long as the wedges were there, the door wouldn't open. She couldn't reach the top ones, but two wedges in the side came out when she worked on them with her pocketknife. She had to push the quad close enough to stand on it and pry out the last wedge.

She jumped down and studied the door. What would she find behind it?

62

After the shock from the Taser wore off, Oliver opened his eyes to see Don Cherry kneeling next to him. His large hand was pressed into the middle of Oliver's chest.

"Do exactly as I say. I don't want to kill you, but I will if you force my hand."

Oliver could only nod. The jolt of electrical current had taken his breath away.

Cherry turned him on his side and bound his hands together with duct tape. He then ripped off a single piece of tape and put it over his mouth.

"Now get up," he said, grasping Oliver by the elbow and pulling him to his feet. Oliver still felt wobbly, but the big man steadied him and led him out the back door. Once there, he sat Oliver down in one of Arthur's Kubotas. "Sit tight. I'll be right back."

Oliver swallowed, wishing he could speak. All of Arthur's vehicles were outside the workshop. He turned his head as best he could when he heard his car being started. Cherry pulled it around and into the workshop.

None of the ATVs could be seen from the street, but Oliver had to wonder who moved all the ATVs from Arthur's garage and why. Had the young man looking after the livestock done it? That made no sense. It also made him kick himself for the drive-bys he'd done, that he'd not walked the property. He owed Arthur an apology.

All of that paled when a question popped into his mind. What on earth was Cherry up to?

He heard footsteps and voices and turned. Two men were walking up from the direction of the Hang Ten. He'd never seen either one before. One was tall and lanky; the other short and stocky, with a nasty-looking scar on his face.

They gave Oliver the creeps as they looked him over.

"Just kill him," the short one said to Cherry when he walked out of the workshop. "We're short on time. The chief is our only loose end; then we're out of here."

Cherry nodded, his face unreadable.

"Where are you putting these bodies?" the tall one asked.

"Millpond," Cherry said. "Weight 'em and sink 'em."

Oliver stared at the man he'd been talking to for weeks. A man he'd believed was not really evil. *Bodies*. Who was he talking about? Bryce and Drake?

"We should just leave after he dumps this one. We have

all the advantage right now," the tall one said as he dumped what appeared to be sunflower seeds into his hand.

"No," the short one said. "I want the chief dead first. And we would have been gone yesterday if you hadn't missed."

"Not like you didn't miss your chance, champ."

For a minute, the two stared at one another.

The tall man blinked. "Well, just do it then, and let's go."

"This is the priest, isn't it?" the short one asked.

Cherry nodded.

"Good. This should bring the chief to us. Go dump him, then get back here. We need to set something up."

Cherry climbed onto the Kubota while the other two men walked back into Arthur's house. As the big man drove them up the canyon, Oliver wished the tape on his mouth would budge. As it was, all he could do was pray.

— — —

"It's okay, Pastor Mac."

Oliver stared at Bryce Evergreen as Cherry marched him into one of the old logging cabins. Next to Bryce was a pale and bruised Drake Harper. Oliver turned to Cherry, who ripped the tape from his mouth.

"Ow. What on earth is going on?" he asked, mouth feeling full of cotton.

"Just sit, padre. No time to explain." He held a bottle of water up for Oliver to take a drink.

His expression stopped Oliver from asking any more questions. This was the dangerous Cherry. After Oliver drank, Cherry pointed to the guys on the floor, and Oliver went to his knees first and then sat next to Bryce, peering at Drake.

"Is he okay?"

Bryce shook his head. "He needs a doctor. His arm is broke, and he might be bleeding inside."

Oliver looked at Cherry. The big man's face was unreadable. He shrugged. "Sorry that happened. Hopefully this will all be over soon and help will come for you."

"What will be over?" Oliver asked.

"The chief will be dead and all of us will be gone." He turned to leave.

"Don, wait. You've not killed me or Bryce or Drake. Why kill the chief?"

"She's a cop. I don't care one way or another about her. You guys . . . well, I got no beef with any of you. Boss wanted you dead; I thought he was wrong. And what he doesn't know won't hurt him."

"But I care about the chief. Don, don't do this. You're not a killer; you've changed . . . you—"

"It's the boss who has a problem with her. He wants her dead, that's on him. He ain't asking me to do it. He pays my ticket. Nothing personal with me. You all sit tight. I'll find a way to let someone know you're here." He pointed at Oliver. "That's all I can promise." Then he turned and left, closing the door behind him. They could hear him pounding it closed securely. Oliver could see there were fresh boards on the door; someone had shored it up.

He turned to Bryce. "What on earth is going on? We've been looking all over for you."

Bryce shrugged. "We've been here since Tuesday." He nodded toward Drake. "This guy came to the Hang Ten. He had a gun and threatened to kill me, said something about his kid. Anyway, he forced his way into the house. I think he wanted to kill Haywood, but Haywood wasn't alone. The Hulk snuck up behind us and got the gun. They fought; the Hulk snapped his arm like a twig."

"Then he brought you here?"

Bryce nodded. "There was a short Mexican dude—he's new to the Hang Ten. He wanted to kill us both right there at the Hang Ten. The Hulk stopped him, said he'd rather we were able to walk to our graves. I thought we were dead. He brought us up here. He's fed us, gave us water and bathroom breaks . . . I don't get it."

Oliver tried to digest this new information and consider the contradiction that was Don Cherry. "I can see why he was angry with Drake, but why did he want to kill you?"

"I got out of my trailer to eavesdrop on the conversation. I saw something I wasn't supposed to see. There was a cop in the house with Haywood, an FBI agent, I think. He's dirty. They didn't want me to tell anyone. Those guys, they all have one thing in common."

"What's that?"

"They hate that chief, man. She's a dead woman."

Oliver leaned his head back against the rough wood plank behind him. Fear shot through him. A dirty FBI agent. That scary little man with the scar. He needed to get free, to warn Tess. But how?

63

"Greater love has no one than this, that someone lay down his life for his friends." The verse ran through Tess's mind as she considered what might be behind the door. Three men were missing. Had they been killed and their remains hidden in this old building? She thought of her dad and she thought of Oliver. They were both praying men.

She closed her eyes. What a hypocrite she'd be right now, to call on the God she'd been so angry with for so long. She wasn't sure she could bear it, to see Oliver stretched out dead in this shabby old building. She would have traded her life for him—she knew it in an instant. If he was dead because of a mistake she'd made, she wouldn't be able to live with herself.

All she could say was "Please, Lord, no. He can't be dead; he can't be."

She took a deep breath and pulled the door open.

There, sitting with his back to the wall, staring at her, sat Oliver. Next to him was Bryce and next to him was Drake Harper.

The shock took her breath away, but Oliver spoke. "Tess! Thank God you're okay."

She swallowed and found her voice. "I could say the same right back at you." She lurched forward, wanting to grab the guy and hold him close for a really long while. But time and place kept her at the task at hand, cutting off the duct tape restraints and finding out how this miracle happened. Drake's pallor stopped her.

"What's wrong with him?"

Bryce told her.

As he and Oliver stood and rubbed their wrists, Tess checked for a pulse. He had a strong pulse, but he was burning up with fever. His arm also appeared to have two elbows; the sight made her queasy.

"You're by yourself?" Oliver asked. "They want to kill you. Can you call for backup?"

"I have my phone. I will. He needs help."

Drake stirred and Tess turned to Bryce. "How long has he been out?"

"Not long. He was talking a little bit ago."

"See if you can get him to drink some water."

He nodded. Tess and Oliver stepped outside, and she reached for her phone, only it wasn't in her pocket.

Fighting panic, Tess rushed to the QuadRunner. Her phone

was nowhere to be found. Then an image formed in her mind. She'd been in such a hurry she'd left the phone in her car, a long, long way away from here.

"What?" Oliver asked.

"I don't have my phone."

"We have to get out of here, Tess. Cherry says his boss wants to kill you. And Bryce says there's a dirty FBI agent with him."

Tess raised her eyebrows. "FBI? What did you see?"

"Two men besides Cherry. A short Hispanic man and a tall, slim Anglo. They both seemed to be in charge."

Something clicked for Tess, random pieces falling into place. The tipped-off raid, the agent's hostility, the long trail of illegal drugs. "It's a DEA agent. That's how the Ghost has been able to be a ghost."

"What?"

"Nothing, just thinking out loud. The short one, what did he look like?"

"He had an ugly scar on his face."

"José Garcia, a very wanted man. He goes by the moniker Ghost."

"Is he the dragon you've been wanting to slay?"

In spite of everything, the reference to dragon slaying made Tess smile. "He sure is."

Just then Bryce emerged from the cabin, supporting Drake, who was awake, alert, and obviously in a lot of pain.

Oliver went to help. They moved Drake to where he could lean on the quad.

Tess tried to think, tried to determine her options. There weren't many. At best, two people could fit on the quad, certainly not four. She wished she'd brought the Kubota.

"How are you holding up, Mr. Harper?" Tess asked.

"I'll live. I was wrong about you, Chief. I was wrong about a lot of things. I—"

"Not important. Do you think you could ride on the quad with Oliver driving?"

He nodded.

"Wait. I'm not leaving you."

"Someone has to get Drake to medical help."

"I can," Bryce offered. "I even know my way out of here. Used to hike up here to get high, back in the day."

Tess wanted Oliver out of harm's way, but she didn't see how to force the issue. There was no time to argue. "All right. It'll be rough, Mr. Harper."

"I'll survive. And it's Drake."

Tess handed Bryce the quad keys and the keys to her car. "Phone is on the front seat, but take the car if you think you need to."

They all helped Drake onto the ATV first. There was barely enough room for the two men, but Bryce was a small enough man and he could easily drive and steer with Drake behind him.

Bryce started the engine. "I'll go as fast as I dare."

"Just get there in one piece."

He nodded and turned the quad, headed back the way Tess had just come.

When he was out of sight, Tess turned to Oliver. She struggled with wanting to run down the hill and confront Garcia, Cherry, and the dirty traitor, Hemmings, and wanting to take it slow and give Bryce time to call for help.

"Any chance I can get you to stay here until everything is under control?" she said.

"Don't you think we should just sit tight until help comes?"

"I can't. There's a drug dealer and a crooked DEA agent down there. They need to be stopped and I plan to do it."

"Then where you go, I go."

"Oliver." Tess stopped. She'd have to find a compromise with the man. "I'm the one who's armed. Will you at least stay behind me and follow instruction?"

"I can do that."

She started down the path toward Arthur's house at a leisurely pace.

"You just plan on walking in on them?" Oliver asked as he fell into step next to her.

"I'm not sure yet. I need to know what they're up to. Did Cherry tell you anything?"

"Just that they planned to kill you and then leave. It sounded like the tall one was going to try to lure you up here because of me."

"That's what bothers me. Suppose they've already lured Bender or Pounder up?"

"It sounded like his main beef was with you, so he might not hurt them."

"Hmm. He's a stone-cold killer, so I doubt that." She lengthened her stride, trying to remember how long it took her and Bender to drive down the canyon. It was a mile and a half. How long would that take to walk? How long would it take Bryce to get help?

They'd walked for several minutes when Tess realized Oliver was very quiet.

"Are you okay?"

He nodded. "I'm praying."

She stopped, faced him, and he regarded her with his stormy green-gray eyes. Tess saw so much there that she knew—his strength, compassion—and there was a hint of what she didn't know and of what she wanted to learn about.

She felt her heart skip a beat. "You know, I better tell you something now, in case I don't get another chance."

"What's that?"

"You were right yesterday. About my dad. Sorry I got angry."

"I took you by surprise. That's okay."

"I . . ." She swallowed, knowing she had to hurry but not wanting to rush this. "I know God is there, he's real. Maybe you can help me catch up on what I've missed after all these years of being angry."

"I'd be happy to." He smiled and Tess wanted to lean into him, throw her arms around him, and not think of anything else. But reality intruded when, in the distance, she heard gunfire.

64

Oliver followed Tess as she flew down the trail. They'd heard a rash of gunfire, *rat-a-tat-tat*, followed by more shots and then silence. He didn't want her to run straight into the mouth of danger but knew there was no way to stop her. He felt a strong connection with this woman, the kind of connection he never thought he'd feel with another woman after losing Anna.

He prayed for clarity, guidance, and most of all, right now, for safety. She slowed as they approached the trailhead. She then cut right, scrambled up a little rise, and he climbed after her. The perch gave them the ability to look down at Arthur's property.

They were both breathing hard when she came to a stop. Dropping to her knees, she leaned forward to peer down into Arthur's backyard. Oliver followed suit.

He could see the back of Arthur's house, the metal garage, and the ATVs and snowmobiles lined up next to the retaining wall. He didn't see any people or movement.

Then he heard voices.

"This piece will work just fine." The short man walked out of the garage. He held what looked to Oliver like an automatic handgun.

"You get her up here, I'll hit my target."

"That might be Garcia," Tess whispered.

As the man walked toward them, Oliver felt Tess tense next to him, but then the man veered to his right toward the house. He'd have to look up to see Oliver and Tess.

"She should be here any minute. Get into position." The tall man appeared, calling after Garcia and then glancing toward the driveway. Oliver couldn't see the driveway from where he and Tess were positioned.

"That's Hemmings," Tess said.

Hemmings walked toward the driveway, stopped at the edge of the garage. He called out, *"Where's Chief O'Rourke?"*

"She'll be along. What happened up here? You said you shot an intruder. Doesn't actually explain why you're here at Arthur's house." Oliver recognized Bender's voice.

"I'm working. This way, Officer Bender," Hemmings said. *"I'll show you. Not sure what the guy thought he was doing trying to steal something, but when I caught sight of him in here, he pointed a gun, so I did what I had to do."* Hemmings stepped into the garage shadows.

Bender hesitated, cautious maybe? Then he started to walk toward the center of the garage. Off to the far left, Garcia had moved. He was now crouched behind a car, poised to come in behind Bender.

Oliver realized Hemmings was setting him up, and he wanted to cry out a warning, but Tess stopped him.

"It's a trap, but I'm too far away. You stay here. I'm going to try to get behind him."

Oliver grabbed her arm, fear spiking. "Tess, there are at least two armed and dangerous men down there."

"Three, and Bender's on my side." She smiled, strength and courage shining through. Oliver felt his chest tighten with emotion.

"I've got this," she said. "Give me a couple minutes, and if you think you need to create a diversion, toss a rock on top of the metal garage, okay?"

He nodded, not trusting himself to speak.

She scurried down the way they'd just come. Oliver turned his attention back to Bender and Hemmings.

- - -

Tess drew her weapon as she reached the bottom of the rise. Hemmings lured Bender into the garage so Garcia could come in behind and shoot him. That was what it looked like to her. She leaned against a tree as the short man with the jagged scar on his face walked past, still several feet below her, concentrating on what was ahead of him. This close, she was certain it was José Garcia. He had a handgun. She had no shot from where she was positioned; she had to get closer, and she prayed that she had enough time. The man was obviously trying to sneak up on Bender. They'd lured him here while attempting to get her, she bet.

As quickly as she dared, she slid down the hill to the edge of the retaining wall.

"Where is he?" she heard Bender say. "I thought you said you shot a thief in here?"

"We need someone to get the chief up here," Garcia said. Tess jumped.

Bender jerked toward the voice. Garcia pointed the gun. "Drop your weapon, Officer."

"What is going on here? Hemmings?"

Tess saw Bender turn as Hemmings hit her officer with a sucker punch. Gabe went down. "He wants the chief, you idiot," Hemmings screamed.

That was enough for Tess.

She leaped from behind the wall, weapon on target. "Both of you, freeze!"

Her attention was on Garcia. He turned, gun pointed right at her, and she fired a burst of two. He went down, shock all over his face.

She moved the weapon to aim at Hemmings. "It's over, Sal. I knew there was a reason I didn't like you. Now you get to be an ex-agent in jail."

"I don't think so." He reached into his jacket and skittered sideways. Tess fired and missed.

He pointed his gun and she moved to find cover. But the snap of a Taser sounded, and Hemmings screamed and went down hard onto the concrete workroom floor.

Tess hurried forward, kicking the gun away from a

motionless Garcia as she did so. Bender climbed to his feet, Taser in hand.

"You okay?"

He nodded and wiped blood from his face. "That jerk. I just got this nose fixed."

Tess smiled, relief coursing through her like cold water, and holstered her weapon. Together they handcuffed Hemmings. She turned to check on Garcia and froze. There stood Don Cherry with an AK-47 cradled in his arms.

65

Oliver never got to throw the rock. Garcia pointed a gun at Tess, and he knew that she had no recourse but to shoot him. When he saw Hemmings fall, he relaxed, believing it was all over. He got up and brushed off his pants, heading down the way Tess had gone. Then he saw Don creeping up from the Hang Ten boundary. The man was looking toward the workshop, so he hadn't noticed Oliver, who ducked. The rifle in Don's hands stopped Oliver from calling out a warning. That would just give his position away and give Don time to shoot.

Oliver scrambled down the hill as Cherry reached the spot near where his boss lay. Oliver peered around the edge of the retaining wall. He saw Tess and Gabe in the garage.

Don had a straight, unobstructed shot; he could mow them down with very little effort.

Garcia was squirming, bleeding. "What are you waiting for? Kill her. Shoot, you big moron!" he yelled.

Oliver crept forward. He could see the surprise on Tess's face. But her hands were empty; her gun was holstered. She couldn't stop Cherry's threat.

"It's over, Cherry. You've got no place to go. Give it up. Drop the gun." Tess stepped forward, hands outstretched. Cherry's attention was on her as Oliver moved steadily forward. He could hear sirens in the distance now. They were getting closer, but would they get here in time?

"Stay where you are," Cherry said and the gun moved ever so slightly.

A surge of adrenaline swept through Oliver. He was not going to see Tess shot dead in front of him.

"Nooo!" he yelled as he sprinted toward the big man.

Cherry turned, a surprised expression on his face. He tried to bring the gun around, but Oliver lowered his shoulder and launched himself, hitting Don at waist level. It was like hitting solid rock and it took Oliver's breath away, but Cherry went down, the gun went flying, and Oliver ended up on top of him.

Oliver scrambled to straddle the big man, prepared to fight and keep him from the gun. He raised a fist, ready to smash it into the man's face if he tried to resist. But his fist stopped midflight when he saw the look on Cherry's face.

He was grinning. His hands were out flat on the ground. "Okay, okay, padre, I give. Your lady's safe. I surrender. Calling uncle."

Oliver sucked in a breath and relaxed as Tess jogged toward him. He dropped his fist as Tess picked up the AK-47.

"Your lady's safe."

Sirens were on top of them, and everything that happened after that was a blur as Arthur's driveway filled with emergency vehicles. There were state police cars, sheriff cars, a Rogue's Hollow car, a Mercy Flights ambulance, and several black vehicles Oliver guessed were federal.

Tess and Bender helped Oliver off Cherry, and the big man was handcuffed by a couple of state cops. Officers in all different uniforms swarmed the area.

Oliver stepped back as officers peppered Tess with questions and paramedics began to tend to Garcia.

Someone asked Oliver if he was all right and he said he was. He watched Tess and knew he was more than all right. She'd slain her dragon, and his heart swelled with love, pride, and happiness. Anna would approve, he was certain. Tess glanced his way as she continued her explanation, and he felt a fiery connection hit him like a flaming arrow. She would be his lady; Oliver would make sure of that.

— — —

Fear had hit Tess like an anvil when she saw Oliver rush Cherry. She didn't dare fire her weapon for fear of striking Oliver instead of Cherry. Then the big man went down under Oliver's tackle and dropped the gun.

Doubting Oliver would survive a fight with the Hulk, she saw the most amazing thing. Cherry gave up. She even heard him say he surrendered. The pastor had slain a dragon of his own. After the big man was handcuffed and she watched

Oliver dust himself off, she fought to keep from laughing and grabbing him in a close embrace as the area filled with cops.

"Chief!"

Tess turned. Agent Ledge jogged her way. "Looks like I missed the party."

Tess shook her head. "You may have, but your partner didn't." She pointed to the garage, where Hemmings was handcuffed, leaning against one of the cars.

Ledge stopped, hands on hips. "Man, I'm so sorry about that. I should have seen the signs sooner. But Sal and I have worked together for so long, I just didn't want to see it. Took me way too long to put two and two together."

"How'd you get here so fast?"

"I figured Sal out, a day late and a dollar short. I amped up a task force yesterday. We hit your station a little while ago and got an earful from some hysterical woman and her brother. When we couldn't find you, and Hemmings called in a shooting, asking for you, Officer Bender wanted to come up and see what was going on."

"It was a trap."

Ledge nodded. "We were right behind him. Now we'll tear the pot farm apart." He gestured to the Ghost. "Never thought we'd get a twofer."

Tess looked at the medics treating Garcia. "Not sure if he'll make it, but he's not a ghost anymore."

"Bet you have a tale to tell."

"I do, but I'm trying to find out where a couple of other people are."

"Bryce and Drake?" Curtis Pounder asked as he came walking up. He'd been off duty and was in plain clothes.

"Yeah."

"They're safe. Drake is on his way to the hospital. Tilly and Bart Dover came to the station with a story about Bryce being missing. Gabe called me and Del in when he couldn't get ahold of you. We decided that Del should take one of the ATVs to check out her story about the logging camp. He found your car at the shed and guessed that's what you had done. He took the Kubota to be your backup and met Bryce and Drake on their way back down."

"Then he called for help," Bender said as he walked up. Ledge had taken custody of Hemmings. "I notified the state cops and the sheriff, and while we were waiting for help, Hemmings called asking for you."

"That's why you came up here?"

"Yeah, he had some story about having shot an intruder here, in Arthur's garage. I didn't tell him where you were. I just pretended you'd be with me and came up 'cause I knew the cavalry was en route."

Curtis nodded. "He'd only been gone a short time when Ledge showed up with all his people."

Gabe grinned. "It's gonna be a fun jurisdiction fight." He waved toward Oliver, who'd come to stand next to Tess. "Little did I know the cavalry was already here. Pastor Mac, I didn't know you played football. That was some tackle."

Tess looked at the pastor and laughed. He smiled back and put an arm over her shoulders. "I'm just glad everyone is okay," he said.

Tess leaned into him, feeling strength, attraction, and some emotions she couldn't even name, not caring what anyone thought or said.

66

Don Cherry asked to speak to Oliver before the sheriff could take him away. Oliver took a seat in the back of the car where Don was secured.

"You want to talk to me?"

He nodded but didn't speak right away. Finally he said, "Padre, you said that you think I do believe in God, that I think we're equals."

Oliver swallowed. Cherry was obviously struggling with something, and it was important to listen carefully and prayerfully say the right thing.

"I do think you know there is a God. I also think you know, or at least have been told often, that if you confess your sins, God will forgive them. I think you're looking for peace. Confession and repentance are the only way to get to what will give you peace."

Cherry chuckled mirthlessly. "You don't know my sins, padre."

"I don't have to know. God does."

Cherry studied his shoes.

A thought occurred to Oliver. "Don, did you kill Hector?"

"No, but I drove the boss there. He was planning on making it look like a murder-suicide, but the chief weren't home. Then he hoped for a frame-up, but that didn't work. He should have just left that day, but, man, he hates that chief."

"Are you going to tell the police that?"

Cherry cocked his head. "You calling me a snitch?"

"What is it you want from me, Don?"

He sighed and shifted in the seat. "I know a lot. And I don't particularly want to go back to prison. But I'll go; I'll do my time and keep my mouth shut. Unless you can prove to me that God is real, that he'll listen to someone like me. If I flip, there'll be a price on my head. I ain't afraid. I can fight that battle, but it just ain't worth the aggravation if all I'm fighting for is a few miserable years waiting for someone to stick me with a knife."

Oliver rubbed his forehead, wanting the right words. "I believe you're asking me to prove something you already know to be true. What you're really asking me is to help you lay down the ego, to show you how to humble yourself before God."

A DEA agent knocked on the window. Oliver held up his

hand asking for another minute. He didn't look happy, but he nodded.

Oliver forged ahead. "All I have time for is a story. In the Bible, the children of Israel had to cross a river, the Jordan, to get to the Promised Land. God was going to part the waters, but they had to show their faith by getting their feet wet first. Once they did that, the waters parted and they crossed the river on dry ground. God is there, he'll show himself, but you need to get your feet wet first, Don. Take the first step. After that, I'll help you any way I can."

The DEA agent pulled the door open, and Oliver had to leave it at that.

67

Tess sat on one of Arthur's snowmobiles and sipped water from a bottle a paramedic had given her while Oliver talked with Don Cherry. The big ex-con was probably their last best hope for answers. Hemmings had screamed for a lawyer before they put him in a car. Garcia was alive but losing blood, and it was anyone's guess if he'd make it. If he did, he was certain not to talk. Would Cherry talk? Would Oliver ask him to?

A late-arriving sheriff's car pulled up and she saw Steve step out. He made his way past the tangle of official law enforcement vehicles and walked toward her.

Tess was glad her anger with him was gone. In retrospect,

she might have acted the same way he had, as painful as that was to admit. She was a cop, and cops were by nature suspicious. There might be no more romantic spark where Steve was concerned, but she would always agree that he was a good officer.

"For someone who's on vacation, you sure do a lot of work," he said with a smile. He sat on the snowmobile next to her.

"Well, I just hate sitting around twiddling my thumbs—know what I mean?"

He smiled. "I do. Thought you'd like to know what's going on at the Hang Ten."

She turned to him and arched an eyebrow.

"DEA came armed with a warrant. They found a bunch of contraband stacked in two outbuildings, along with pill-making equipment and even more stuff in one of the bedrooms in the house."

"Contraband?"

"Um, white powder, likely fentanyl, more stuff that is likely heroin, and homemade pills marked as oxycodone, but who knows. And there's a bunch of steroids and banned sports performance-enhancing drugs."

"Steroids?"

"Yep, and a boatload of weapons and stuff to make bombs."

"Gaston was storing all that there?"

Steve shook his head. "No, Haywood is singing like a bird. He claims most of the stuff appeared after the raid in Yreka. Haywood says it's all Garcia. He even says that he thinks Garcia killed Hector."

"He thinks?"

"He wasn't there. But he gives Garcia motive. Garcia hired Hector to bother you. But Hector wanted to leave and stiff Garcia a lot of money. They argued, and Garcia beat him up and threw him in a car. Next thing Haywood knows, Garcia is giving him a letter Hector supposedly wrote—"

"Saying that I threatened to kill him."

Steve nodded. "And Hector was dead. It would help to find the gun and maybe a little more corroboration, but it looks like Belcher is going to have to back off where you're concerned. Oh—" he reached into his pocket—"I almost forgot. Del gave me your phone to give you. You have a couple of messages."

"Thanks." Tess looked down at the phone and then asked the question that had been bugging her since the day she found Hector's body. "Why was Belcher pursuing to convict me so aggressively?"

He hiked a shoulder. "On the surface, you were the only one with motive. He's not a bad guy; he had tunnel vision. If it's any consolation, I think he'll see the light and be reasonable." He stood. "I'd better go, make sure Belcher is updated on everything going on here. I'm sure he'll have to call off the grand jury."

"Thanks, Steve, I appreciate it. I appreciate everything."

He nodded and left. Tess listened to the messages on her phone. Two were from news organizations and she deleted them. One was from Jonkey.

"Chief, I cleared up that photo, and I ran the plate. You won't believe who it belongs to. Please call me back."

Tess grinned and gave a fist pump, then played the last message.

That message brought her to her feet.

"*Chief O'Rourke, this is Phillip Whitman's girlfriend. I spoke to you a while ago, and I have to tell you now that I wasn't being truthful. I haven't been able to sleep, but I'm not a liar. For my own mental health, I have to tell you the truth. Yes, Phillip did come to see me that weekend. But he didn't get here until well after 10 a.m. And when he did get here, he was aggravated and upset. I don't know what he did, but I can't lie for him anymore.*"

68

Tess needed to get to the station.

"What's the matter, Tess?" Oliver walked up. He'd finished speaking to Don Cherry, and that distracted her for a minute.

"I have to do something. What did Cherry have to say?"

"He's . . . I'm not sure. Well, he said Garcia killed Hector."

"That's Haywood's story too. Will he testify?"

"That I can't say. He's struggling with himself. It's kind of like he's standing on a fence—step one way and it's the lawless life; step the other way and it's the law-abiding life. I pray he steps the right way."

Tess nodded, realizing that thinking about prayer didn't make her angry anymore. It might just work. "I never really considered that Cherry could be redeemable. But maybe the fact that you guys are still alive proves he is."

"I believe everyone is redeemable," Oliver said.

Tess saw Agent Ledge coming their way. She'd noticed that he was in a jurisdictional dispute with the state cops and the sheriff's office. It looked as if he had won.

"We need to interview both of you," Ledge said. "My agents are going to be combing through everything here, including taking a run up to the logging camp. How about we head back to your station?"

As much as Tess wanted to run off and finally close Tim Harper's case, she knew she had an obligation to give her statement regarding what had happened here today. She had, after all, shot Garcia. There would be an investigation of that. She noticed the state cops leaving; soon the sheriff deputies would as well. DEA agents were everywhere.

"Okay," she said, casting a glance toward Oliver. "You're probably exhausted."

"Starving, actually. Think we can get the Feds to pop for pizza?"

— — —

It turned into a long night of interviews and questions. Saturday morning Tess got the word from Addie.

"I can't put you back on official duty, especially since there's a shooting investigation going on. But if you want to travel somewhere with one of your officers, I have no problem with that."

"Thank you. There's something important I need to take care of."

Jonkey was waiting for her at the station. She had the enhanced photo in her hand. It was still a little cloudy, but the letters and numbers on the Oregon license plate were readable. Jonkey also had a printout of the registered owner's information.

"Ready?"

Jonkey nodded and together they climbed into Jonkey's patrol car. They were going to make an arrest in the murder of Tim Harper. Tess felt it right that Jonkey be the one to make the arrest; it had been her call, after all. It took them about thirty minutes to arrive at the small, nondescript home in Medford, on Delta Waters, just below Foothill. A four-door sedan was in the driveway. As Tess walked past it, she noted scratches in the front bumper.

Tess took one side of the door and Jonkey the other. Jonkey rapped on the door. A moment later, Phillip Whitman answered the door.

"Yes?" Fear flashed across his face when he recognized Tess. "Ah, Chief . . ."

"Mr. Whitman, we need to talk."

He stared at them for a moment. Tess knew he was her killer, but the why eluded her. She'd decided on a course of action: Ask first. If he denied, she'd get a warrant and be content to prove the case in court. But she wanted a confession and a reason to give to Drake and Eva Harper as to why Tim Harper was dead.

She was about to speak again when he stepped back and opened the door. "Sure, come in." There was defeat in his voice.

"First, you need to know your rights. You have the right to remain silent. If you give up the right to remain silent, anything you say can and will be used against you in court. You have the right to an attorney, and to have him present while you're being questioned. Do you understand these rights as I've explained them to you?"

"I get it."

"Having them in mind, do you waive your rights? Will you talk to me?"

"I'll talk."

"Mr. Whitman, I checked out your alibi for the night Tim Harper died. Your girlfriend called me. Do you know what she told me?"

He swallowed; she could see his Adam's apple working. He gave a slight nod. "I didn't think she'd stay quiet." He sat down hard on his couch, put his elbows on his knees, and held his head in his hands.

"What happened after the party that night?"

His head rolled back and forth. Then he looked up. "I'm sorry it happened. I'd take it back if I could. I went to Rogue's Hollow that night to contact Howard."

"Howard Delfin?"

"I didn't know the boys were going to be there. The last thing I wanted was for them to see me with Howard. I improvised, told them I was just there to wish Greg well. I did that and I was able to give Howard a message to meet me out at Smugglers Cove."

"Tim found you there."

"He was after photos. I didn't even know he was there. I mean, he rode up on his bike, went out to the picnic tables, where I was waiting for Howard. Tim heard our whole transaction. He . . . I asked him to be quiet, but . . ."

"You didn't think he would."

"No. I panicked. He rode off and I went after him and knocked him off his bike. And then it all went south from there."

"You took him home."

Whitman was crying now. "I couldn't leave him in the ditch . . . I couldn't. I thought if he died in his room, in his bed, there'd be less questions, less investigation. I wanted it to look like an accident. That's what it was, really, an accident."

"You injected him with drugs." Jonkey glared. She had no pity for the man's tears, Tess could see.

"Because it was humane."

"He wasn't a dog. And his clothes? Why did you take his clothes?"

"DNA, man. I cried, I cried. I'm sorry it happened—really, I am."

"Stand up. You're under arrest for the murder of Tim Harper."

He stood and Jonkey cuffed him.

"Were you distributing fentanyl for Delfin?" Tess asked.

He shook his head. "That was for my personal use. I got steroids from Howard. They're more lucrative than the other stuff, as far as I'm concerned."

Jonkey put Whitman in the back of the car while Tess called to see about a warrant for the residence. They'd be here all day, but she was bound and determined to charge Whitman with everything she could.

After the warrant came through, she found a little bit of fentanyl and boxes of illegal performance-enhancing drugs. She also found some shorts and a T-shirt matching the description of the clothes Tim was wearing the night he was killed and an iPhone with Tim's initials carved in it. It would be small consolation, she knew, but she was glad she had something to return to the Harpers after she told them that Tim's killer was in custody.

Finally.

69

TWO WEEKS LATER

The election results came in and Tess breathed a sigh of relief. Pete Horning was the new mayor by a wide margin. And the initiative for pot sales failed by twenty-five votes.

"No recount for the mayor's race or the pot initiative," Casey Reno said as Tess poured her coffee. "I think peace will reign in the valley once more."

"Hear, hear." Tess sat and raised her coffee cup. Her shooting had also been cleared, and Tess had returned to work after seven days off. It was the vote of confidence she needed from the townspeople. They were all on her side and she was ashamed that she even imagined that they weren't.

"You've had a lot of downtime," Casey said as she looked around Tess's eat-in area. Tess followed her gaze. Boxes were gone; decorations, books, and knickknacks were in their proper places.

"Have you finally unpacked everything?"

"I have. I hate just sitting around, so I made good use of my time off. This place is home now. My guest room is ready for the next time I have out-of-town visitors. I even have a new heat pump."

"Sergeant Pounder did a good job running the PD in your absence."

"Never doubted it. Curtis is a good cop." He'd done a great job with the firestorm that had erupted after the shoot-out at Arthur's house. It had everything the news media could want—a dirty federal agent, a violent drug lord, and piles of contraband and weapons.

Casey left for the restroom, and while Tess sipped coffee, she recollected the past few days. Her first day back her colleagues had done something Tess hadn't done since she was fifteen.

They celebrated her birthday. Oliver brought the cake. Gabe shared how he and Jonkey both had worked to help Tess.

"It was Becky who figured out how the e-mail message Hector had was faked," he said.

"It was easy. They weren't very good at hacking. They used an address one character off, so at a glance, it looked as though it was from you, but it didn't hold up to any scrutiny."

Tess couldn't speak. She felt different. There was no crushing sense of loss when they sang "Happy Birthday," and the dream had not returned. There had even been a surprise attendee: Drake Harper. He was thinner, and his arm was in a heavy cast, but he looked better, like he was on the road to recovery and acceptance. Whitman wasn't going to fight the charges, so there would be no sordid trial to wade through for the Harpers.

"Thank you, Chief. I'm sorry I gave you such a bad time."

"You have nothing to apologize for. I'm just glad we caught the bad guy."

He nodded. "It was so senseless—that's what I struggle with most. I know why, but it's a nonsense reason. But Tim was a boy full of hope and optimism. I can't let that be forgotten."

"I understand."

"I know you do."

Tess had even been to a Sunday service. Oliver was mesmerizing behind the pulpit. His voice sang with a little Scotland as he spoke, and Tess could see why his congregation was so large. He'd preached on trust, and it brought back memories of her father, good memories.

Trust.

Tess pondered the word for the whole time she was off. She'd finally put her finger on how Oliver had changed after Anna's death and his visit home: he was stronger. There was no knocking him over; his faith and trust in God rooted him. Tess had been knocked off her feet when her father died—whether because her faith was weak or because she'd never really had any, she didn't know. And she'd always believed that she had picked herself up and moved forward—without God.

Now she wasn't so sure.

She'd been reading her father's Bible. Not the text, but his notes strewn throughout. Just about every page had at least one note written in her father's crisp, clear block printing. She cherished every bit she read, hearing her father's voice as she read them. There was a lot about trust, and there was a lot about Tess. She kept the Bible by her bedside and turned the pages every night, often brought to tears by her father's insight and love. One note in particular touched her. It was in the margins of Psalm 139 and it was a prayer. *"Lord, please help Tessa to know with certainty that your presence is always with her no matter what pain and heartache this world may bring."*

She'd read that prayer over and over, wondering if it was true even though she'd been angry with God for so long. She wanted to ask Oliver about it. She wanted to talk to Oliver about a lot of things. Casey returned to the kitchen and grabbed her purse.

"You have a visitor, and I have to run. See you later."

Oliver Macpherson had followed her.

"Hello, Tess." He stopped in the entryway. She knew he'd been to the jail. Don Cherry was still in custody in Jackson County but would be remanded to federal custody at some point. Hemmings and Garcia were already in federal custody. Cherry was accused of state crimes, but because of Sal Hemmings, the Feds were going to take their bite first. Oliver believed there was something in Don worth redemption. A week and a half ago Tess would have argued with him. But now she just didn't know. And it puzzled her—Cherry could have added to the death toll and killed Drake, Bryce, and Oliver as ordered, but he didn't.

Tess smiled, glad to see Oliver. He'd been updating her

regularly on the aftermath of the shooting and keeping her apprised of any news on the Rogue telegraph.

"Hey. Have a seat and some coffee."

"I will." He stepped into the kitchen and pulled a mug down from the cupboard. He poured the coffee and sat in the chair Casey had left.

"Anything new to report?" Tess asked.

"Aye, Jackson County Sheriff's officially indicted José Garcia for the murder of Hector Connor-Ruiz. He'll likely be tried after the Feds finish with him."

Tess arched her eyebrows. "Yeah? That's great news. I wasn't certain that Belcher would buy Don Cherry's explanation of things."

"Well, Don's had an awful lot to say. To borrow a phrase from old film noir movies, he's singing like a canary. He's giving detailed statements; he even helped close the murder of Howard Delfin."

"Garcia again?"

Oliver nodded. "According to Don, Garcia had a singular focus: kill you and avenge his brother. Then he'd tie up loose ends and flee the country. That's why Hemmings was here. He was leaving with Garcia because he believed his cover was blown."

"Why'd he stockpile all that stuff at the Hang Ten?"

"His first plan was to get rid of you—that's why he hired Hector and set up operation there, thought the location would be good. Eventually he'd buy Arthur out or just get rid of him. But when you proved too hard to get rid of, according to Don, he went ballistic. Arresting Carr lit the fuse; Carr did a lot of Garcia's dirty work."

Tess considered this. "Did Cherry ever tell you why he didn't kill Bryce and Drake when they told him to?"

"I've asked. He gets coy."

"You have a guess?"

"He's working out his faith. I think he's truly changed, just not ready to shout it from the rooftop."

"He'll testify against everyone?"

"He says yes."

"My guess is the Feds will try to get a plea deal going and avoid trials for Garcia and Hemmings. They have enough evidence. Don might not have to testify in court."

"I'm praying that he'll get a lenient sentence whatever happens."

Although she doubted she'd ever trust him, Don Cherry had filled in a lot of blanks. He was an accessory to at least two murders in Oregon. He claimed to have driven Garcia to Tess's house and watched him kill Hector. Likewise with Delfin. After Delfin was killed, he drove Garcia back to Arthur's, which was where Garcia had been hiding.

Cherry claimed it was Hemmings who drove Garcia back to Delfin's looking for Tess and planning then to kill her because they were certain the grand jury wouldn't indict her for Hector's murder. Of course, Garcia called Cherry a liar. But Ledge had told Tess there was some evidence to lend credence to what Don had to say; they'd recovered several guns, and one had been positively identified as the gun that killed Hector and Delfin. The only prints on the gun were Garcia's. In fact, other than the AK-47 and a Taser, Cherry's prints weren't on much.

And there'd been a little cooperation on the Delfin murder

case from Dustin, still in the hospital but on the mend. He claimed he was hiding in the house when Delfin was killed.

"You like the guy," Tess said, referring to Cherry.

"I'll admit I got used to our little talks. He's a complex fellow."

Oliver had faith that people could change. Would she ever get there?

"By the way, Bryce Evergreen paid the last of his fines and has decided to stay in Rogue's Hollow."

"No kidding."

Oliver gave a nod. "He accepted a job working at Dover's orchard."

"Good for him. I heard that Haywood is going to try to keep the Hang Ten." No charges had been filed against him.

"He is. Maybe he'll make a go of it."

Oliver peered at her over the rim of his coffee cup, peace in his stormy gray eyes. And that gave Tess peace.

"Guess I'll have to get used to pot farms in my jurisdiction."

He smiled. "Grand. The Hollow could use a good dragon slayer."

Tess laughed and they clanked coffee cups. He reached his hand out and gripped hers. She held on tight, not wanting to let go, knowing that she'd found more than a job and a home here; she'd found a life. A tingly warmth crept through her. Oliver's presence and his trustworthy friendship filled the room. Tess liked the feeling. It was steadying, just like the feeling of being home.

ABOUT THE AUTHOR

A former Long Beach, California, police officer of twenty-two years, Janice Cantore worked a variety of assignments, including patrol, administration, juvenile investigations, and training. She's always enjoyed writing and published two short articles on faith at work for *Cop and Christ* and *Today's Christian Woman* before tackling novels. She now lives in a small town in southern Oregon, where she enjoys exploring the forests, rivers, and lakes with her Labrador retrievers, Abbie and Tilly.

Janice writes suspense novels designed to keep readers engrossed and leave them inspired. *Lethal Target* follows *Crisis Shot* in her latest series. Janice also authored the Cold Case Justice series—*Drawing Fire, Burning Proof,* and *Catching Heat*—the Pacific Coast Justice series—*Accused, Abducted,* and *Avenged*—and the Brinna Caruso novels, *Critical Pursuit* and *Visible Threat.*

Visit Janice's website at www.janicecantore.com and connect with her on Facebook at www.facebook.com/JaniceCantore.

DISCUSSION QUESTIONS

1. In the opening scenes of *Lethal Target*, Chief Tess O'Rourke is called to a death investigation, possibly caused by a drug overdose. Some residents of Rogue's Hollow are pointing fingers at the legal pot farms in her jurisdiction, claiming, "One drug leads to another." Where do you stand on this issue? Are there any benefits of marijuana or a legal opioid painkiller that might outweigh the drugs' negative associations or abuse?

2. When Oliver Macpherson calls Tess a dragon slayer, she says she wishes she could take away the desire for drugs, and Oliver replies, "Only a heart change can take that away." Do you agree with his statement, or is there more to the issue than a heart change? Where do you start when you want to conquer addictions in your life?

3. How did you feel when you learned that Tess is reluctant to go deeper in her relationship with Steve Logan? Is Tess being prudent or too cautious in

following rule #12 ("Keep work professional, and personal life, personal")? What do you think about her realization that she feels more comfortable around Oliver than around Steve?

4. A familiar face from Tess's past shows up in Rogue's Hollow to stir up trouble. How does she handle Hector Connor-Ruiz's presence in town? What could she have done better?

5. Oliver thinks of Tess as a warrior for justice but notes that she seems motivated by the belief "I need to do this because *God won't*." Do you believe there are situations God removes himself from? Why might it appear as if he has done so? Are there circumstances in your life or the lives of those around you that seem unjust or as if God is uncaring? What might you do in those cases?

6. After about a year of living in Rogue's Hollow, Tess begins to truly feel at home. What gives her that sense of peace? How long does it take you to fully settle into a new place? How do you know when you're home?

7. Oliver compares Tess—the law—to his wife, Anna, who embodied grace. When might one situation call for more of a certain trait than the other? Do you consider yourself to be more like Tess or Anna? Or do you walk the line between the two characteristics like Oliver?

8. In his grief, Drake Harper lashes out at Tess, berating her for failing to do her job. What makes his outbursts

understandable? Can you relate to him? How does Tess handle this? Anger is sometimes considered a secondary emotion, a safer outward expression of what a person might truly be feeling. What underlying fears or emotions or physical conditions might be masked with anger?

9. When trouble is quite literally dropped on Tess's doorstep, how does she respond in that moment? What about earlier, when her ability to perform her duties is called into question by some of the townspeople? And later, when Logan calls her to ask about her interactions with Hector?

10. After finding it in a box filled with long-forgotten items, why does Tess carry her dad's courage card around, though it offers her little comfort? How can a simple reminder, a promise of truth, offer encouragement, even when we least expect it? What can you do today to extend a simple comfort to someone?

11. Tilly Dover has overcome a challenging past and seems to be in a good place, but her brother has a hard time believing she will remain drug-free. Is he right to keep his distance and protect his family, or should he extend grace time and again? Are some people lost causes, or should we always hold out hope?

12. Oliver recognizes how easy it is to get stuck in the past, caught by the unanswerable question of "why." What has he done to set aside the search for an answer and

move forward? What does Tess need to do? Have you ever experienced a time when you felt caught up in looking for an answer to "why"? How are you able to move forward?

13. Don Cherry shares a bit about his colorful past with Oliver, who eventually tells the ex-con, "You're asking me to prove something you already know to be true." What does Oliver tell Don to do? Why is getting your feet wet so difficult sometimes? What does fully humbling yourself before God look like to you?

14. Toward the end of *Lethal Target*, Tess spends time reading her father's Bible, finding comfort in the notes he wrote in the margins. How do you imagine her story playing out?

Turn the page for an
excerpt from *Crisis Shot*,
the thrilling first book in
the Line of Duty series.

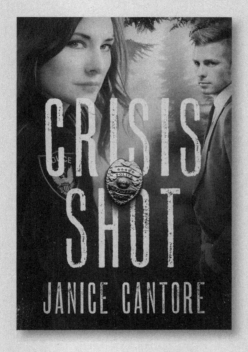

Available now from your favorite retailer

Join the conversation at

1

LONG BEACH, CALIFORNIA
FEBRUARY

"999! 999—" Click. The voice cut off.

Commander Tess O'Rourke was halfway to the station when the emergency call exploded from the radio. The frantic transmission punched like a physical blow. A triple 9— officer needs help—was only used when an officer was in the direst emergency.

Adrenaline blasted all the cobwebs from Tess's brain. Dispatch identified the unit as 2-Adam-9, JT Barnes, but had no luck getting the officer back on the air.

She was early, hadn't been able to sleep. Seven months

since Paul left and she still wasn't used to sleeping alone. After a fitful four-hour nap on the recliner in the living room, she'd given up, showered, and decided to head into work early in predawn darkness, at the same time all hell broke loose.

Tess tried to get on the radio to advise that she was practically on top of the call and would assist, but the click and static of too many units vying for airtime kept her from it. Pressing the accelerator, Tess steered toward Barnes's last known location.

A flashing police light bar illuminating the darkness just off Stearns caught her eye. She turned toward the lights onto a side street, and a jolt of fear bit hard at the sight of a black-and-white stopped in the middle of the street, driver's door open and no officer beside it. It was an area near the college, dense with apartment buildings and condos, cars lining both sides of the street.

She screeched to a stop and jammed her car into park as the dispatcher wrestled to get order back on the air.

Tess keyed her mike. Voice tight, eyes scanning. "Edward-7 is on scene, will advise" was her terse remark to the dispatcher.

She drew her service weapon and bolted from her unmarked car, cold air causing an involuntary inhale. Tess was dressed in a long-sleeved uniform but was acutely aware that she was minus a vest and a handheld radio. As commander of the East Patrol Division in Long Beach, her duties were administrative. Though in uniform, she wore only a belt holster, not a regular patrol Sam Browne. It had been six years since she worked a patrol beat as a sergeant in full uniform.

But one of her officers, a good one, was in trouble, and Tess was not wired to do nothing.

"JT?" she called out, breath hanging in the frigid air as her gaze swept first the area illuminated by yellow streetlights and then the empty car.

The only sounds she heard were the gentle rumble of the patrol car engine and the mechanical clicking of the light bar as it cycled through its flashes.

A spot of white in front of the car caught her eye and she jogged toward it. Illuminated by headlights were field interview cards scattered in front of the patrol unit as if JT had been interviewing someone and was interrupted, dropping the index cards.

Someone took off running.

She followed the line of cards between two parked cars and up on the sidewalk, where the trail ended, and then heard faint voices echoing from the alley behind an apartment building. Sprinting toward the noise across grass wet with dew, she rounded a darkened corner and saw three figures in a semicircle, a fourth kneeling on the ground next to a prone figure.

"Go on, cap him, dawg! Get the gat and cap him!"

Anger, fear, revulsion all swept through her like a gust of a hot Santa Ana wind. Tess instantly assessed what was happening: the black boots and dark wool uniform pants told her Barnes was on the ground.

"*Police!* Get away from him!" She rushed headlong toward the group, gun raised.

In a flood of cursing, the three standing figures bolted and ran, footfalls echoing in the alley. The fourth, a hoodie partially obscuring his face, looked her way but didn't stop what he was doing.

He was trying to wrench the gun from Barnes's holster.

Was Barnes dead? The question burned through Tess, hot and frightening.

"Move away! Move away now!" Tess advanced and was ignored.

Sirens sounded loud and Tess knew help was close. But the next instant changed everything. The figure gave up on the gun and threw himself across the prone officer, grabbing for something else. He turned toward Tess and pointed.

She fired.

Watch for the exciting
conclusion to the
Line of Duty series.

Available summer 2019!

TYNDALE

CP1408